THE JUDGMENT ON
HIGGINS AND HUNTER

Also by George V. Higgins
available now from Ballantine Books:

A CITY ON A HILL

THE FRIENDS OF RICHARD NIXON

The Judgment of Deke Hunter

George V. Higgins

BALLANTINE BOOKS • NEW YORK

Library of Congress Catalog Card Number: 76-10215

ISBN 0-345-25862-2

This edition published by arrangement with Little, Brown and
Company in association with the Atlantic Monthly Press

Manufactured in the United States of America

First Ballantine Books Edition: February 1978

MANY OF THE PLACES in this book are real and exist. None of the characters does. There are, I believe, actual people who have done some of the things which are done by the characters in this story, but I have no idea of their identities, nor any interest in them, for that matter. This is a story. If in reading it there is found resemblance between its characters, and people living or now dead, then, perhaps, it is a good story. Perhaps, if only because we are not very imaginative animals, and are no more skilled at getting into trouble than we are at getting out. But it is still a story, and that is all.

The
Judgment of
Deke Hunter

PART ONE

☐

The Quarry

The Holgates

☐ 1

IN EARLY 1965, Edmund K. Holgate of East Bridge-water, Massachusetts, purchased two homes for himself and his wife, Judith. For $27,500, they bought a one-bedroom condominium in Coral Gables, Florida. The other place was a three-bedroom wooden-frame cottage at Weekapaug, Rhode Island; it cost $31,900 to buy, and about $5,400 to winterize. They sold their farmhouse and land in East Bridgewater for $67,800, paying off a mortgage debt of $8,005, and he sold his seventy-five percent interest in Holgate Realty for another $45,000.

Edmund Holgate, then, was sixty-one. Judith was sixty-two. Late in 1963, while flying between Boston and Augusta, Edmund had experienced sharp pains in his chest; while electrocardiograms taken at the Cardinal Cushing Hospital at Stoughton (he rejected medical assistance in Boston that night, because he wanted to go home) were inconclusive, the doctors did point out that he was slightly overweight and did not get enough exercise. They also said he was working too hard.

Edmund, who wore a blue blazer and a red-and-blue-striped tie four out of five days a week, went home and talked it over with Judith. Judith agreed that he was working too hard, and had been doing so for nearly thirty-nine years. She saw no further major responsibilities of theirs for their daughter, Andrea, who had married a man named Hunter, against their wishes, in late 1962. She said it was time they began to spend some time enjoying themselves. He said he was not sure they could afford it and he would miss Andrea.

He had never made less than $3,000 a year in commissions. In 1954 he had hit a prosperous period, which he did not fully trust, and made $9,600. In 1955, he had made $11,700. In 1966, just over $12-000, and he stayed in that bracket until 1961, when he managed to put together a shopping center plaza that brought him a personal gross income of $217,000, in addition to the $13,000 that he made from other business. He was thoughtfully advised by his accountant; he managed to keep most of it. Thereafter he averaged about $19,000 a year, until he retired. When he made that decision, the day after the cardiogram, his books showed a net worth of nearly $300,000. Judith told him that they could afford time for themselves, and suggested a summer house in New England, which Andrea could visit while Hunter was working. Edmund said that he could probably find something on the Cape. Judith said that she'd prefer something father away. Edmund said he saw her point. In the farmhouse, in East Bridgewater, the light from the flames in the fireplace shone dully on the black surfaces of Judith's trivet collection, and brightly on the surfaces of the maple colonial furniture, and they celebrated their decision with a glass of Christian Brothers sherry, which the doctors had recommended for Edmund's tension.

□ 2

IT WAS REALLY the last house in Weekapaug, on a small sandy point near the boundary of the Misquami-cut State Beach. It was only six years old, done in gray weathered shingles, but then all of the houses on that point were newly built, or reconstructed from the ground up after 1959, because the land was precariously close to the sea, and the tides cleared out the buildings whenever a hurricane came through. That made the house cheap to buy, and it had been built cheaply, for those very reasons.

The land behind the Holgate house—on the side that the highway was on—sloped down gradually to a small salt pond. There was a deck on the ocean side of the house, where the owners and their guests could watch the sea. There was a screened porch on the highway side, where they could sit and watch the headlights of the GTOs and the motorcycles and the other vehicles operated by people who made Edmund and Judith nervous. The people in the cars and on the bikes went down to the carnival grounds across the street from the State Beach pavilion. They made a lot of noise and sometimes threw beer bottles into the scrub on the highway side of the property, and late at night, when the Holgates were trying to sleep, the people at the carnival grounds and the adjacent bars came out and ran drags, which attracted cops and sirens and made restless the sleep of the Holgates. But although they did not like the people that they observed from the porch, they used the porch instead of the deck because it protected them from mosquitoes.

The Holgates, moving into the cottage at the end

4

of June, 1965, got indifferent enjoyment from it that summer. Mrs. Holgate was not satisfied with the speed with which furniture was delivered, and missed the Women's Club in East Bridgewater (she attended two meetings, at considerable inconvenience, and discovered that her old friends now thought her an outsider). She drove past the farmhouse once, and saw that it had been painted yellow. Mr. Holgate missed his daughter, who rejected invitations to spend July and August with them; she explained that Deke was spending three days at the State Police Barracks and only one at home, and, with Sam newborn, she wanted to be at home in Canton when Deke got his days off. She did agree to come for Labor Day, when Deke would be on duty for the whole of the holiday weekend.

In the evenings of that weekend, Andrea sat with her parents on the porch, while what her father called "the hooligans" went by on the road, and she nursed her baby, and explained several times that Deke did like his work, and did not regret playing baseball, and believed that they would have security from what he did. Edmund Holgate said he hoped so, and Judith Holgate went to bed early while men who fished at night sneaked over onto the beach on the ocean side of the house, and cast metal jigs into the dark water.

Deke Hunter

□ 3

WITH PACKING LEFT to do, Andrea Hunter left the porch around ten-thirty on the evening of September 2, 1973, leaving her father and her husband on the porch. The wicker rocker creaked when Hunter shifted his weight. In the salt pond down the slope, a small animal swam audibly.

"Ducks're out late," Hunter said. He was thirty-one years old. He weighed one hundred and ninety pounds, and only six or seven of them were fat. He had his hair cut short, and he wore chino pants and a pullover shirt, blue, and a pair of old penny loafers.

"I don't think so," Edmund said. His face had pinkened and firmed up in eight years. He was almost seventy, and he looked closer to fifty than he had when he was sixty. He wore a green Lacoste shirt and white slacks and sandals, and a permanent tan. "Sam's been tending to your little project with them, and he found something down there the other morning that he thought were muskrat tracks. But when I looked at them, it looked like a regular rat to me."

"Oh good," Hunter said. "Nothing I like better'n a nice big brown water rat for company. Damnit, when did the rats get here?"

"Well," Edmund said, "it was fairly recent that the ducks got here, and stayed, at least."

"They don't stay much after Columbus Day, I remember," Hunter said.

"I wouldn't know that," Edmund said. "But they weren't here when we got here. I'd imagine it's hand-

6

outs. People down at the beach feed them, I suppose. All of them on handouts, too."

In the darkness to the north there was a ferris wheel turning, with white lights. They watched it for a while. Around it there was a glow from the other rides and attractions. They could not hear the music. A Karmann Ghia went by on the road, quite slowly.

"Ducks'd draw rats," Edmund said. "Come after the eggs. When we kept chickens for a while, at home? We tried it, back when the war started. We didn't even have gas for the car. I had to put it up on blocks. Ration stamps. It was awful. We had the barn, and I got some wire and we built a coop. Andrea was just born then. My wife'd feed her and then come out and help me with the coop. It was really hot that summer, too. No air conditioning in those days, no sir. And then we got ourselves two cocks and ten hens, Rhode Island Reds, because we were going to have eggs and chicken to eat. And pretty soon we had rats. Never had rats before. We had rats then. Looking for the eggs. Ducks drew the rats."

"I saw a rat once in the dugout at Binghamton," Hunter said. "I came back from a sacrifice and I sat down, we were short about three guys that night, and I sat down and this big rat ran right across the floor in front of me. Scared the shit out of me."

"You afraid of rats, Deke?" Edmund said.

"They're not my favorite people," Hunter said. "No. I guess, if I was prepared for a rat, I could probably take care of him all right. If I was in a slum or something, in an alley, I'd expect to see a rat and the rat wouldn't bother me much. Or down by the waterfront. We pulled a floater out of the Quabbin Reservoir a couple years ago, one of the Macklin gang, six shots in the head and the rope broke on the cement blocks so he surfaced after about three weeks. Now lemme tell you, that's a great big blue disgusting sight, a body all filled up with gas like that and bloated like a blimp, and I didn't drink anything that came out of a faucet for about a month. But I was doing all right with him, and while we're hauling him out, this big rat ran out of the bushes and off into some

other bushes, and it scared the shit out of everybody. I
thought somebody was gonna get shot. See, we weren't
ready for rats. Dead bodies, yeah, but nothing nasty
like a rat. I dunno how those guys can do autopsies
the way they do."

"We had rats when the plaza first opened," Edmund
said. "You never know what it is. The first fellow saw
one, he ran the ice cream shop, and the place was
brand new. The whole place was absolutely brand
new. And he was almost a fanatic, he was so clean. I
mean, he was meticulous. I saw his food preparation
areas. They were cleaner after the lunch business than
they were before it, in most places you'd go into. The
place was spotless. This was before we turned it over
to the owners, and I was still technically in charge. He
was almost in tears. Droppings in the storeroom. 'Get
an exterminator,' I said. 'Nothing else you can do.
And don't worry about it.' There was a bakery next
door, and I suppose they got some mice with their
flour. On the other side there was a supermarket.
'Don't be surprised if you see another one of them
some day, either. Some truck'll come in and a rat'll
get off, and it won't be your fault when that happens.
You just call me if somebody complains.'"

"This is civilization," Edmund said. "Motorcycles,
people driving their cars too fast, rats that come
around looking for bread crumbs and duck eggs.
Doesn't matter."

"I wonder if there's somebody around here's got a
twenty-two I can borrow," Hunter said. "Give me a
little project of my own to do, while Sam's taming the
ducks. Shoot the bastard."

"Don't you always have to carry your own gun?"
Edmund said.

"Oh, sure," Hunter said. "I'll let off that thirty-
eight, if I can ever get close enough to hit the son of
a bitch with it, and your wife'll jump right out of her
skin."

Edmund laughed. "That's right," he said. "Of course,
you fire a twenty-two, and she'll do it then, too."

"Yeah," Hunter said, "but I can do that from further away from the rat, and still hit him. I use the

two-inch on him, I'll miss, and then I'll have to do it again, and that'll be twice she jumps."

"Maybe drive the ducks away, too," Edmund said.

"Well," Hunter said, "everything's a trade-off, you know? But maybe not. One shot? They might go away, but they'd come back."

"They were smart enough to stay in the first place," Edmund said. "They get fat here, with no real effort. You know what that kid's done? Sam's got them coming up to under six feet, now. He's really taking it seriously. Out there by six-thirty, every morning, got his stale bread and his crackers. The free-loaders wait for him."

"Works the morning shift too," Hunter said.

"Absolutely," Edmund said. "He's religious about it. 'Dad's got them trained. They expect it.'"

"He's a good kid," Hunter said.

"He really is," Edmund said. "For a kid his age, he's the most responsible kid I ever saw. If I were still in business, and it weren't for the Child Labor Laws, well, if it weren't for them, I'd go back into business, and put him to work."

"Except that sometimes," Hunter said, "I wish maybe he wasn't quite so serious. This young, only eight, eight and a half, it seems to me like you oughta be a little more, I dunno. . . . You're supposed to be a grown-up for an awful long time. Shouldn't start so early, you can help it. It comes on soon enough as it is."

"Michele doesn't seem like that, Deke," Edmund said.

"Michele doesn't," Hunter said, "and neither does Nicky. But Michele's not gonna be six until after Thanksgiving, and Nicky's just turned four. They didn't come into the world as serious as Sam, but they're not as old as he is now, either, and maybe when they are, they will be. Maybe not. I'm home more, now. More'n I was when Sam was a little kid. Maybe that's got something to do with it."

"I know it has," Edmund said. "When Andrea was young, before she went to school, I mean, I was home every night for supper. It didn't matter what I could've been doing, instead. I was scrupulous about that. Every night. I bet I didn't miss three in a month. Pick her up, hold her, my God but she was a beautiful child."

"In my line of work," Hunter said, "what I had before, they didn't let you come home every night. Every fourth night."

"I know that," Edmund said.

"I hadda make a living," Hunter said. "I still do."

"But you can come home more, now," Edmund said.

"Put it this way," Hunter said, "I don't have to stay in a barracks, now that I'm in plain clothes, if I haven't got anything to do. But if I've got something that's gotta be done, I still have to do it, and if it's night, I got to work nights. Simple as that."

"I just worry about Andrea," Edmund said. "When she was in high school, when she was in college, she was such a pretty girl, so lively. And now she looks so worn. So tired out. I worry about her. I'm sorry that I do it, but I do."

"Look," Hunter said, "do you mind if I blow out that damned candle?"

Edmund chuckled. "It's all right with me."

"Well," Hunter said, "that's maybe because you're not the one that's going to be sleeping out here. Stink as they do when they're going, they stink even worse when you put the things out. Damned citronella. My mother used to burn those things, too, and I hated them then. You don't need it anyway. There's no holes in the screens here."

"You can't convince Judith of that," Edmund said. "I personally got myself used to it, long ago. She's always used them. Then for a while she was using those No-Pest strips. But we left here for a weekend two years ago, when a friend of mine died up in Avon, and we were gone for five days when the weather was hot, for the wake and the funeral, and when we came back here and opened it up, the fumes nearly knocked me over. I thought I was going to have another attack. So, Deke, I think you're probably stuck with the candles until Judith goes to bed, and better off with them too, as far as that goes. I'll put it out." Edmund got up from his wicker chair and snuffed the candle with his fingers.

"How do you do that?" Hunter said.

"What?" Edmund said.

"Put out a candle with your fingers," Hunter said. "I knew a guy in the Eastern League who could swallow a lighted cigarette. How do you do things like that?"

"I don't know how you do it with a cigarette," Edmund said. He sat down again. "My guess is, like the fire-eaters. They fill their mouths with saliva, and when the torch goes in, the spit takes all the heat and it turns to steam and it doesn't even sear the skin. I read about that in *The Reader's Digest,* a long time ago. I don't remember the book. But with candles, your skin's just not there long enough where there's heat. You just pinch, and there you are. Before there's fire enough to burn you, the heat's out."

"It's a hell of a thing," Hunter said. "I couldn't climb a rope, either. I was convinced, when I was a kid, that I was doomed for the rest of my life because I couldn't climb a rope. Shinny up a goddamned rope. The things you worry about."

"With me," Edmund said, "it was money."

"Well," Hunter said, "either you're a better worrier'n I am, or else you just put longer into it."

"I didn't quit," Edmund said. "I'm still worrying. We've got a large amount of money under financial management, stocks and things, and every day I get up and go and get the paper to find out what those stocks are doing. I wanted to put it in banks. I should have. It would've been much more relaxing. The way it is, I'm still scared all the time, scared I'll be wiped out."

"Is that likely?" Hunter said.

"I hope not," Edmund said. "Not that hopes matter."

Four large miller moths moved around on the sunporch screens. There was a cricket under the floorboards, and he sang from time to time. On the ocean side of the house the waves broke, making a faint noise on the highway side. A Honda went by, with two people riding, making a laboring sound.

"They better matter," Hunter said.

"Why is that?" Edmund said.

"Well," Hunter said, "I'm looking for a guy, and I haven't got very much time to find him. And I'd better find the son of a bitch, because his buddies're going to trial in a couple months or so up in Salem, and if we're convicting them, which we're gonna do, we're gonna have to use a guy that the guy I can't find doesn't know about yet, and as soon as we use him, if I haven't found the guy, the guy we got to use is dead. So either I find the guy, or the other guys hit the street, or, shit, I dunno. I got to find this guy."

"What's his name?" Edmund said.

"Donnelly," Hunter said. "Teddy Donnelly."

"I don't know him," Edmund said.

"I didn't expect you would," Hunter said. "Or where he is, either."

"What did he do?" Edmund said.

"He robbed a bank," Hunter said, "with the rest of them, the guys that we've got. And I lost a case that the federals brought right down here, not so long ago, and I better not lose this one."

"What happens if you do?" Edmund said.

"I start hoping again," Hunter said, in the dark.

Madeleine St. Anne

☐ 4

IN LATE SEPTEMBER OF 1973, there was still enough business on the Post Road in Warwick, Rhode Island, to keep the Henry IV Motor Inn operating. Its rooms were rented by salesmen and other people, who stopped there instead of at the plentiful competition because they had decided that they could go no farther, or because they had no other place to go. Its restaurant, the Tower of London Mead Hall, got its trade from people who did not require very much, and did not have very much to pay for what they got, and because there were many more of them than there were people who needed rooms badly, the restaurant supported the rest of the operation. On March 8, 1975, shortly before three A.M., a passing motorist saw flames in the dining room. Quick action by policemen and firemen saved the seven guests asleep at the motel, but the structure was gutted.

On the evening of September 26, 1973, Deke Hunter and Madeleine St. Anne arrived at the Henri IV in separate cars. He got there first, and waited for her, out of the rain, under the canopy. She parked her Camaro near the door, and did not bother with her clear plastic umbrella. When she was under the canopy, she shook her hair, and smiled at him. At the restaurant desk, the Tower Hostess, an overweight blonde woman in a tight black dress, with rose-tinted white hair and rhinestones on her glasses, smiled at perfect strangers as though they had been regular customers, and seated Deke and Madeleine near the King's Ransom Salad Bar, where there were pieces of

13

lettuce and chopped Bermuda onion on the red and black carpet. They put their coats on the benches with them in the booth. Madeleine got up immediately and made a salad.

"Maybe if we'd've had kids," she said, pausing between bites of cucumber seasoned with vinegar. She had dark red hair, cut short. She wore a white body shirt and tight red pants and white vinyl boots with stacked heels. She was twenty-eight. "I dunno. You can't tell. But, still, it might've helped if we'd've had kids. Isn't that something? Me saying that? And I was the one that always didn't want them. Boy, you never know."

Hunter had a beer brought to him, and he drank from the silver-colored, plastic stein, decorated with lions rampant. He wore a basket-weave blue blazer, and blue-and-white-checked slacks that would have been more comfortable on a warmer evening, and a white broadcloth shirt, open at the collar. "We had kids," he said. "Didn't help us much, I can see."

The glass in the windows of the restaurant was divided into red and blue diamonds by thin strips of wood, inside and out. The glass was textured, and the rain took odd courses down the ripples.

"It's my fault as much as it's his," she said. "He's a very nice guy, actually. You know what I mean."

"I like him myself," Hunter said.

"Everybody does," she said. "Everybody likes Freddie. He's a hell of a nice guy. You know how long he was up there? At the courthouse?"

"Shit," Hunter said, "I was only there about six weeks myself, all told. I thought, I was just visiting, myself. One trial. I wished I had been. No, I don't know."

"He was there," she said, "well . . . , you were there when? When was Lion's trial? Two years ago?"

"Year ago last spring," he said.

"Year ago last spring," she said. "Okay, April. He came there, he started at the courthouse right after, it was right after we went down the Bahamas on our vacation, and that was July, so it was, it was August he was, he started there. Yeah, they laid him off, down at Groton, and I talked to the Judge, and I said: 'Look, my husband got laid off down the submarine base. Can you do anything for him?' Well, the Judge likes me. 'What can he do?' What the hell can he do? Anything he wants, actually, but I don't know what to say. 'He's, he's a foreman. He was a foreman. Now he's not a foreman. He was an assembler foreman.' So, okay, the Judge'll see what he can do.

"All right," she said, "and they bring him in. Court officer. Put him on right after Labor Day. He's there less'n a year. Less'n a *year*. About six months, actually. And, you know something? People're still asking me: 'Hey, where's Freddie? How's Freddie doing these days?' "

"I believe it," Hunter said.

"I dunno why it is," she said. "I dunno how he does it. Guys come and guys go, and guys hang on forever, and nobody ever pays any attention to them. You get somebody that spent his whole life around that place, and he finally retires, and they give him a party, and the next day everybody's got a hangover and the day after that, nobody knows he was ever even there. Freddie was there was less'n a year, and that was two years ago, and Freddie they remember. Still. Why is that?"

"I don't know," Hunter said.

"Neither do I," she said, "and that is a strange thing. I been married to the guy for almost six years now. We had some hard times, well, what we had, I thought we're going to have some hard times, sometimes, but we never did, and we always had a lot of good times, and you'd figure: I'd know him by now. I'd know what makes him tick.

"Well," she said, "I don't. Well, I *know* him. But what makes him tick, I don't know. He ticks, that's for sure. He ticks like a clock. But I sure don't under-*stand* him. No *sir,* I don't. He just baffles me. I wonder why that is."

"I don't know what makes Andrea tick," Hunter said. "I lived with her lots longer'n that. I still don't know."

"That isn't it," she said. "I know lots of guys. I

know how they think. I sit there and I take down what they say. I can tell. There're guys, guys're supposed to know a lot more'n Freddie. You know McGonigle, you met him, right? In the trial. Magoo."

"He was the one that had Lion?" Hunter said.

"Nah," she said, "Leonetti had somebody else. Wait a minute. I dunno. Magoo was Cronin's lawyer. Lion had, who the hell did Lion have? He had that motion to suppress. Big guy, nice dresser, pissed the Judge off something terrible, and he knew it and he didn't give a shit. It doesn't matter. Magoo's in that court all the time, and if it wasn't for the way he talked, you'd never even remember him at all, and this is a very successful guy that's made a lot of money and he's been coming in there probably for a hundred years, and I got to stop and think before I can tell you something about him. That's what I'm saying. Freddie's different."

"Magoo was the guy that had the goddamned motion to suppress the stuff we got on Cronin with the wiretaps," Hunter said.

"*Right*," she said.

"And he didn't win it when he could've," Hunter said. "I thought he was a lousy lawyer."

"He's got his good days and his bad days," she said. "I sit there every day, and that's the way it is with most of them. At the trial he had some of his good days."

"He had a whole lot of them," Hunter said. "I remember that kid they had, the Strike Force had, prosecuting those guys, and he went through those motions and everything like he was making sandwiches. 'This one I can't wait for, the trial.' And I told him, see, I was, I knew enough about Cronin, he's not gonna hang his hat on somebody, isn't gonna get his hat back to him, it's over, and I said: 'I'm not so sure.' But the federal guy was, boy, he was surer'n shit. And then we had the trial, and Cronin got his hat back, better'n brand new."

"You see what I mean?" she said. "What'd you spend with those guys? How many weeks?"

"The trial was just over five weeks," Hunter said.

"And they're killing you, right?" she said.

"Not me, so much," he said.

"They weren't doing you any good," she said.

"It would've been nicer if I'd had somebody up in front of me that could've won it," he said.

"And still," she said, "you had trouble remembering who was doing it to you. But not Freddie, and all he was was a guy standing around in a suit."

"Watching me," Hunter said. "Watching me very close."

"Nah," she said. "He doesn't watch guys. Freddie doesn't pay any attention to anybody. Just to Freddie. And maybe that's why it is."

"He's got a great line of shit," Hunter said.

"I don't think that's it," she said. "There's lots of guys with a great line of shit. And that's all they've got. They haven't got anything else going for them. All they can do is go around all the time, glad-handing people and acting like jerks, and nobody remembers them five minutes after they see them.

"And there's lots of guys too," she said, "that haven't got a great line of shit, but they know a lot of things, and they been to school and everything, and nobody remembers them, either. But there's very few guys that didn't finish high school, even, and then they were welders for a while down at Groton, and then they got to be foreman and then they got laid off, and didn't go back when they could've, and then on top of that, they dropped something else that was steady and're still making out better'n what they would've done if they did what everybody else would've done, like that. It's more'n a great line of shit, Mister Hunter," she said. "I don't know what it is, but it's surer'n shit more'n that. You know what he's making now?"

"A hundred grand," Hunter said.

"He's making over thirty-five thousand dollars a year," she said. "Thirty-five thousand dollars a year. The guy's a natural salesman, is all. He doesn't have to go out on the road and go after people. They call him up. He just sits there in his nice office and he talks on the phone. *He talks on the phone.*

"You know what he's doing?" she said.

"Making book, sounds like," Hunter said.

"He's getting fat," she said. "All he does is sit there and take the calls. People call him up, and the other guys, that're selling the same kind of things that Freddie's selling, all they get is what's left over after Freddie gets through answering the phone. When people want something, no matter what it is, if they know Freddie, they call Freddie. Look, if you wanted to buy a new car, maybe, or borrow some money, you think you'd go and call a guy that sells tape decks and tapes and stuff like that? A clean car? A genuine loan?

"You would not," she said. "You know why you wouldn't? Because *you* don't know Freddie. They, the people that Freddie knows, when they want something, they call him. I don't care what it is, they call Freddie.

"He's getting commissions on Cadillacs, now," she said. "He's sold so many of them. 'I told him,' he said to me, 'I called up Harry and I told him, I said: "Harry, look: I sold, I sent you five sure customers this month, and three last month, and every last one of them I seen driving around in a Coupe de Ville or better. There's two El Dorados in that group. And you're a very nice guy and everything, you take me out to dinner and buy me a few drinks. Not enough. Now on, I want a finder's fee." '

"So," she said, "now he gets a commission. One-half what the guy gets, from selling a Cadillac to a guy that called Freddie and wanted a Cadillac. Same thing with this guy he knows that sells real estate. Gets half the commission on the house. He's amazing. It's absolutely unbelievable. Everybody he knows, that calls him and wants to buy something, and he's got the money for it, Freddie knows some guy that's got it to sell and couldn't get rid of it until Freddie called him. He didn't even finish school. Look at me."

"Look at me," Hunter said.

"I graduated high school," she said. "I graduated, it was two years I was in business school. I graduated from that. Then the steno school. I've got, I went around asking people. And they told me, and I listened to them and everything, and I did what they said, and . . . I'm not bad-looking."

"Madeleine," he said.

"I'm not," she said. "I did everything they told me, and everything, except for one thing, about Freddie. And they all said: 'Don't marry the guy.' 'He doesn't know anything.' 'Just another guy.' 'Madeleine, you're special. You made yourself special if you weren't before.' 'He's nothing.' 'What is he? Another working stiff. You got an education. Worked hard for it.' My father said that, and he didn't even pay for it. 'Cost a lot of money. Play your cards right, you're gonna *make* a lot of money. Security. Probably, maybe as much's twenny thousand dollars a year.' 'Whaddaya want with a guy like this?' You should've heard my brothers. 'That what you're going to school for, all this time? Have a lot of babies for a bum like that? He's nothin', Mad, just nothin'. Just an ordinary guy.'

"Okay," she said, "he's an ordinary guy, then how come I'm so interested in him, huh? I can't leave him alone. How come that, I wonder.

"So," she said, "I did it. What everybody told me not to do, I did it. I went and married Freddie. It was, I'm not even sure he even ever asked me, but it was all right with him. The only thing was, I told him: 'I'm not having no kids, no kids whatsoever.' I told him, I said: 'Freddie, if all I wanted to do was, I wanted to spend all my time having babies and everything, then I would've done it instead of spending all that time doing the things I did. Because I didn't. But I did them. So, if you're not gonna like that, all right, and that's the way it is and everything. It goes. And another thing,' I says to him, 'I didn't do all of them things on account I wanted to support somebody, all right?'

"Get that," she said, "me saying that, to him. When he goes out in the rain, money falls on him. I didn't know that, then. 'You're gonna have to work. What you make's yours, and what I make's mine.' That was a great idea I had. 'You got to look out for yourself, all right? I'm willing to be your wife. You want a mealticket, get your ass someplace else.'

" 'Goes the other way too, I assume,' he says to me," she said. " 'Oh, sure.' I haven't got any brains. 'Sure it does.' Because, see, I didn't know anything. 'Okay,' he says, 'what you got is a deal.'

"I didn't quite frankly believe it," she said. "Not for one minute did I believe it, I was thinking: Boy, what I really should do here is get it in writing. But I didn't. I figured: We're gonna get married, and then in about a year, here's this guy, he's down the submarine base, all those guys ever think about's having kids and going bowling and stuff like that, and he's gonna start raising hell. But, all right, he says it's all right with him, I'm gonna take him at his word. And, you know something? He never, he never bothered me again about it. He's an amazing guy. I can't figure him out."

"He's probably got a girl," Hunter said.

"Uh, uh," Madeleine said. "Not him. Freddie doesn't need a girl. If he wants a woman, okay, all he's got to do, he's . . . , he hasn't got a girl."

"Okay," Hunter said.

"He doesn't need a girl," Madeleine said. "He's got at least fifty women, a hundred women, if he wants them. You remember Dickie Colisemo?"

"Was he on the Lion's case?" Hunter said.

"Yeah," she said. "He was Rossi's lawyer."

"The sharp-looking guy with the watch," Hunter said.

" 'Da warch,' " she said.

"Yup," Hunter said, "him I remember. You know something? I was going to buy one of those things. The dial keeps changing colors and everything."

"Yeah," she said.

"And you know why I didn't?" he said.

"Cost too much," she said.

"You know something?" Hunter said. "You know something, Madeleine?"

"I," she said, "I know a lot of things."

"Yeah," Hunter said. "Well, I know a lot of things I could say, too. But, no, it cost thirty-nine bucks, is what it cost. Thirty-nine American dollars. And here I was, there was a time when I figured, all I hadda do was hit some doubles, and it wasn't that long ago, either, I thought that. Just hit some doubles, and

maybe ten, a dozen homers a year, and . . , I just
didn't know anything. I thought if I could go to my
right where I was playing, I could go to my right fast
enough to play anyplace else, and that's when I found
out, there's faster leagues, and I couldn't go any faster.
But what I used to think was if I just kept on doing
what I was doing, I'd probably make about sixty or
seventy grand a year. I used to think that. But Jesus
Christ, I thought he was some kind of classy guy, and
he's got a forty-dollar watch. For Christ sake. Shit."

"Deke," she said, reaching out with her left hand
to touch his right wrist, "what kind of watch you wear,
that doesn't matter, you know."

"Does to you," Hunter said. "Does to everybody
else I know. Does to me."

"If it mattered to me . . . ," she said. "Look: it
doesn't matter. You know what Freddie wears? A
Timex. An electric Timex. And Dickie Colisemo, what
I was starting to say, you know what he drives? A
Mark Four. A cocoa Mark Four. New, every year. And
you know what his wife's got?"

"A bicycle," Hunter said.

"Another Mark Four," she said. "A silver Mark
Four. Now this is a guy that's got money. You ought
to see *her* when she goes out. The silver fox jacket,
the whole thing, I think she gets her hair done every
day. I mean, she is really done up. Platinum. *Nice*
figure. If you could see Dickie, and you didn't know
from seeing Dickie that Dickie had money, and
then you saw Lisa and you knew Lisa was Mrs. Dickie
Colisemo, you would know then that Dickie had
money."

"He's wired in," Hunter said. "Of course he's got
money."

"Around the end of December," she said, "lots of
people go out and buy evergreen trees and they bring
them back home and they put colored lights and stuff
on them, and then they give each other presents."

"Okay," Hunter said.

"Everybody doesn't have to be a cop in this world,
you know, Mister Hunter," she said.

"I know," he said.

"There's some people," she said, "that think there's another way to live, and as long as they don't do anything that's against the law, or anything, well . . ."

"That anybody can catch them at," Hunter said.

"Okay," she said, "that anybody can catch them at. It's all right. So what I started out to say, Dickie got this case on in front of the Judge, and he's in the other day, and afterwards he comes up to me and pretends like he's waiting for everybody else to get through, ordering transcripts, and then they all leave, and he says to me, Dickie says: 'You know, your husband there, you ought to do something about him.' So I told him: 'Gonna take more clout'n I've got, do something about Freddie.' And he says to me: 'I got more clout'n you've got.' And then he told me, he sent Lisa down, there's something the matter with the tape deck in her car, and the dealer told her, she was gonna have to wait a week for him to get the parts, and maybe Freddie could do something faster.

"Now that guy goes to the track with Freddie," Madeleine said. "When Rockingham's the only place that's open, he's got this kid he hired, and they take one of those brand-new Town Cars, and they have to leave about five o'clock in the morning, and this kid comes around and picks them up. They're not even awake. And they've got Thermos bottles of coffee, and Danish in the back, and they go up there and they watch the horses work out, and then they stay there all day and they watch the races and the kid waits with the car. The car's got a phone in it and everything, and then, when they're coming back, they start calling their offices and doing the whole day's business between four o'clock and dinnertime. So naturally, he's got this good customer of his, that he can't do anything for, and the guy only buys two Mark Fours a year from him, and he can't do something for him and he doesn't like telling him that. That he can't fix the guy's wife's tape deck. So, he doesn't. He sends him to Freddie.

"Her," Madeleine said. " 'You know what?' Dickie says to me. 'Freddie had the parts in stock. Son of a bitch. And I get out of court early, here, the other day, and I go home, and there is he, the son of a bitch, he's backing out of my driveway on me.

" 'Now,' Dickie says, 'he's not supposed to be doing that. Nobody asked him to do that, go around and start backing out of my driveway on me, the fucker. This friend of mine asked him, he didn't say anything about coming down and backing out of my driveway. He asked him, he told my wife to go down to Freddie's place and get her tape deck fixed, and that's supposed to be all. So, because I didn't want to have to listen to her anymore, her tape deck doesn't work, she can't listen to her Platters' tapes. "He was checking it out," she tells me. Oh, sure. I know what he's checking out. That son of a bitch. You better tell him, I don't go for this stuff, that he's really checking out. I know what he's checking out, and the next time somebody's tape deck gets fixed, it's gonna be *his* tape deck.' "

"Uh huh," Hunter said. "Lemme tell you something, that's gonna be more amazing: when a couple hard guys show up to shoot him, and the bullets bounce off."

"Never happen," she said. "Dickie is a gentleman."

"What's he got," Hunter said, "be such a gentleman about?"

"Deke," she said, "come on, now."

"Just out of curiosity, Mad," Hunter said, "and it's none of my business or anything, and you can tell me that if you want, but just out of curiosity . . ."

"Yeah?" she said.

"I dunno how curious I am, all of a sudden," Hunter said.

"Oh," she said.

"Well," Hunter said, "look: there's the Congressman. You're awful, you know an awful lot about how the Congressman thinks, and everything. You must've spent a lot of time with him, sometime or other. Then there's this guy, this Dickie. Him, too. And there's Freddie, and there's somebody else, and well, you know, I've been down here two times in the past month, and this is the third time, and once, *once,* I can see you."

"The Judge's been sitting late," she said. "There's a big backlog."

"On Sunday nights," Hunter said. "I would make book on this: I would bet more money'n I've got, he's the only federal judge in the world, holding court, Sunday nights."

"It's the trials, Deke," she said. "They sit day and night all week, and they all want the transcripts right off, and I have to come in and dictate my notes so they can have it. And they're all guilties, they're all convictions, so even the ones that don't want it every day, want it right after, so they can appeal."

"They're not *all* guilties," Hunter said.

"You had some bad luck on Rossi and Lion," she said.

"Okay," Hunter said.

"It takes time," she said.

"Turning out transcripts," he said.

"Cut it out, Deke," she said. "You haven't been down here that much."

"This is the third weekend," he said. "It will be."

"That isn't much," she said. "I didn't see you for a long time, this summer."

"Except for a couple of times," Hunter said.

"Twice," she said.

"Which I hadda practically break my ass to get," Hunter said.

"Deke," she said, "all right? Look, I'd rather see you'n anybody else in the world, all right? But, two times?"

"I was doing things," he said.

"I know that," she said. "I didn't say I didn't understand or anything. It was you that was complaining about me. You oughta understand too. I'm doing things."

"I couldn't get free," Hunter said. "I had three scumbags that went to trial on a mess of shit that they should've pleaded guilty to, and the Assistant DA that had it just fucked around with it and fucked around with it and fucked around with it some more, and then he finally won it and I was supposed to be grateful. And the family's down here, and I'm tearing down here every weekend and getting shit because I'm not tearing down here every night or something, I guess is what it was, and in the meantime what I really should be doing, I haven't got time to do, and that's find a guy that wants to stay lost. It's just like Lion's case: if there's something that's gonna end Friday night, it'll be my case, and it'll go to the jury, and it'll always be at least midnight before they come back with a verdict. *If* they do. It never fails. I never seen it to fail."

"That much I do know," she said.

"You oughta," he said. "That jury in the Lion case was out two days, it took them to ruin me."

"I didn't mind that," she said, smiling.

"Well," he said, "I did have something to take my mind off my troubles."

"In addition to which," she said, "it was a hell of a lot warmer in that hotel'n it was where we were tonight."

"The heat's been off there," he said. "It's chilly for September, and nobody's been there for a couple weeks."

"I'm not saying I minded," she said. "It was, it was just damp, was all."

"It's supposed to be damp," Hunter said.

She began to laugh, and the hostess, passing with the twelfth and thirteenth dinner customers of the evening, automatically smiled.

Sgt. Horace Carmody

☐ 5

THE SUPERIOR COURTHOUSE at Salem, Massachusetts, is old, and includes displays of the paper war-
rants issued for the hangings of witches. On the
morning of September 27, 1973, Deke Hunter found
a space for his unmarked, pale green cruiser on the
slanting part of the lot behind the granite Registry of
Deeds next door, and set the handbrake with minimal
confidence that it would hold. He went across the
asphalt driveway and up the stone steps and into the
brick courthouse, down the tiled hall between the pale
green walls, through the varnished doors, and into his
cubicle in the Office of the District Attorney.

There were two old veneer desks in the cubicle, and
two chairs. Horace Carmody, at fifty-one, sat in his
chair and observed Deke Hunter put his sport coat on
the hook. Carmody, five-feet-ten and one-eighty-one,
in a tweed sport coat and dark green slacks, pushed
his swivel chair back until it touched the varnished
wooden part of the partition. Then he leaned back
until his gray crewcut touched the frosted glass of the
upper half of the partition, and clasped his hands
across his belly. "What you oughta do," Carmody said,
"you oughta get yourself a job in a bank. You'd do
great inna bank. You work in a bank, hell, nobody
knows what the hell he's doing in a bank. You come
staggering in around noontime, like you do here, nobody'd even notice."

"It's not even ten," Hunter said.

"Nothing happens in a bank, is why," Carmody
said. "The bastards haven't even got anything to do,

26

unless they're getting held up or something. You come in late in the morning, everybody just thinks you're some kind of a wheel or something. You'd do great in a bank."

"I had enough stuff to do with banks," Hunter said.

"Around here, on the other hand," Carmody said, "certain people tend to get a little pissed off."

"Like who," Hunter said, sitting down. "Tell me who's pissed off."

"Mister Shanley is pissed off," Carmody said.

"Oh," Hunter said, "for a minute, there, I thought it'd be something important. He knows what he can do, and if he doesn't, I can tell him. And it won't take me long, either. Little shapers like that. Prick. I don't worry about things like that. I had some things I hadda do."

"Brave words," Carmody said. "He's got some things he's got to do, too. So he said, anyway. Like, one of them is, he was in about nine-fifteen, looking for you. He was trying to find you, was what he was trying to do. Seems like he's got a couple attorneys and counselors-at-law, upstairs there, hollering and yelling at the Judge about how their fellows got this, what is it, this constitutional right to go to jail right off, instead of stalling around all the time and running around on the street doing more things they oughta get put in jail for."

"He say who it was?" Hunter said.

"Fat John Killilea," Carmody said, "and the equally learned Sam Wyman."

"Uh huh," Hunter said. "Well, it was bound to happen, I guess. The question was just when it was going to happen."

"Fat John's ordinarily not that eager to say bye-bye to his boys," Carmody said.

"Shit," Hunter said, "neither's Sam Wyman. But they know something about this one, and it's different."

"Is this the Peabody thing?" Carmody said.

"Nah," Hunter said. "This is the Danvers National, last March twenty-second. Three guys inside, one guy outside, a little over forty thousand dollars."

"Leaper Donovan?" Carmody said.

"Leaper Donovan with a shotgun about a foot long in his paws, and a couple pounds of cotton in his cheeks, and a bright red stocking hat on his bald old head," Hunter said. "Andy Marr with his trusty Buntline Special Thirty-Eight and a big white bandage on his nose and the collar of his jacket turned up so you almost couldn't see that big purple birthmark he's got on his neck under his right ear. And Teddy Donnelly with that forty-five automatic he's used about nine different times to make withdrawals and it's gotten so familiar to guys now that they use the pictures of it when they train the new tellers now: 'Now, you assholes, this here's a picture of Teddy Donnelly with his mirror sunglasses on and his felt hat and his windbreaker, and if you look closely at his right hand, you'll see he's got a gun in it that's about the same size as, oh, a Studebaker. Now when you see Teddy, or somebody that looks something like Teddy, or even somebody that maybe isn't quite as big, or doesn't have a gun that's quite as big as this or a different color or something shiny, you can be pretty sure that you are getting yourself held up. Now the sensible thing to do, when you see Teddy or somebody like Teddy, is give the guy what he wants, which is the money. Because old Teddy has been known to take that thing and make a loud noise with it, and I am here to tell you, ladies and gentlemen, that item can cut off your phone service for you, on a permanent basis, and it won't do your vacation plans any good either.'"

"You got pictures of them," Carmody said, "or is Danvers another one of those nice refined little banks where they don't believe in the twentieth century and people that rob banks?"

"No," Hunter said, "they had the cameras all right. We got pictures up the yin-yang, and they're good pictures, too. Leaper's're so good he should order enlargements for his mother. And I saw Andy down at the House of Correction, there, and I told him: 'Andy, they're beautiful. Very good likeness. You want, I'll get you some blow-ups and you can send them out to the drugstore and have them tinted for your personal use. Tell you what: I'll get two copies, and that way you can give them to all of your friends.' Teddy's're pretty good, too. Specially good of the gun. We didn't get any of Billy, of course, since he was out in the car all the time, listening to the radio and admiring the walnut dashboard, but then we did get Billy himself, and Billy made a good Act of Contrition and he's gonna testify, so we don't really need much in the way of pictures of Billy."

"So what's the problem?" Carmody said. "Go to trial with the bastards and put them away."

"You mean: the problem in addition to Assistant District Attorney Richard J. Shanley?" Hunter said. "Keeping in mind that that guy could fuck up a two-car funeral, you mean: some other problem? Very simple. We got pictures and we got eyewitnesses and we got a rat to tell us everything the other people didn't see, and we got lots more stuff besides, but we haven't got Teddy Donnelly. We just have not got Teddy. We grabbed Billy right off, because he went where he always goes after he does something, and that's the only time he goes there: down to the Indian Club off of Winter Street in Lawrence, and gets himself stiff as a boot. We got Leaper and Andy because Billy's not careful when he's getting over being scared by getting stiff, and he told us where to find them, and we went to the Howard Johnson Motel in Natick and knocked on the door of Room One-Twenty-Six, and there were the two of them, sitting inside and counting the fives and tens that they got for seventy-five cents on the dollar from the guy that bought the actual loot from them. And we arrested them, too. Then we counted up all the guys we arrested, and we looked in the closet and everything, under the bed, in the trunk of the car, everywhere, and the most we came up with was three. And not one of those three guys was Teddy Donnelly. Nope, you can't fool us. We have three guys, and it was four of them that did it, and one of them was Teddy, and Teddy we did not get.

"Now," Hunter said, "I wouldn't want you to start thinking that your diligent and hardworking Massachusetts State Police are not conducting a full-scale,

no-holds-barred investigation to determine the present
whereabouts of the said Edward M. Donnelly, wanted
for questioning in connection with the said robbery.
Or that we are not being aided by the full and complete cooperation of the Federal Bureau of Investigation, which has a warrant for his arrest on charges of
unlawful flight to avoid prosecution for bank robbery
while armed. Why," Hunter said, "we've even got a
Prevent Departure, Detain On Arrival notice with
the watchful officers of the United States Customs
Service, who stand guard at all points of exit from the
United States of God-blessed America.

"We know what he looks like," Hunter said, "and
he's the kind of guy that doesn't exactly blend into
a crowd, with that big nose of his all decorated with
rum-blossoms and that scar he got on his cheek when
he got in a fight in Cherry Hill, and that tattoo that
he got on his left arm, the one of the fire-breathing
dragon, when he was in the Marines in World War
Two. He's six-two, almost, and he goes about two
hundred pounds, when he's thin, and more'n that when
he isn't, and he's been known to play the horses now
and then, and he's got a girlfriend in addition to his
wife, that he hasn't seen for about a hundred years,
and her name is Lenore and she's a cocktail waitress
in Haverhill and she hasn't budged out of Haverhill in
the past six months. Which we know because that's
how long we've been watching her. The only thing,
really, that your tireless State Police don't know about
Teddy Donnelly is where the fuck Teddy Donnelly is.
That's what we don't know, and that's why we've had
Billy Gillis sweating large droplets in a safe place since
we caught him in the Indian Club with his belly full of
Carstairs and his brains all scrambled on the evening
of last March twenty-second."

"Uh," Carmody said.

"And I personally," Hunter said, "am plumb fucking
out of ideas of things to try next. First, right after we
got his buddies, there, I figured if we didn't get him in
a week or so, we'd get him in a couple months, or at
least he'd surface, because he'd run out of money.
Teddy couldn't've had more'n eight or nine grand in

his pants when he screwed, because Billy and Andy and Leaper had almost twenty-three on them when they got tossed. And Teddy has been known to spend a dollar or two in his time, which is very hard to do if you haven't got it. So I thought: in a couple or three months, Teddy's gonna smoke himself out and go rob another bank or something with some new guys that he doesn't know so well, and maybe then we'll get him. It was March, like I say, when I figured that, but if Teddy's been out on a job since then, it must've been Kansas because I sure didn't hear about it."

"He didn't even send you a postcard," Carmody said.

"Didn't write, didn't call, I've been in tears every night," Hunter said. "I've also been talking to some guys, asking around, you know, if anybody's seen my old pal Teddy and how come he never drops around to see me no more, and I haven't gotten shit for it."

"So try the two guys you got," Carmody said. "Shit, if you haven't got him, you haven't got him. Three out of four ain't bad."

"Not such a hot idea, when you think about it," Hunter said. "It looks okay, when you start. What the hell, you go with what you got. These guys're in custody. You don't try them, you lose them. But the first time I heard that idea, it was from the eminent prosecutor, Mister Shanley, and when Richard Shanley says something, and it sounds good to me, I start wondering if maybe all of a sudden I'm not traveling with a full seabag anymore. So I start thinking about Billy, and how scared he is, that Teddy's gonna jump out of the bushes the day Billy comes in to sing for us and make a big hole in old Billy. And then about how Billy's gonna react when he finds out it's not just once he's gonna have to do it, it's twice.

"Now how the hell Billy ever got into the bank-robbing business, I'll never know," Hunter said. "He just isn't your basic hard-nosed desperado, that eats nails and fishhooks for breakfast and washes them down with horse piss. He's a pretty good hand with a wheel, but there's lots of guys that drive cars pretty well, and don't get to thinking they oughta start driving them for guys that rob banks, because that's risky. Billy doesn't like risks. 'Why'd you do it, you jerk?' I asked him. 'For the money.' he says, which is logical, I guess, but there's no money in what he's got to do now if he wants to keep his three-to-five in out-of-the-way places and not get twenty big ones in Walpole with the guys that hired him and now they don't like him anymore. The trouble with throwing separate parties for Leaper and Andy and then one for Teddy, if we ever catch the bastard, is that we've pretty much got to invite Billy to all of them, and I really don't think he can deliver it twice without blowing something."

"Plus which," Carmody said, "if he's really scared of Teddy . . ."

". . . he can change enough stuff the second time through to make it look like he was lying the first time, or he's lying the second time, and walk the bastard and save his own skin," Hunter said. "Exactly what's worrying me. Billy's not really scared of Leaper. Leaper's had guys beaten up, but he doesn't like bloodshed, or something, I guess. Andy's a fresh little fucker, but he doesn't shoot people. Andy's done a lot of time, and he takes it as it comes. But Billy's scared of Teddy, and there isn't much that's true that I can tell him to make him feel better. And he won't believe the lies I could make up. Teddy's a bad bastard from the word Go, and Billy's not stupid enough to buy any story that Teddy's joined the convent.

"Now Shanley," Hunter said, "you know how he is. He never sees anybody else's difficulties. I said that to him, about how Billy's liable to blow his lines in the first trial, if Teddy's still on the loose, looking around for someone to shoot, and it didn't make any impression on him. You know something? The more I see of that kid, the more I don't like him."

"He was all right when he came in," Carmody said. "I had a couple of things with him, and he handled them well."

"That's when he was hungry," Hunter said. "When he came in, I thought the same thing. Just as eager as he could be. But now, I think, he's turning out different. All of a sudden he's running around, and he's doing this and he's doing that, and if you want to talk to him today, he can't do it. He's got to be over in Lynn, or something, making a goddamned speech.

"You know what I did last week?" Hunter said. "I tried to see him last week, because after all, it's not exactly news that there's a new session coming up, and it just might happen some of the cases we've got indicted, well, maybe somebody might want to try some of them. So, and I've got about six files that've got his name where it says 'Prosecutor' on them, okay? Now you know me, Horace. I'm a respectful guy. I know he's got plans to be Attorney General, or Pope or something. How do I know that, about this guy that's an Assistant and he's supposed to be trying cases only he hasn't got time? Because he told me. 'Deke, some day I am gonna be the Attorney General.' Right, and I'm gonna be Queen Wilhelmina of Holland if I can just find a guy to do the operation and put the silicone in.

"So," Hunter said, "last week, and I haven't got a whole world of confidence in this kid either, you know? I thought . . . , it doesn't matter what I thought. He didn't have time to go over the cases. Now tell me: how'd he look when he came in this morning, huh?"

"Very worried," Carmody said. "Said he might have a problem with this thing."

"Because last week, when he should've been thinking about it," Hunter said, "he was spending all his time in the civil session, trying that case with the tenement fire that he's gonna make a nice fat fee out of. See, that's what I mean. When he first came in here, he got all the shit cases, and I bet he put fifty of those lowlife Puerto Ricans in the jug for beating on their wives and each other, and they got to thinking he was Charlie Tiger. So the building goes up and all their pet rats die, and who's the guy they hire to get them at least five thousand dollars a rat? Richard J. Shanley, the great courtroom lawyer.

"You give that guy one of his own cases," Hunter

said, "one of those private cases that he never would've gotten if he wasn't in here, making a lot of noise, and he will work his ass off. But the criminal stuff that got him the cases, that you got to spoon-feed him. He makes twelve grand a year off of this job, and thirty grand a year off the other stuff, and he doesn't give us any time whatsoever, and I think it stinks."

"He's won some things," Carmody said.

"He did," Hunter said. "He'll win again. He'll win this one, probably. Shit, my dog could try this case and win it, and I haven't even got a dog. I hadda fight the Bureau to a standstill to keep this State. You think there's some reason, they wanna make it federal? Like, maybe, it's a sure winner? Course he'll win some more. Because he gets good stuff. So, consequently, he now thinks he's a regular magician, and he can roll around in shit and come up smelling like aftershave.

"I hate guys like that," Hunter said. "Look, tell one he won, that you had or anybody else had, that really did you some good, all right? Tell me that. One case he won, that you were really worried about, that maybe somebody else would've lost."

"That's the way George Samuels used to talk, when I knew him," Carmody said. " 'Don't come in here, you're bragging around you convicted some guilty bastard. When I'm gonna listen to you all full of yourself is when you convicted somebody that was *innocent*. Some fox in the grass that *didn't* do it. Then talk to me.' No, I only had Shanley on some small shit. But he was all right, though."

"When was that?" Hunter said.

"Couple, three years ago," Carmody said. "Maybe, actually it was almost three years ago. When he first came in here and they were breaking him in on misdemeanors."

"Yeah," Hunter said. "That's what I thought. Before he decided his hands're quicker'n everybody else's eyes. You know what did it to him? You know what did it to him? You know what ruined Shanley? It was the thing with the four coons, there, the gang bang. Remember that? Four coons, grabbed a girl up at Lowell Tech. That was the one that wrecked Shanley."

"Ryan was gonna try that case, I thought," Carmody said.

"It was Ryan's case," Hunter said, "and did he ever have the wind up him."

"Never saw anybody like Ryan for hating boogies," Carmody said.

"I know it," Hunter said. "He's almost sick about it."

"Ryan's an old man," Carmody said. "That's what he is, and that's all he knows. He's about sixty years old, and he never got married, and he stayed home and took care of his mother, and the same thing happened to him that happens to all the women that do the same thing. The guy wouldn't know how to get laid if you gave him a book about how to do it. What he'd do is nail you for distributing the book."

"He knows how to go after guys, though," Hunter said.

"Ryan thinks everybody in the world's getting laid except him," Carmody said. "I see him. He takes up the collection down to Saint Margaret's. Every Mass. That's the kind of thing that Ryan likes, so he can go through the envelopes out in the vestry and see how much everybody else gives. Reads every single one of them. I remember once, somebody was talking about how Ryan was trying a bad check case, and they had about nine hundred pieces of paper for exhibits, deposit tickets, all that shit. And Ryan's going through them like they're just pages in the morning paper. He knew them all cold. 'How can he do that?' guy says to me. I knew how: got his practice memorizing what everybody in the parish gave in the envelope. Ryan doesn't think there's any such thing as something you don't need to know because it doesn't mean anything.

"Also," Carmody said, "he is dirt cheap. Ryan don't use no envelope, not on your life. Ryan drops in a quarter, and he doesn't pay seat money, either. 'The hell, Horace, I contribute the labor, right?' I caught him at it one day, I came in late and used the side door."

"He can still go after those coons," Hunter said.

"He thinks they're getting laid," Carmody said. "He thinks they're the principal guys that're getting laid, and he never did. I remember, boy, if you wanted to see a guy go after somebody, about eight years ago we had this lockpicker in here. Took us about three years to do it, too, you think Donnelly's giving you trouble after six months.

"Everybody knew who she was, and what she was doing," Carmody said. "It was this woman, this big, fierce-looking, mean woman. About, I dunno, fifty-five or so. Looked almost like a man. And she was doing it in this crummy motel about six miles out of town, everybody knew it, and god*damned* if we could catch her at it. She'd rent the room, and the girl'd show up and go in, and we just never got enough to get a warrant and go in and grab her at it. And the girls wouldn't talk, either, afterwards, and I bet we tried to get it out of a dozen of them. Because, sooner or later, one of them was going to bleed to death in there. It's a wonder they didn't all get infected anyway. Filthy goddamned place.

"Well," Carmody said, "she finally slipped up, and we got this kid that was about sixteen and her boyfriend knocked her up and the lockpicker hurt her so she hadda go in the hospital. She was a very tough kid. She was pissed off, is what she was. So she gave us some names, and there were a couple more that'd talk, too, and we grabbed the old bitch, and did Ryan ever have a time with that one. Jesus. It was enough to scare you, the way he went after her. I mean, it's okay to win. It's a hell of a lot better'n losing. But with him? I dunno. He made me nervous."

"He made those coons nervous too," Hunter said. "You know something? When it was Ryan's case, they weren't even gonna try the thing till Shanley got it."

"Was that when Ryan had the prostate?" Carmody said.

"Yeah," Hunter said.

"That's from not getting laid," Carmody said.

"Well, if I'd've known that, and known what that case was gonna do to Shanley," Hunter said, "I would've fixed the guy up with something. Because that was the end of the Golden Dream. Before, Shanley thought he was supposed to come in here and put guys in jail for doing things. After, all he wanted to do was get his name in the paper."

"Dave Wyatt was on that," Carmody said. "Poor son of a bitch. Never knew he had a thing wrong with him, and then he wakes up one day and his chest is tight, and the next thing you know, they're closing him up, because he's so full of it. Didn't hesitate to talk about it, either. 'Did the right thing. Might's well go this way, let them cut me off, inch by inch.' Great guy he was. Wyatt told me the kid did a good job."

"Look," Hunter said, "it would've been hard to do a bad job. You would've hadda work at it. You ask him, you go up to Shanley now, though, and you ask him, and he'll tell you he won it and it was a damned close thing. Which is bullshit. Utter bullshit. Look, right? The head nigger had Jimma Dacey."

"Oh," Carmody said.

"Jimma Dacey," Hunter said. "And the rest of them had some other guys. One of them had a guy from Boston that's a very classy coon himself. Although, and Dave said that to me at the time, it probably wasn't the brightest thing the guy ever did, getting himself a colored lawyer for a case like that in this county. But anyway, they all let Dacey run it."

"That beauty," Carmody said. "There is something I will never figure out. He's got to make about nine million dollars a year, stomping around and foaming at the mouth, and the stupid guys think he's great, and he is. He's the best thing, on defense, ever happened to the Commonwealth's case. Can't do one damned thing for anybody except rant and rave. He gets the jury so pissed off the only reason it takes them an hour to find the guy guilty is, they stay out forty minutes after they got a verdict, make it look good."

"That was the second time I worked a case, had him on it," Hunter said. "The first time, I was scared shitless. Six years in a bluebird, hiding in the bushes and waiting for dentists to go by me too fast in their Jaguars, grabbing guys for driving under so drunk they couldn't even ask me what the problem was, and then trying to convince me, I should let them drive home and kill themselves and a few other people so I could spend the rest of the night watching people cut them out of wrecks. Now I'm finally out of the cruiser. I got a jacket on and everything. I'm gonna be a god-damned *detective*. No more pulling guys over in the middle of the night and wondering when I walk up behind their cars if this's gonna be the one that shoots me in the belly when I ask him for his license. Oh my God.

"So," Hunter said, "I got this shitty little gas station stick-up. There was no way in the world the guy's gonna get off. I went in his house. I had everything on him. Prints. Positive make. Everything. I could've put this guy away if he'd had Flee Bailey sitting next to him. And I go in, with a warrant, naturally, and you know what he does? He jumps me. So I beat the living shit out of him, and then when he comes up for trial here, I'm all lathered up again. This's my first real trial. I want to win it. Jimma's defending the guy.

"So," Hunter said, "they tried it. They didn't have any business trying it. Ryan told me that. That made me jumpier. I started thinking: Well, then, they must have something we don't know about, if they're trying it. See, I didn't know Jimma then. He always tries everything. Whether he's got anything to try or not.

"And the jury goes out," Hunter said. "I see the old deputy standing around in the hall. I was practically pissing down my leg. I thought I was gonna throw up. So I went up to him, and I said: 'You been around. How's it look?' And he looks at me. 'Look,' he says, 'when you got Jimma, they find the guy guilty on the way up the stairs. I figure they'll hold out for lunch. If they're still out at one, they get a ham sandwich and a paper cup with coffee in it. From the drugstore. This is an experienced jury, and it's a cheap one. There's five of the guys on it that sat on a Breathalyzer thing last week, a Driving Under, and the defendant had a point-eighteen. He was practically in a coma when they arrested him, and those guys stayed out for an hour and a half for the god-damned sandwich. Forget it. They'll hook him. They'll just make you wait for it.' And he was right," Hunter said. "That's exactly what they did."

"That girl?" Hunter said. "The one the coons got. She was in the hospital for over two months, after those vicious cocksuckers got through with her. They hadda practically rebuild her box. She had a broken arm. They finally decided, they couldn't save any of her teeth, and they put in a complete set of false ones. She had her cheekbones broken and one of the broken ends come out through the skin. She had to have plastic surgery on her face, and she almost lost one of her eyes. Detached retina. Multiple hematomas. About three concussions. Subdural hematoma. They got her when she was going home from the library and they dragged her off into the woods, and then when they were through with her, one of them took this tree branch and stuck it up her cunt.

"I think she was still a mental case when they tried the thing," Hunter said. "They had to take a recess about every ten minutes, even when she was on direct. And I will say that for Shanley: he handled her very well. Very patient. Very calm. Very low-key. But she was crying and everything. It was awful. They pulled me off what I was working on, so I could help Dave with that thing, and I really wished they didn't, it was so bad. That poor kid. The only thing she ever did was go to school and study hard, and for that she won those bastards. The whole group of them didn't have the intelligence of a chimpanzee, sat there staring at her and making faces when she said something. Bastards.

"Dacey gets her on cross," Hunter said. " 'And now, Miss Whatchamacallit, is it? No? It's Mrs. Whatchamacallit? Well, Mrs. Whatchamacallit, it wasn't Mrs. Whatchamacallit at the time of this alleged incident, now, was it? It was Miss Whatchamacallit then, wasn't it?"

"The jury couldn't believe it," Hunter said. "You're not fooling old Jimma, no sir. He knows the victim was living with a kid when his coons throttled her.

He's gonna try the case on *consent*. 'No rape at all, ladies and gentlemen of the jury.' Just a sex-starved white girl that was living with her boyfriend for about three months before the night the coons did it to her, and they're engaged and everything. . . ."

"You know what I did?" Carmody said. "I got born too soon, is what I did. You could get a piece of ass when I got out of the service. You could. You hadda practically wear yourself down to a nub to do it, or else you could pay for it, or else you could do without it. And if you got it, and you didn't pay for it, you hadda sweat like a bastard for a month, she had her period. Twenty years too early, was my problem. I never got anything right."

"You know what that kid did?" Hunter said. "After all that? She's practically useless. She's under some kind of drugs all the time. She can't have kids. God only knows what she thinks about when she's going to bed with a guy after that. The kid *still* marries her. Just like they planned."

"He'll regret it," Carmody said.

"Hey," Hunter said.

"He will," Carmody said. "That's a dumb thing to do, go around borrowing trouble like that. Look, the surest way in the world that I know about, make a broad hate your guts, is get her pregnant and then marry her. They never forgive you for it. The ones that don't forgive you the longest are the ones, they weren't pregnant at all, just late on their period.

"What he did," Carmody said, "what he did is worse. Every day she looks at him, she'll be thinking about what happened to her, and then he did this, and she'll hate him for it, is all. Just hate him for it."

"She wasn't pregnant," Hunter said. "When they got her to the hospital, they flushed her out."

"Worse," Carmody said. "That's what I said. It's worse. I pity him. I pity that kid. She's gonna spend the rest of her life getting even with him for what him and them niggers did to her."

"I thought it was a damned decent thing to do," Hunter said. "I still do."

"That kind of damned decent thing can take a lot

out of a man," Carmody said. "You spend your whole life doing somebody a favor, it can get to you after a while. Wears you down."

"Yeah," Hunter said. "Well, you should've heard old Jimma anyways. She led them niggers on, is what she did. She went out and she scouted up those four coons that're total strangers to her and all about ten years older'n she is, and she snuggled right up to them guys and said to them: 'Come on, fellas, take me out in the woods and stick your big black hogs in my mouth and fuck me about twelve times and then break every bone in my body. That's what I go for.' He actually *said* it to her: 'Are you quite sure, Mrs. Whatchamacallit, you didn't lead them on?'"

"Maybe she did," Carmody said.

"Come on," Hunter said.

"There's more'n one way of doing things like that," Carmody said. "That's what I mean about Ryan. You think nobody ever led Ryan on? She didn't know she was doing it, but she did it. She knew she was doing it, but she didn't mean to do it. Something. Them guys, most guys've got a way of watching people pretty close. Particularly them spades. That's how come they can hook all those cameras and stuff the minute somebody goes out for a few minutes and doesn't let the dog in. They can tell. They probably found out, she was living with a guy, and they probably figured, they could do it and if she did call the cops, they could beat it."

"Oh for Christ sake," Hunter said.

"I didn't say they were smart, thinking that," Carmody said. "I said they were probably thinking that. They watch all the time. That doesn't make them smart. It just means they're always on the lookout. Sometimes they get things wrong. They don't understand what they're watching. They see it, but they don't get it right. They don't understand what it means, but they know what it is. They're still watching, just the same.

"You take a look around those METCO towns," Carmody said. "All the goddamned liberals started bringing the black kids out in buses, so they can learn how to play polo and everything, just like we did. Take a look at them, because the next thing they did, they got all the black kids' mothers out there for tea and cookies, and their boyfriends, too. Parent-Teachers'. And them spades go riding around out there in Weston, they never saw anything like that before in their lives. They didn't even know Weston was *there*. 'Man, look at all this good shit these guys got.' And the next thing you know, they're back on the holiday weekend with a pry-bar for the back door and a dent-puller for the ignition on the Thunderbird. You want to learn something about human nature, you just go and check the B and E stats they got in those towns, for before they had the boogies in, and for after."

"I played a lot of ball with black guys," Hunter said. "I ate a lot of greasy food with black guys, and drank a certain amount of cheap beer with them, too, and I always got along with them all right."

"Okay," Carmody said, "don't make any difference to me. But I still say, there's some scouts around in this world, and when somebody starts getting ideas about making things easy for them, well, I don't like things where you just go out and start something and get everybody all stirred up when they weren't, before. And you don't know what you're doing but you go ahead and do it anyway. She probably got those guys all stirred up."

"She practically had hysterics on the stand," Hunter said.

"Maybe she was also dumb," Carmody said, "dumb like them. I been at this a long time. I've seen lots of people that got themselves into a whole mess of very dangerous shit that somebody like me had to go around and drag them out of, because they were too damned dumb to see they were getting themselves into the shit in the first place. It still counts even though the only reason you did it was that you're too goddamned stupid to know what was going to happen to you. Probably walking around all over the place with one of those miniskirts on, and no bra, tits bouncing around, you get a gust of wind and you can see the promised

land, and it just never went through her head, maybe
some big strong bastards're gonna get a look and figure she's good for it. There's lots of dumb people,
Deke. That's what keeps me and you in business.
Never catch the smart ones."

"Lemme tell you something," Hunter said, "if I ever
do run across a smart one, I'm gonna do my best to
make damned straight sure Shanley doesn't try him.
Because that's the thing that made Shanley the big
honcho trial lawyer. It was all Ryan's fault, getting
sick like that. He ruined the kid."

"The kid don't know he's ruined, though," Carmody
said. "What're you gonna tell him when he comes
down here and says the case's set down for trial and
where the hell were you this morning when he needed
to talk to you?"

"Horace," Hunter said, "I had car trouble. Even a
cop can have car trouble. I checked the regulations
and it's right in there."

"What's the matter with your car?" Carmody said.

"What's the matter with my life?" Hunter said.
"My father-in-law's the problem with my car. You remember last year, I tore the muffler out? I went down
to Weekapaug and got his goddamned boat and hitched
it onto my car and started pulling it up here, and
there's this huge crown on the beach road where the
sand blows away from the ruts. Well, that load on the
back was just enough so I tore the muffler out, and it
cost me a hundred bucks."

"Yeah," Carmody said.

"I went down there yesterday afternoon," Hunter
said. "Guess why: I was closing up my father-in-law's
cottage and bringing his boat up. Called me up last
Friday. All over me like a new suit. Didn't I think it
was pretty near time when we might get some frost
and maybe I better shut the water off. Appreciate it if
I'd put kerosene in the crappers. Suppose I could
tighten the hinges on the back door. I finally said to
my wife: "Whyn't he do some of those things himself,
you know?" It's his stuff, not mine.

"Well," Hunter said, "he can't. He's in Florida. He's
been in Florida since the day after Labor Day, or

headed there, at least. He likes to watch spring training, so he gets there by the middle of September before they've even played the World Series, for Christ
sake.

" 'You wanted him to leave,' she says to me. I did.
He was driving me nuts. He drives me nuts every
year. She's always telling me, it'll be ours some day,
and what a great guy he actually thinks I am. Which
he does, like shit. And I'm fixing the roof, and I'm
painting the porch, and I'm putting putty on the goddamned windows, and what's he doing? He's 'keeping
me company.' Every night I get to stand guard, the
little shits that come down to Misquamicut on the
bikes don't get stoned and come by and rape everybody in their beds. Because I'm a cop, see? 'Feel a
heck of a lot better when you can join us for
the weekends, Deke.' Oh, it's beautiful. He had this
heart attack about ten years ago, when he was going
someplace on some big deal, or else maybe he was
sitting next to a guy on a plane that had it, and he got
frightened. I dunno. But the result is, he can't do
nothing heavy. So he's sitting on the porch, with the
ballgame on, and I'm running around like I was three
guys or something. Sure, I'm gonna get the place. The
wife and kids, they get a nice summer, they go swimming every day and they take the boat to the pond
and go fishing and it's very nice for them. But during
the week I can cook my own food and wash my own
drawers, and Friday nights I get to sit in traffic for
about four hours and sweat my balls off, so I can do
the same thing coming back Sunday night. So I can
spend all the time in between doing work he can't do
and 's too cheap to pay somebody to do it for him.
You know what's the best thing to do? Get yourself a
nice heart attack while you're still young enough to
enjoy it. It's great. It's better'n having slaves.

"So the boat was still there," Hunter said. "I've been
dodging it and dodging it and dodging it, and I figure,
I wait long long enough, he'll hire somebody go put
the thing away for the winter. It's not like anybody's
gonna be using it, for Christ sake, and I don't want the
fucking thing sitting in my yard for the next eight or

nine months. But, nope. No such luck. And he out-waited me putting the boards up on the windows, and I said to her: 'Why didn't he take the fucking boat? You bitch every time it snows, I haven't got it in the garage instead of my own car, which I paid for. How come I'm supposed to take care of his stuff all the time and let my own stuff just go straight to hell? Well, he didn't take the boat because he got himself a new Grand Ville last year and somehow it always slips his mind, he's gonna need a trailer hitch on the thing if he's gonna take the boat out. And the stuff in the place that gets all mildew if you leave it there in the winter, the blankets and everything, he didn't do anything about that stuff, either. No room for it. Besides, he's going to Florida. He doesn't need blankets.

" 'I tore the muffler out of the car last year,' I says to her, 'snaking that fuckin' boat out of there.' 'There's no need to swear,' she says. See, that's another thing he doesn't do. Once I think he said: 'Damn.' I'm not sure. Of course he doesn't swear. The hell's he got to swear about? I do all his dirty work for him. So, and this and that, and I finally said, 'I'll go down there.' And I did.

"As a result of which," Hunter said, "I tore the muffler out of my car again. And in addition to which, it was raining. Everything I couldn't get in the car, I put in the boat. I put the tarp over it. The tarp didn't fit right. The rain went in around the tarp all the time I was driving, and everything got all wet. Ever smell a wet pillow?"

"I tell you what," Carmody said, "if the urge ever comes over me, I'll call you up."

"Do that," Hunter said. "I got, I think, nine of them. And there's some curtains and tablecloths and stuff, and a whole box of cereal and canned goods that I took out of the cupboards, and that's all wet. Every mile I drove, the rain was blowing in under the tarp, and the carbon monoxide was coming in through the windows, and I'm getting sicker and sicker and wetter and wetter because of course I got to drive with the windows open, and when I got home, she wakes up. Tells me I'm late. I knew that. Did I board up the windows? No, I got to go back down there next week-end and do that, and she tells me how the vandals'll get in before I do. Then this morning I went down to Beach's, and Wally wrote me up a new muffler on the warranty, which he is not supposed to do, and you know something? If Shanley wants to be pissed off at somebody, he couldn't've picked a worse guy than me."

"Look," Carmody said, "do me a favor, all right? Do this: when Shanley comes down here all in a sweat, tell him you and me're gonna see Charlie Thomas and maybe find out where Donnelly is for him. Okay?"

"Is he out again?" Hunter said. "What the hell's Charlie want?"

"Dunno," Carmody said. "Called me up and said there's a couple things I might be interested in. Charlie wants to see you about a couple of things, you go see Charlie. He's a little daffy, but he doesn't lie."

"Bet he doesn't know shit about Teddy, though," Hunter said.

"Almost certainly doesn't," Carmody said. "But Shanley doesn't know that, and it'll calm him down and give you a little more time to think of somebody who might know something, which is better'n where you're headed now."

"True," Hunter said. "Right now I'm not headed anywhere."

Andrea Hunter

ON THE EVENING OF SEPTEMBER 27, 1973, Andrea Hunter gazed through the doors of the Sears store at the Dedham Mall, and gnawed at the inside of her right cheek. She was thirty years old. She weighed just over one hundred pounds, as she had when she was a cheerleader in a heavy white sweater and a short red skirt and red tights at East Bridgewater High School, starting in the fall of 1956, and her muscles, when she was not moving purposefully, seemed also to have retained the vivacious mannerisms she had learned then. There was always the trace of a smile at her mouth, and when someone spoke to her, she tilted her head to the right and raised her eyebrows, and her blonde hair flipped at the ends. She wore white blouses with small, round collars, and blouses with small prints of clocks, and antique cars, and strawberries, and apples. She wore a gold circle pin with those blouses, and she wore slacks in public, instead of jeans. "What we really need," she said, "is a new one."

"Look," Hunter said, "what we really need is the money to pay off the one we got, that isn't paid for yet, and then some more money, to fix it with."

"It's paid for, Deke," she said, as people went by with sleeping babies in their arms and crying children in strollers and surly children held, protesting, by the hand. The sound system played selections from *Oklahoma!*, interrupted frequently by announcements of special bargains on anti-freeze, and disposable diapers.

47

"You know that. I bought that and paid for it with my own money, that I had from when I was working."

"Well," he said, "nothing else is."

"The Lockes got a new one," she said. "Diane really likes it."

"Barney can afford it," he said. "Barney makes about eight times as much as I make, by the time he gets through with everything. Plus which, I think his mother left him some money."

"It's got one of those things on it that makes ice cubes and then chops them up," she said. "Diane said it's really nice for drinks and stuff."

"We still can't afford it," he said. "Besides, Barney works all the time. When's he got time to have drinks?"

"We've got to have them over," she said. "We owe them about three times."

"Barney's working this weekend and next," Hunter said. "And it seems to me, there's something I've got to do this weekend myself, you might've mentioned to me once or twice. I saw him down the liquor store and I was talking to him. He just got three more details on the Turnpike."

"We could ask them over next Friday night," she said.

"We'll have to throw them out at eleven o'clock, if you expect me to get down the cottage early enough to get half the things you want done, done."

"That's all right," she said.

"Maybe it's all right," he said, "but it's not my idea, much of an evening."

"Well," she said, "we've got to do something."

"You used to tell me," he said, "I thought you couldn't stand Diane."

"I changed my mind," she said. "I wonder what they call those things."

"What things," he said. "Come on, willya? I don't want to spend all night standing around here. I had a bitch of a day. I wanna relax. Bruins're playing Rangers, for Christ sake."

"You don't have to spend all your time watching television," she said. "You can spend some time with me, without killing yourself."

"Andrea," he said, "I'm not complaining about spending time with you. What I don't like is spending it staring into a goddamned department store. I'd rather spend it watching the hockey game."

"Not talking to me," she said.

"I'd just as soon talk," he said. "We can talk at home."

"I'll just have to make another trip, then," she said. "You never talk to me, and when I want to do something, to save myself some time, you want to rush me."

"Andrea," he said, "what do you want to do?"

"I want to get some of those things that you use to dry things out," she said. "You know those things."

"I don't know those things," he said.

"Well," she said, "maybe you should. It's your fault, everything got wet and everything."

"I didn't buy that thing," he said. "He bought that tarp, and it doesn't fit right. It leans."

"You should've thought of that," she said, *before* you put everything into it."

"I didn't have any choice, for Christ sake," he said. "The car was full before I put a single thing into that boat. If I'd've left it there, I'd have to make another trip, and in the meantime, I'd be hearing from you all the time about that."

"We'll be lucky if it isn't ruined," she said. "All that stuff. It's worth a lot of money, you know. You're concerned enough about it when it's your own money, but when it's somebody else's, well, it just doesn't concern you very much."

"Look," he said, "for at least three weeks, you've been after me, get the stuff out of there."

"I didn't want it all covered with green stuff, next summer," she said. "Is that so unreasonable? I'm the one who has to clean it up, you know. Not you. When we get down there and the blankets and everything're that way, it's something I just have to do."

"So," he said, "I got it out."

"Well," she said, "that didn't mean I wanted you to ruin it, getting it out. I didn't want it to rot, but that didn't mean I wanted you to get it all soaking wet, instead."

"Look," he said.

"You should be able to tell when it's raining," she said.

"Goddamnit," Hunter said, "I had a hard day, and it was a hard day after a hard night and there's gonna be another hard day on top of it tomorrow. Now I am not gonna stand around here all night in a goddamned shopping center and have a goddamned argument with you. You wanna fight, we'll go home and fight. You don't wanna fight, also okay. We'll go home and won't fight. But either way, I'm not gonna stand around here when I got to get my ass in gear tomorrow morning and go rassle nine Majors to get some skindivers who aren't gonna find anything after I get them."

"What's that for?" she said.

"I talked to a guy today," Hunter said. "Horace took me to see him. And I don't think the guy knows shit from Shinola about my case, but he says he does and the fuckin' thing's down for trial the first week in November, and I'm not in any position to take any chances. And he says the guy I've been looking for's probably a guy that he happens to know's down at the bottom of a certain quarry in Quincy, which I don't for one fucking minute believe, but I've got to find out and that's gonna be another waste of goddamned time I haven't got. And it pisses me off."

"You've got a filthy tongue in your head, you know that?" she said.

"Another in a long list of things I don't give a shit about," Hunter said. "Come on. Decide what you want and go get it, or decide you don't know what the hell you want, but either way, do something and let's get the hell out of here. This place drives me batty."

"Well," she said, "how can I go in there and ask for it, if I don't know what they call it?"

"Go in and tell them what it looks like and what it does," he said.

"It's one of those little white cloth things that've got something in them," she said. "All I can think of is the rice that goes in the salt-shakers. I want, that's not what I want, only the kind I want are the big ones.

They look like bags of sugar, or flour, or something, and when you put them somewhere, they dry things out. They absorb the moisture."

"The stuff's already wet, for Christ sake," he said. "What good's that gonna do, if the stuff's already wet?"

"I don't want them for that," she said. "I want you to put some of them around when you go down there, so when we go back next spring, everything won't be all damp and musty inside."

"Who's paying for that?" he said.

"All I have to do is ask them," she said. "You know that. Just tell them what it costs and there'll be a check in the mail the next day. It's not going to be very much, you know, when you start thinking about what you save in free vacations for us."

"It's never very much," he said. "The oil and the gas and the wear and tear on the car? Those're all free too. They're so free I haven't got any money left for a vacation that I could take, too. Keep that in mind too, Andrea: it's only a free vacation for some of us."

"We had a nice summer down there," she said. "If that's all it cost us, I don't think you should complain."

"You did have a nice summer down there," he said. "I had a lousy summer up here, and going back and forth, and the only thing that was different about the two places was, I did a different kind of work down there'n I did up here. I thought it sucked, and I bet next summer'll suck, too."

"Don't complain to me," she said, "if you didn't want to take a couple of weeks. That wasn't my idea, for you to spend the whole summer working. You could've come down with us before Labor Day, and he would've left you alone, if you can't stand him so much."

"I don't see any vacation in working for no pay instead of working for pay," he said.

"Before you're through," she said, "the kids're going to forget what you look like. They never see you.

"First you were gone all the time last year when you were down in Providence with that case," she said. "Which you lost. Then when *we* went down to

Rhode Island, you wouldn't come, and now I suppose you're going to think of something else to be doing, next year."

"Sooner or later," he said, "the house's gonna have to be painted."

"Uh, huh," she said, "I knew it."

"How long're we gonna stand here like this?" he said.

"Someday," she said, "you're going to wake up and it'll dawn on you. You'll realize all the things you missed, and then it'll be too late."

"Like the Bruins game, for one thing," he said.

"Then," she said, "when that happens, don't come running to me, and expect me to feel sorry for you."

"Okay," he said. "How about this: I meet you at the car. You go in there, and when you're through, come to the car and I'll meet you there. All right?"

"All right," she said. "On your way, there's a pet shop down there that we passed when we came in. I forgot at the supermarket. See if you can get some fish food, all right?"

"Fish food," he said.

"Is that too much to ask?" she said. "Sam's out of fish food, and after all you've had to say about how much they cost, the fish, I'd hate to have to hear you if they starved to death."

"I took care of them all summer, you know," he said.

"I think it's good for a boy to have interests," she said. "I think it's a good thing. If you had to take care of his fish for him while he was away, I still think that's all right. You probably didn't get home until it was so late, and you were so drunk. That's probably why it bothered you so much."

"Fish food I got to get," Hunter said. "Bullshit I already got. Anything else?"

"No," she said. "I got Vickie to take me shopping. I went shopping with Vickie this morning when I didn't know if you were going to be able to get home in time tonight. She said Marshall heard you come home last night. You woke him up, too."

"Wouldn't be surprised in the slightest," Hunter

said. "No muffler and all, must've sounded like a B 17."

"You can say what you want," she said, "they're still nice people."

"Very nice people," he said.

"They're good neighbors, Deke," she said. "I have to live with those people while you're off all day and staying out of town all the time. I need to depend on them."

"Yup," he said. "One, two, three . . ."

"I can't depend on you," she said.

The Sanderson Quarry

7

AT EIGHT-FIFTEEN on the morning of September 28, 1973, Deke Hunter in chino pants and a windbreaker stood seven yards from the brink of the Sanderson granite quarry off Liberty Street in Quincy, Massachusetts. He drank coffee from a white Styrofoam cup. The remains of the night mist rolled slowly around the edges of the quarry, where there were discarded condoms and Schlitz cans, and pieces of broken glass in the scant weeds.

The supervising sergeant from Troop F at Logan Airport was named Finch. He was a short, muscular man with clear blue eyes, and the muscles in his arms were noticeable under his blue jacket.

There were two separate streams of bubbles on the surface of the green water in the quarry. They popped quietly in the morning sunlight.

"Takes a while, doesn't it?" Hunter said.

"These things're like chimneys, most of them," Finch said. "You get a pond a hundred yards across, it's pretty unusual if it's deeper'n thirty or forty feet. You can go over the thing pretty fast and see what's down there.

"These things," he said, "they're liable to go down a hundred feet or so, and they're narrow, you know? So you get a lot of stuff in there and it's all piled up, and it's pretty hard to get around and see what's in it and under it. Takes a while."

"Yeah," Hunter said.

"You got a fortunate thing in one respect about this one, at least," Finch said, "and that is, it's a pretty

54

new one, and it looks to me like there's probably a spring down there or something. You get one of these things that it just petered out, it got too deep for the people to work or something, and it's about a hundred years old, all the water that's in it's gonna be stagnant."

"I wouldn't care to swim around in that much myself," Hunter said.

"Ahh," Finch said, "the guys're used to that. They don't like it, but they're used to it. It's just hard to see in it. You take a light down there and there's so much silt and shit and algae in the water all the light does is reflect off of it, right back in your eyes. It's like swimming in vegetable soup. You can't see anything. But you get one like this, that's spring-fed and your surface evaporation and the spring, they sort of keep things a little clearer, you know? So you can see what you're looking at, better."

"Yeah," Hunter said.

"You still get the run-offs from the snow, and the rain of course," Finch said, "but when you got that spring working down there, it keeps everything more or less moving around, and you can see what you're doing."

"Yeah," Hunter said.

"What do you figure," Finch said, "assuming the guy's in there and all, how long's he been there?"

"I doubt if he's in there," Hunter said, "you want the real truth. He's a son of a bitch we can't find, and I'm damned if I can tell you why. He's the kind of guy that's got to do something every so often, or he gets himself restless and does something anyway. But for six months we've been looking for him, and we're getting to the point where we really need to find him, and there's just not any sign of him and I can't understand it.

"I've been everyplace," Hunter said. "I've been to places where he's been before, I got people watching people that he hangs around with, we've had an APB out on the bastard, we got the federals looking for him, everything. Nothing.

"Now my rabbi, Carmody, comes up with this guy,"

Hunter said, "Charlie Thomas. Maybe you heard of him."

"If I did, I forgot it," Finch said.

"North Shore," Hunter said. "Charlie's been known to do a little time now and then, for some stupid mistakes that he made. Fat guy. Dresses up in those blue suits with white stitching on them, wear a big hat and he looks like a fuckin' cowboy all the time. He's a gaffer. Checks now and then, a few stolen goods, nothing very big and nothing very small. Claims he knows a lot.

"Charlie just got out," Hunter said, "and he evidently got wind of something that made him think maybe somebody was making up his bunk for him again, so he got in touch with Horace and he said he'd like to have a chat.

"Now I am fresh clean out of ideas on where my guy is," Hunter said. "So Horace says to me: 'Come along. Charlie knows lots.' And I went. Can't do any harm. And right off of the bat, Charlie tells me he knows exactly where my guy is, and this is where he says.

"Charlie's reliable," Hunter said, "but he's made a mistake or two now and then. And I frankly think this is another one. But Charlie was in Norfolk for almost two years this last time, on account of he ripped off a guy for ten grand, didn't go for that shit, and he swears a guy in there with him told him that Donnelly's under that water."

"And you just don't know," Finch said.

"Well," Hunter said, "Donnelly's some place. And if he's not robbing banks, then he's stopped spending money or else he's found another line of work, or else he's dead. If he was robbing banks, somebody would've made him. He's a very distinctive-looking fellow. So he's not robbing banks, is what I think, or if he is, he's changed his style enough so people can't recognize him, and that I find hard to believe.

"Another line of work," Hunter said. "Also hard to believe. The guy's around fifty, and except when he was in the service he's been either robbing banks, the same way, and living high off the hog with the dough, or else he's been doing time for robbing banks. He don't know anything else. He couldn't run a con if it killed him, and he didn't get enough from the one I want him for so he could live off it for six months the way he likes to live.

"Then there's his girlfriend," Hunter said. "Not a bad-looking gash, and she really likes Teddy. The broad doesn't move for six months. So where the hell is he, and what is he doing? Teaching school? Taking in laundry? Stealing hubcaps and jimmying parking meters? The bastard has gotta be somewhere, but I'll be fucked if I know where he is."

The air bubbles traveled randomly around on the surface as the divers worked. Finch gestured toward the exposed walls of the quarry, twenty feet tall on the other side. "At night's when these things're rough," he said. "See them holes?"

"No," Hunter said.

"There's holes in the newer ones," Finch said. "Where they used dynamite, I guess. I dunno. There's holes in them, anyway. Bats live in them holes. You get one of these things at night, some asshole rolls his car in while he's humping some dolly and they're both out of their minds, you got bats flying all around you while you're waiting. They got that radar, or whatever it is that they got, so they don't hit you, but Jesus, they're swooping around, catching bugs and stuff, and it's downright spooky. I hate bats. Drive you crazy."

"Suck your blood," Hunter said.

"Sure," Finch said, "make you inna fuckin' vampire. First thing you know, you're not going home when it's dark, you're gonna go out and bite some chicken on the neck or something. Your teeth start getting longer and when you're not hanging upside down to sleep, you're lying down in a casket. Freaky, weird stuff."

The two areas of bubbles converged. "They're coming up," Finch said.

"Wanna bet on the grappling hook?" Hunter said.

"Hey," Finch said, "don't worry about it. You never know what you're gonna find in these things. They oughta go into them once a year on a general principle. We don't find what you're looking for, maybe we find what somebody else's looking for. Maybe we find something nobody even knew was missing. You never know."

The divers in their black wet suits, with vertical yellow stripes, broke the surface and shoved their masks up.

"Get anything?" Finch said.

"Depends," said the one on the left. "Depends on what you had in mind."

"Bodies," Finch said.

"Got, I think it's a fifty-one Plymouth convertible," the diver said.

"Human bodies," Finch said.

"No human bodies," the diver said. "Tell you what we have got, though, you want it: we got about, oh, forty or fifty cats."

"Cats?" Finch said.

"Cats," the diver said. "There's at least forty cats down there, and every single one of them's got a brick tied around his neck with a piece of sash cord or something."

"Son of a bitch," Finch said. "A mean kid." He turned to Hunter. "Want some cats, Corporal? That help you at all?"

"I guess not," Hunter said.

□

PART TWO

Tango Zebra Whiskey, Three Niner Niner

Madeleine's Attitude

□ 8

"IT WOULDN'T BOTHER ME if he did," Madeleine said on the evening of October 8, 1973, in the Spanish Galleon Lounge of the Seven Seas Motel in Cranston, Rhode Island. She wore a short, blue-and-white knitted dress, and silver shoes that looked gold in the orange light of the plastic lanterns. "I mean, I wouldn't actually go some place that I knew Freddie was going to be, or anything, but if he was to come in here, well, what could he say? He'd have to be in here with somebody himself, since he told me he hadda go to Worcester tonight."

Hunter drank beer from a pewter flagon. "It'd bother me," he said.

"Look, Deke," she said, "forget it, all right? I'm cold. It's not raining? All right, but it's still cold. I'm going to have, it's going to take me at least three drinks to warm up, and there's no way you're gonna talk me out of having them."

"I'm not trying to talk you out of anything," Hunter said.

"The more I think about it," she said, "you know something? I must be nuts. You could've at least brought a sheet with you. If I'd've known, I would've brought one myself."

"You were with me the last two times," he said. "You saw me throwing the stuff in the boat. You saw what was there that weekend. Nothing."

"I didn't think of it," she said. "Jesus."

"Well," he said, "what the hell was I supposed to do? Maybe I should've called you at home, so you

60

could walk out the door with a blanket or something?"

"I could've bought one," she said, "and left it in the car. He never looks in my car. That's *my* car. Shit." She brushed her hair back with her right hand. "I mean, I've tried it lots of ways, Deke, but that was *cold*. You didn't tell me it was gonna be so cold."

"The heat was set down," he said. "It takes a while for it to come up."

"I'm not gonna go and do that again," she said. "If you wanna see me again, you just better make up your mind: you've got to get a motel. Those mattress covers're rough too. I don't think I got any skin left on my elbows from this outing."

"That'd be nice," he said. "Somebody goes by and sees my car outside a motel. What am I doing, sleeping over, I came down to take care of something at the cottage?"

"Your car's outside here," she said. "Somebody could see it here, too."

"I'm having something to eat," he said, "and a couple of drinks. And if the question comes up later, I can prove it."

"With a woman," she said.

"There's no law about that, that I know about," he said. "Not even in Rhode Island."

"Okay, Deke," she said, leaning back in the chair, "now I'm gonna tell you how it is."

"I'd get spotted," he said. "That's the kind of guy I am. I'd get spotted coming out of the room. When I do something, I get caught."

"It's the ten bucks," she said.

"It's not the ten bucks," he said.

"It's the ten bucks," she said. "Deke, you can spare, *every*body's got ten bucks."

"I've got ten bucks," he said. "It's not that."

"What does she do, Deke," Madeleine said. "Does she go through your pants? Do you have to account for your money to her? Is that what it is? Say you lost it through a hole in your pocket."

"No," he said. "My expense money? That comes to the office. She doesn't know how much money I got on me."

"You're really fucked up, aren't you, Deke?" she said.

"No," he said. "There's nothing the matter with me."

"Sure," she said. "You think . . . , look, what're you doing right now? Tell me exactly what you think you're doing, right this very minute."

"Sitting in a bar," he said, "having a drink, talking to a woman."

"With your life, Deke," she said. "What're you doing with your life?"

"I'm a cop," he said.

"Being a cop," she said. "That's the best thing you can say. Being a cop."

"Putting guys in jail," he said. "Yeah. That's what I'm doing."

"Well," she said, finishing her Southern Comfort, "I don't think that's very much to be able to say, you know that?"

"It's not bad," he said. "It suits me."

"It's nothing," she said.

The waitress came over and Hunter ordered another round by pointing to the empty glasses. The waitress went away.

Madeleine leaned toward Hunter. "What am I, Deke? Tell me that: what do you think I am?"

"I know what you do," he said.

"Yeah, yeah," she said. "I'm a court reporter. What am I, though, to you? What am I doing?"

"I thought we went through that a couple times," he said.

"Oh, Christ," she said, leaning back again, "I don't mean that. Get over it, willya? I'm nobody's god-damned girlfriend, and I never will be."

"Then I don't know what you're talking about," he said.

"I," she said, "I am getting, I am getting some *pleasure* and some *satisfaction* out of my life. Just like the beer ads. Gusto. What I do in court is just my job. You know something, Deke? I'll tell you something, and you should really think about it.

"You," she said, "are gonna be dead a long time.

You got to realize that. And once you realize it, once you start to get so you know up from down, then go and get some pleasure out of your life, and go and have some fun. Because nobody's gonna feel sorry for you, if you die and you didn't do it."

The waitress brought the drinks.

"I don't know," he said. "I thought, that's what I was doing."

"Nah," she said, drinking. "You're not having fun. You're too nervous all the time. You don't get any enjoyment out of it, you know? You're worried all the time."

"No," he said.

"You don't," she said. "You're scared all the time. I can tell."

"How can you tell?" he said. "What can you tell? Tell me that: what makes you think that I'm not enjoying myself?"

"Oh," she said, "I didn't mean that. You can get it up all right. You can do that. But it's like, you're desperate. You know?"

"No," he said.

"Sure," she said. "When I first started seeing you, you know? I couldn't put my finger on it. I knew it was something, but for a long time I couldn't figure it out, and then for a while I just stopped thinking about it. Because it just didn't seem like it was very important. What the hell, you're a good-looking guy. There's no reason . . . I thought: 'Boy, here's a guy. I bet he's been around.' I was the most surprised thing in the world. You know what I worry about, when I know I'm gonna see you? That some time, you're *not* gonna be able to get it up."

"Now," Hunter said, "that's where you're wrong."

"And if you can't, sometime," she said, "well, I got a strong idea you're the type of guy I wouldn't be able to do anything for. Blow job or anything. If that was to happen. Some guys . . . , I knew a guy once, and he had that kind of trouble every so often, but he was just tired or he was thinking about something else, and if I did the right things to him, well, he was all right. But you I don't think I could do that for. You're different."

"Madeleine," Hunter said, "it'll never happen."

"Well," she said, "I really hope you're right. Because really all you've got going for you right now is that. You can always get it up. And if you couldn't do that, well, that's the only thing I know about that you're not worried about. The only thing. And you're not very good at doing things to fix things that you're worried about."

"All right," he said, "next time we get a motel room."

"That's not what I mean," she said.

"I thought that's what you were talking about," he said.

"I was," she said. "Now I'm through talking about it. I'm not going back into any cold place with the windows all boarded up, if that's what you mean. No, sir. But, it's *you,* you know? You've got to loosen up some. Start enjoying yourself. See what there is. Like me, you know? You can't hang back from anything. You've got to do everything. Never mind what might happen. Just go ahead. Or else, *don't* do anything, and go back home to her, and stop seeing me, and do it that way, if you can't stand it. Because the way you are, you're just in-between, and it stinks. It isn't anything. You know what I mean?"

"I guess so," he said.

"My girlfriend Eleanor," she said. "You never met Eleanor."

"I don't think so," he said.

"She's married to this really neat guy," Madeleine said. "I really like Dougie, and so's Freddie, and we all get along together really great, you know? So, we went out. Last Friday, I'm getting through work, she calls me up and she says: 'Hey, you and Freddie, let's have dinner and stuff.'

"So we did," Madeleine said. "We went down the Oaks and we had dinner, and, you got to wait a long time there, specially on the weekends, so we had lots of drinks, and we ate, these really good steaks that they have which everybody in the world knows about and that's why you got to wait so long, and we had wine, and then we had some more drinks, and when we got through, we were *bombed*.

"So the guys," she said, "this is Doug and Freddie, they wanted to go over this place in Johnston, that's got topless. So Eleanor says: 'Oh, no. There's any topless shit going on, we're gonna do it. You're not gonna spend the whole night spending all kinds of extra dough on drinks to look at some other boobs when you can look at mine at home for the regular price.'

"You oughta see Eleanor," Madeleine said. "She has got really big boobs. I mean, *really*. Mine're pretty good, I mean, but hers, boy, even when she hasn't got a bra on, which she likes to do now and then, they stick right out to here. She wears, she wears a thirty-six-D, but I don't see how she can get them into it.

"So Doug says: 'Look, they got this girl down there that's got a snake. You haven't got no snake.' And this, and that, and we . . . , I didn't know, you know? But I was absolutely *bombed*.

"So we go back to their place," Madeleine said, "Eleanor and Dougie's. And she makes them sit down. We're gonna be right back. Now I used to, I've known Eleanor since I was in the fifth grade, you know? So I trust her. But I don't know how I feel about this. Because, I got pretty good ones, but next to her, I dunno.

"Well," Madeleine said, "she wouldn't listen to me. 'Come on,' she says, and we go in the bedroom. I was wearing this pants suit, and she makes me take off my blouse and bra, and then we go back out. 'You wanted topless?' she says. 'You got topless.' And then we have to wait on them, get drinks for them and everything, and Dougie put a buck down my pants, and then he says: 'I still don't see no snake.'

" 'I tol' you,' Eleanor says," Madeleine said, " 'there's better things'n watching some broad let a snake crawl over her tits.'

" 'Like what?' Dougie says.

" 'Like having them in your mouth,' she says, and she goes over to Freddie, and he's sitting down, and she takes her right one and sticks it in his mouth. 'See?' she says.

" 'Fine for him,' Dougie says, 'but how about me? Don't do a fucking thing for me.'

" 'Oh no, you don't,' I says," Madeleine said. "Because I could see what they're leading up to, you know? And I was kind of scared, actually. I never did anything like that before."

"That's terrible," Hunter said.

"Oh no it's not," Madeleine said. "So Dougie says to her: 'Anyway, you got too many clothes on.' And the next thing, she goes back in the bedroom, and she comes out, and all she's got on's her white boots, and she lies down on the coffee table just like in the doctor's office, and I watched them. And they get all through, and she says: 'Now Madeleine.' And they hadda fight me, you know that? The three of them hadda fight me. That, that was what was terrible about it."

"Jesus Christ," Hunter said.

"No," she said, "because, in the best way, it was good. Because I was the only one, and there was three of them, and that made it better. It was more exciting. But, and this is the thing, I really wanted them to do it to me. I didn't want to do it myself, like I was agreeing to it, because I was afraid, but I wanted them to do it to me because I really wanted to do it. I really did. They had me down, and Freddie was getting my boots off, and Dougie was holding my arms down, and then Freddie took my pants suit off, and then, it was Eleanor, that took my pants off. *'I'm* gonna do this,' she says. 'The last time I saw this thing it didn't even have hair on it.' And I was glad, you know, even though I was crying. I had on my red pants, you know? The ones you saw that time, that you can see through? And . . ."

"Shut up," Hunter said.

"No," she said. "That's what I mean, see? I was glad. Because she liked it, and so'd they, and pretty soon I liked it, and we didn't stop till it was after four in the morning. You think you and me could ball all night? But, you get something going like that, and then you can. And if they hadn't've made me do it like that, like they did, well, I wouldn't've. I wouldn't've done it if somebody asked me to, somebody that I knew. They had to make me. So, and they did, and I was lucky. But everybody isn't, probably. I doubt anybody'd ever do that to you."

"Fuckin' double-A right, they won't," Hunter said. "I'm disgusted. That's the worst thing I heard about, that somebody that I actually knew was doing, since I was playing ball, for Christ sake, and we got back from Springfield pretty late one night and the guys hired a black whore and a white whore to eat each other in a back room and than blow the whole bunch of them. Jesus Christ, Mad, they used to arrest people, did that kind of thing. Put them in jail. Just cheap, dirty, shitty people that have to do things like that to get their rocks off. Guys that want women to drive nails through their dicks. I think it's fucking horrible."

"Deke," she said, "there's only two things you can do, that you can have fun with. You get old, and then there's only one. I know people. I've seen people, some people, not many, that're really happy, because what they like to do, they like to think. The Judge's like that. And that's good. And some of the lawyers, too. Because nobody's ever gonna want to see their body, or do things with them, and they probably don't want to either. Because they're ugly.

"Maybe they didn't used to be ugly, or something," she said. "Maybe they got to be ugly. I don't know. But I always feel sorry for them, and then I think: 'Well, I'm the other kind. I can do that. I can take my body and I can get satisfaction, you know? And I can give it to other people, too. It makes me feel good. And if I didn't know that . . . , well, I always knew it.

"And you," she said, "you're the same kind of person that I am. Only you don't know it, and you're much more afraid of being it than I ever was. And you're not gonna get the kind of help you're gonna need before you can do it, *because you've got a tight asshole*.

"So the way it'll end up, is," Madeleine said, "you'll, it'll be the same as it would've been if you'd've been the other kind, except you're not, and you'll never be happy."

Hunter said nothing.

"That's what I mean," she said.

She put her left hand on his right hand. "Deke," she said, softly, "that's what I'm telling you: time goes by. There're *things* . . . . It doesn't matter what you do, you know? If you haven't got money or something. That doesn't matter. It really doesn't. What matters is that you feel good. That you're doing things that make you feel good. And you're not scared about them. And you don't *worry* about them. You don't go around saying: 'Well, is somebody gonna see my car or something?' Because, what if they do? Who cares? You just tell them: 'I was doing something that made me feel good.' You know?

"You got to have something, Deke," she said. "You've got to have something that you can do, besides just running around and working and everything, and never having any fun and feeling lousy about things all the time. See? And then, that's yours. And you forget about all that other shit. It doesn't matter."

"Did you make that up?" he said.

"What?" she said.

"That story," he said. "Did you make that up?"

"No, Deke," she said. "No, I didn't make that up."

"Is that what you do?" he said. "You go to orgies? You let guys . . . How many cocks've you had in your mouth? Do you know? Or've you lost count?"

"Deke," she said, "look, you know? If there was one thing, if somebody could come up and say to you, and make it be true, you could have anything in the world that you wanted, one thing, and all you hadda do was ask for it, what'd you ask for? A million bucks?"

"I dunno," Hunter said. "Yeah, yeah, that'd be all right. A million bucks."

"Okay," she said. "Fine. But you're probably not gonna *have* anybody come up and ask you that, that can deliver. That can give it to you. That's what I mean. You're always gonna have to work, and as a result you're always gonna be this way, you know? Always thinking about what you want, and what you're not gonna get, and you'll never even notice

what you have got that'd, well, it might not make
up for it, but it's a hell of a lot better'n nothing.

"You're never gonna get what you want, Deke,"
she said. "And what's worse, you're never gonna appreciate what you've got, and I feel sorry for you. If
you think, if you think what you said, that people
like me're disgusting . . . isn't that what you said?"

"That's what I said," Hunter said.

"You poor fuckin' sorry dumb shit," Madeleine
said. "You meant it, too, I suppose."

"I meant it," he said.

"And you," she said, "you're the guy that puts his
cock in my body every chance he gets, and then
when I try to put something into your mind, this is
how you react? I'm disgusting? You think that, because I told you and I'm trying to help you?"

He stared at her. "I never heard anything like this
before in my whole life," he said. "I used to arrest
guys for selling pictures, for Christ sake."

"Deke," she said, "you know me. Is that, is what
you said, is that what you think?"

"Yes," he said. "That's what I think, and that's
what you are, too. Jesus H. Christ."

The Hamden Tolls

☐ 9

ON THE MORNING OF OCTOBER 10, 1973, at 9:05 A.M., Sergeant Horace Carmody, at his desk, received a telephone call from Captain Ellsworth Mooney of the Connecticut State Police.

Carmody and Mooney had met in 1960, during the Kennedy presidential campaign. Captain Mooney was then in charge of security arrangements for a visit to Boston by Governor Abraham Ribicoff of Connecticut. Sergeant Carmody was assigned by the Massachusetts Commissioner of Public Safety, at 1010 Commonwealth Avenue, as the liaison officer to Captain Mooney. Captain Mooney, a mistrustful man and a humorless one, was favorably impressed by the diligence and gravity of Sergeant Carmody, who enjoyed the advantage of familiarity, apparent familiarity, with Captain Mooney's scholarly papers. The captain, who retained his Reserve commission as lieutenant colonel in the 101st Division, Airborne, ran six miles a day and took offense when someone called it *jogging*, was a national expert on methods of interrogating suspects, and had contributed three articles on the subject to the *Journal of Criminal Law, Criminology & Police Science*. He had lectured to the State Police and Highway Patrol academies in Illinois, Michigan, Wisconsin, Ohio, Nebraska and California, and was a member of the night school faculty of the University of Hartford. His cordial, though intermittent, correspondence with J. Edgar Hoover had begun when he attended the FBI police training school at Quantico

70

Virginia, and continued as he received and accepted invitations to address later sessions. After his experience with Sergeant Carmody, he wrote a letter commending him, to Commissioner Leo L. Laughlin, who saw to its inclusion in Carmody's file. Detective Lieutenant George Samuels, informed of this, told Carmody he expected a round of drinks and a dinner for briefing Carmody on Star Cops in general, and Captain Mooney in particular, and Carmody responded by delivering to Samuels a small and rather bedraggled geranium in a clay pot, together with a valentine that he obtained with some difficulty in August of 1960.

On the morning of October tenth, Captain Mooney reported to Sergeant Carmody that a Connecticut trooper named Belcher, on duty the previous evening at the Hamden Tolls gate of the Connecticut Turnpike, had had his attention attracted to a Buick Centurion hardtop, color blue, carrying New York registration tags Tango Zebra Whiskey, three niner niner. Trooper Belcher had observed the subject vehicle first at about twenty-hundred-eighteen hours, proceeding at a rate of speed too great for existing conditions, and in excess of the posted limits, in the southbound lane. Trooper Belcher had observed that the vehicle was operated by a white male Caucasian. Trooper Belcher further observed that the subject motor vehicle failed to come to a complete stop at the toll plaza, and that the operator did not place the required amount in the toll basket, but dropped the coin on the pavement and at once departed from the toll plaza at a high rate of speed.

Captain Mooney said that Trooper Belcher reported his position and gave a description of the subject vehicle on his official frequency, and then proceeded to give chase. In the ensuing pursuit, Trooper Belcher clocked the Buick at speeds in excess of ninety miles per hour, and observed that it was being operated in an erratic fashion. Four point three miles from the toll plaza, Trooper Belcher brought his vehicle alongside the subject vehicle, while signaling with his lights and by hand signals, to the operator, to pull over.

Captain Mooney said that the operator at first did

not obey either Trooper Belcher's hand signals or those made by his lights, but at length did so.

Captain Mooney said that the operator of the subject vehicle at first refused to exit the vehicle as directed by Trooper Belcher, but at length complied. He said that Trooper Belcher observed that the operator was a white male Caucasian, about forty-five years old, with black and gray hair. He was wearing a sports jacket and gray slacks and a white shirt open at the throat. Trooper Belcher observed that the subject's eyes were glassy, and his speech was slurred, and he detected a strong odor of alcohol. The operator had to be assisted from the vehicle, and he used his hands to steady himself upon the fender. When he was asked for identification, he was unable to produce any. Trooper Belcher, having formed an opinion as to the sobriety of the subject—that he was drunk—placed him under arrest for reckless operation, operation while intoxicated, and operation without license and registration in his possession. The subject then refused to state his name, and was taken to the nearest place of confinement, where he was booked under the name of John Doe, and fingerprinted and photographed. The Buick was then driven to the Troop B barracks at Chiltonville, for safekeeping, where, using keys confiscated from the operator, it was searched. Nothing of importance was uncovered. As a matter of routine investigation procedures, the vehicle identification numbers were sent out over Telex, and the fingerprints of the operator were compared to Connecticut files and dispatched also to the FBI.

Captain Mooney informed Sergeant Carmody that Vermont State Police responded at one hundred-twenty hours that the Buick Centurion, hardtop, color blue, New York registration tags Tango Zebra Whiskey, three niner niner, had been reported stolen from the parking lot at the Hamilton Inn at Brattleboro, at nineteen-hundred-oh-five hours on October ninth, and that the desk clerk had described the thief as a white male Caucasian, about forty years old, wearing a sports jacket and gray trousers. The operator, at one hundred-twenty hours, was asleep in his cell and could not be awakened. He was snoring heavily, and appeared to have passed out. An additional charge of possession of a motor vehicle, knowing it to have been stolen, was placed against him. Vermont advised that a complaint and warrant for grand theft, auto, would be sought in the morning against John Doe. The FBI Field Office at Hartford was advised, and responded that a prosecutive opinion would be sought in the morning from the office of the United States Attorney, as to whether federal charges of knowingly transporting a stolen motor vehicle in interstate commerce should be filed.

Captain Mooney further advised Sergeant Carmody that the subject operator awoke at oh-six-hundred-thirty-five hours and requested water and aspirin. He gave his name as Kenneth W. Mooney, of no permanent address, last permanent address being 17 Payson Avenue, Rochester, New York. He said he was a baggage handler for Trans World Airlines until he was discharged two years previously for absenteeism. He said he had lived at odd jobs after his unemployment compensation ran out, and that his last job had been that of a laborer in a commercial laundry in Burlington, Vermont. He said he was forced to quit that job on October seventh, because the work of pulling industrial linens out of the machines had caused him a severe back strain. He said that he had hitch-hiked from Burlington to Brattleboro, and there had been picked up by a white male, about twenty, who was driving the Buick Centurion. He said that the youth said he was driving to New York, where he lived, and offered the subject a ride to La Guardia, where, the subject said, he hoped to find work with one of the airlines. The subject stated that the operator of the vehicle had offered him a drink from a quart of whiskey which he had in the car with him, and that they both had several drinks. The subject stated that the youth, at his request, stopped in a rest area in Holyoke Massachusetts, at approximately nineteen hundred hours, so that the subject could relieve himself. The subject stated that when he returned to the motor vehicle, the youth had unzipped his trousers and was displaying his penis, and that he made homosexual advances to the subject. The subject said that he, although drunk, refused, that the youth then pulled a knife on him, and ordered him from the vehicle. The subject said that he became enraged, and took the knife away from the youth, subdued him, put him out of the car, and himself drove the vehicle away. The subject said that he was sorry for what he had done.

Captain Mooney said he had been intrigued by the identity claimed by the subject, when he reported at oh-seven-hundred hours, and had intended to have the subject brought in. But at oh-eight-hundred-oh-ten, Captain Mooney said, the FBI reported that the fingerprints submitted as those of John Doe had been positively identified as the fingerprints of Edward M. Donnelly, DOB 2-15-24, New Bedford, Massachusetts, and that there was outstanding for him a warrant issued by the United States Magistrate, Boston, authorizing his arrest for unlawful flight to avoid prosecution (bank robbery).

Captain Mooney said he had caused the subject to be advised that he was now under arrest on such charges, and that he had notified the FBI, Hartford, that the State would waive its jurisidiction in the event that Massachusetts authorities intended to commence extradition.

"Captain," Sergeant Carmody said, "that is what I call excellent police work."

Hunter came into the Salem office shortly after nine-thirty. "I got what I think is some good news for you," Carmody said. "They got the fucker Donnelly in irons in Connecticut."

Hunter sat down without taking off his coat. He grinned. "For so early in the day," he said, "it isn't bad."

PART THREE

□

The Alibi

Charlie Thomas Had Called Again

☐ 10

ON THE AFTERNOON OF NOVEMBER 15, 1973, Horace Carmody picked his teeth in the office at the courthouse. He said: "How's life with Fat John and all them other learned counsel?"

"My friend," Hunter said, "it's beautiful. It's like the guy that didn't want to hurt the dog, so he cut off his tail an inch at a time. Fat John's up there, hollering and yelling, his man's been in the cooler seven months and he wants his goddamned trial. Sam Wyman agrees with Killilea. Teddy Donnelly sits there looking like somebody rubbed shit on his head . . . , you know, I don't really think Teddy planned to attend this performance. He acts like he doesn't really want to be here at all. And so for revenge, he hired himself Tommy Hart."

"Oh, Jesus," Carmody said. "Hart calls his mother before he decides to sit down or get up. He's a terrible staller."

"Plus which," Hunter said, "we got old speedball himself, Richard Shanley for the Commonwealth, and I swear to God, Horace, he's about as hot to try this thing as I am to go and get my foot cut off. I think he's scared of it, is what I think. When he's going fast, he's pretty slow, and when he stalls, it's like watching the grass come up. He's got Fat John and Sam yelling 'Trial trial trial,' and Billy shaking in his boots in the safe house, praying that it never comes to trial, and Tommy Hart yelling 'Prejudice, prejudice, I haven't had time to prepare, my client's not gonna get a competent defense.' And there sits Teddy, like a big, pissed-off stone. What the hell're you doing?"

"I had one of those goddamned veal cutlets that they give you down at the Villa," Carmody said. "They put that creole sauce on top of it, so you can't see what you're getting, and a good half of it's this old tough toast they put under it to jack the thing up and make it look thicker. There's about as much veal on that plate as there's clams in the chowder, but I already knew about the chowder because I had that once before, and I didn't have the veal so that's what I had. And now there's two things I know about down there. I'm gonna keep trying, though. The place's full for lunch every day, so they must have something there that a man can eat. It's just a matter of finding what it is. It's not the veal, though. My teeth're all full of celery."

"I hate to see guys sucking shit out of their teeth," Hunter said. "Makes me sick to my fuckin' stomach. You oughta quit eating things you can't see, and if you can't do that, at least go clean your teeth in the goddamned Men's Room, so I haven't gotta watch you do it. You Polish, for Christ sake? Lemme see you scratch your balls."

"You're never gonna make sergeant," Carmody said. "You're gonna be a corporal for the rest of your natural life. I meant to tell you that before. You got this habit of showing disrespect for senior officers. It's all right to have it. Not all right to show it. Some day it's gonna get you in a whole mess of shit, and then you're gonna come whining around to me, looking for sympathy and everything, and I'll have to tell you: 'Remember, you're climbing all over me? I had something in my teeth that was driving me nuts and you wouldn't leave an old man alone that was just lucky he still had his own teeth to get things in? Remember that? Well, I ditched you on the fitness report, is what I did, Corporal.'

"That'll teach you some manners, smart ass," Carmody said. "I'm beginning to think Shanley's right: you're an uncooperative little prick. You oughta be out on Route Nine in full pack, freezing your ass off and learning respect."

"When did Shanley say that?" Hunter said. "That

little shit. When he'd sooner fuck around anytime than do something? When'd he say that?"

"You didn't even take the exam," Carmody said. "You haven't even got enough on the ball, take the exam. How do you think they make sergeants, anyway, some angel comes down, whacks you onna back? 'Good going, kid, you made sergeant'? You got to do something first, you're ever gonna amount to anything in this world, you know."

"When'd he say that?" Hunter said.

"The hell do you care?" Carmody said. "What difference it make, when he said it?"

"I don't like the way he's acting with me on this thing, is why," Hunter said. "He acts like he knows something I don't, that I probably should. He's a shifty motherfucker anyway."

"He always says that," Carmody said. "You got no idea how many times I hadda go to bat for you, and this is what I get for my trouble. Disrespect. You going to trial or not?"

"Judge's got it under advisement," Hunter said. "Said he'd be out until three, and he'd come back in then and tell everybody what he decided."

"How's it look to you?" Carmody said.

"I think the guy wants to try it," Hunter said. "Look, he's gonna try some of it, anyway. I figure the most he can do's sever Donnelly's case from the other guys', and he probably doesn't want to do that anymore'n we want to try it twice in front of him and somebody else, either."

"That'd figure for old Peter," Carmody said. "Judge Macarthur's no dummy. Look, tell you what: soon's you know if Donnelly's in or not, willya come down and tell me?"

"Whadda you care?" Hunter said. "It's my problem and Shanley's, if it has to go twice."

"Because I had another call from Charlie, this morning," Carmody said, "and he said he hears, if Donnelly's part of the package, he thinks he oughta see me."

"Shit," Hunter said, "tell Charlie we found Teddy in the quarry down in Quincy with a hundred feet of two-inch chain around his middle. No way can we try

Teddy. He's dead. That guy we got sitting up there's just his double, that we hired to confuse everybody."

"That was unusual," Carmody said, "that Charlie was wrong like that. Usually, if the horse tells you: 'Charlie's wrong,' go with the horse. Otherwise, go with Charlie."

"Charlie's just a cheap crook with a big imagination," Hunter said. "Look, what's he doing these days, besides telling fairy stories to us so a lot of guys can go swimming on their days off?"

"Charlie's still a little vague about what he's doing," Carmody said. "But Charlie's always been a little vague about what he's doing. What other guys're doing, that he's pretty talkative about. He's maybe stealing a few things, although I doubt that. He knows a few guys that're stealing a few things, and he's always had a pretty good list of things that you could buy if you were in the right place at the right time with some small bills, but that's all. I think, maybe, Charlie might possibly be doing something with a loan officer that he shouldn't be, but not much else. He's been out since August, and he's got a new Marquis, and he told me he went to Bermuda last week. 'I felt like it,' he said, which is nice to be able to say if you're apparently unemployed. He's got a fine tan."

"Charlie's gonna go back in again," Hunter said, "he doesn't look out."

"I dunno," Carmody said. "He's a big boy, now, and there are guys that can make a pretty good living, reading the *National Armstrong* and picking the proper horses. Not many, but some. I told him, I said: 'Charlie, it's nice to have you back again, see you in the sport coat and all, have a cup of coffee with you, talk about what's in the newspaper.' Didn't bat an eye. Told me, he's not going back. 'I got one of those Water Pics, Sarge, and they haven't got the right outlets in the cells for them. I'm getting to the edge of the place where a guy's got to look out for gingivitis, and then they take a shiv and start carving your gums up. Or else your teeth fall out. Like your hair did.' I told him: 'Better watch it, Charlie. We got a real tiger in there now, they get you again and the guy won't belt it out for less'n fifteen, more if you try it.'

And that's when he said he heard I got a guy trying Donnelly, and he heard something that he's only gonna take a chance on telling me if Donnelly's really going. So tell me as soon as you know, all right? I had some very interesting chats with Charlie over the years. I'd hate to think I missed a good one."

First Thing, Second Thing

☐ 11

IN THE COLD DARKNESS before six in the morning of November 16, 1973, Deke Hunter kept the 1968 Chevelle steady at sixty on Route 128 southbound toward the Ridge Arena in Braintree.

"You don't mind this, do you, Dad?" Sam Hunter said. He wore the black and gold traveling colors of the Boston Bruins; his sweater was number 10. He had black rubber guards on his skate blades, and he wore the wide-cuffed, ribbed black gloves at all times.

"I don't mind," Hunter said.

"Mom said," Sam said, "you have to get up early and everything, and you have to work late."

"It's all right," Hunter said. "I'd tell you if it wasn't."

"If it was just practice or something . . . ," Sam said.

"I know," Hunter said. "Look, a couple times it's been four in the morning, and there was one gawdawful time it was three-thirty. Don't worry about it. I don't mind."

"Sharon's leading the league," Sam said.

"They've got a good club," Hunter said.

"They shouldn't be leading," Sam said.

"If they've got a good club," Hunter said.

"They have," Sam said. "They've got a very good club. They've got all big guys. I heard Coach. He was saying, he thinks some of their guys're at least twelve. They've got to be."

"Sam," Hunter said, "never mind all that stuff, all right? That's kid stuff, saying things like that, and it's

81

for kids 'way younger'n you are, that don't know any better. Never mind how big they are, or how old you think they are. Just get in and play hockey the best way you can."

"They're Rangers," Sam said. "How come they did that? Rangers. Who'd want to be Rangers?"

"Your club was first in the league," Hunter said. "The first club in the league, around here, naturally, is going to be the Bruins. Don't worry about that, either. It's how you play that counts."

"Vad's doing better, isn't he?" Sam said.

"Last I saw," Hunter said, "Vadnais was going very good. Probably go even better without that goddamned moustache."

"He's getting much quicker," Sam said. "And, his passing's a lot sharper. I used to be embarrassed last year. He was always getting fooled, and then they'd take the puck and score with it. And then, the next day, I'd have to go out there and listen to all the guys."

"You're not Vadnais," Hunter said.

"I've got his number," Sam said.

"Who's got Orr's?" Hunter said.

"Driscoll," Sam said. "He's just got it because his father's an assistant coach."

"How do you think he feels?" Hunter said.

"Who?" Sam said.

"The Driscoll kid," Hunter said. "Can he do the things that Bobby Orr can do? Do people expect that?"

"No," Sam said, "of course not. The only reason that he's even on the team is his father."

"Come on, Sam," Hunter said. "Is he the kid that takes the shift with you?"

"Yeah," Sam said.

"He's a very good little skater," Hunter said.

"You never played hockey, Dad," Sam said.

"Nope," Hunter said, "I didn't. But my vision's all right, and I remember watching the two of you pretty closely when you played Weymouth that night."

"You didn't see us, the night we played Wollaston," Sam said.

"I know it," Hunter said. "You know where I was. I hadda go down and close up the cottage."

"Or the time we played Stoughton Red Wings," Sam said.

"And that was either the same thing," Hunter said, "or else I hadda work. You know how it is, Sam. Everybody has a nice time down there all summer, swimming and everything, and everybody wants to do something, and then somebody has to close up the place when the cold weather comes, and go out and make the money so everybody can do the things they want, and so far, nobody's given me a number I can call to find the guy who's hanging around waiting to do those things instead of me."

"Well," Sam said, "you still didn't see them."

"No," Hunter said, "no, I didn't."

"I played good in those games," Sam said.

"I'm sure you did," Hunter said. "You did all right in the one I saw."

"I kept getting caught up-ice," Sam said.

"You did all right," Hunter said. "You won, didn't you?"

"You said that, Dad," Sam said. "I kept getting caught up-ice. You're the one that said that."

"You won the game, didn't you?" Hunter said.

"Sure," Sam said, "but you said I was too interested in getting goals, and that was why I was always getting caught up-ice."

"I did not," Hunter said. "I said I thought you might be more interested in getting goals than a straight defenseman would be, and that as a result you had to skate awful hard all the time to get back when your team lost the puck."

"Mom said you said that," Sam said.

"Okay," Hunter said, "two things, all right?"

"All right," Sam said.

"First thing," Hunter said.

"First thing," Sam said.

"First thing is: you wanna know what I think, check with me, and ask me what I think, okay? Not Mom. You want to know what I think about something, you ask me and I'll never bullshit you. But you got to ask me."

"Okay," Sam said.

"You mother's all right," Hunter said. "She's a good woman and you oughta be proud of her. But she doesn't decide what I think, and she doesn't always know what I think. Got it?"

"Ten-four," Sam said, "message received."

"Second thing," Hunter said.

"Second thing," Sam said.

"Second thing is: hockey's a team thing," Hunter said. "I never played hockey, except a little pickup stuff down the pond. Nobody I ever knew really played hockey, and they didn't have hockey when I was in high school because there weren't any rinks, and my father couldn't've afforded the gear if they'd been playing someplace else anyway. But it's still a team sport, and I played a lot of those things, and there's not that much difference between them. You know something? You're young. You're gonna be alive for what looks like a long time, to you, now. Maybe you're not gonna be playing hockey all that time. Maybe it'll be something else. Maybe it'll be nothing else. Doesn't matter. Even if you turn out to be a cop like me, you're gonna have to learn it: everything, almost everything you're ever gonna do in this life, is going to be that you got one job to do and there's another guy next to you that's got the next job to do, and you both better do the jobs you're supposed to be doing.

"This case that I'm working on, that keeps me out late," Hunter said, "it's the same kind of thing. If the prosecutor's no good, then we probably lose. If I'm no good, then we probably lose. If I try to do his job, I haven't got time to do mine. If he tried to do my job, he's not in a position to do his. Who scores the goals in this game you got here," Hunter said, "who gets the assists, it's nice if you're the one, but it really doesn't matter. Long's the Canton Bruins've got more goals'n the Holbrook Flyers when the game's over. That's all. And that thing about whose number you're wearing, and who's wearing somebody else's? Forget it. The guy that's wearing the number can matter, but it's not gonna be because he had one number on instead of another one. It's what he does. Got it?"

"Yeah," Sam said.

"Now," Hunter said, "as a matter of fact, the night I saw you play, before, you know something? You did spend too much of your time in the other team's zone, and you know why."

"I was forechecking," Sam said.

"Why're you forechecking?" Hunter said.

"That's the style we play," Sam said. "Keeps the other guys off our goalie."

"Who's supposed to do the forechecking?" Hunter said.

"Everybody," Sam said. "That's the way we play the game. You've seen us. What we do is, we don't go right back. We sag back and bunch on the lines."

"I saw you get one," Hunter said. "You stole that thing like the guy wasn't even there, went right around him, deked the goalie onto his ass and hit it by him. How long did that take?"

"I dunno," Sam said, smiling.

"Well," Hunter said, "it wasn't very long. And you know why? Because when that forward swung his own net and came out, you were waiting for him at the edge of the face-off circle in the attacking zone. Isn't that right?"

"Yeah," Sam said.

"And you poke-checked it off his stick right *in* the face-off circle," Hunter said, "and I bet you didn't take more'n three steps before you were looking right down the goalie's throat and he just didn't have time to get set. Which is how come you got him the way you did. It happened too quick for him."

"*Yeah,*" Sam said.

"Well," Hunter said, "I don't think you're supposed to do that. When I was playing with the Giants in Springfield, we were out in Reading one night, and we had one hell of a dull game going on and all anybody there wanted to do was get the damned thing the hell over with and hit the road. I forget where we were going next. Pawtucket, Rochester, I dunno. So, of course, that was the night everybody picked to get a tie game going, and I guess it was about the thirteenth inning or something, and I'm leading off, and I hadn't done a damned thing all night. I think I booted one that should've been a double play, and everything I hit was nice and soft and right at somebody, and it was just a lousy night.

"So I was leading off," Hunter said, "and they had a new pitcher in, and all I could think about, and all anybody else could think about, was getting on the bus and cracking a beer. It was hot and muggy and everything else. So the manager tells me to bunt.

"Now that wasn't a bad idea for a manager to tell me to do," Hunter said, "because I was a very wristy hitter even when I was going good. My hands were okay, but I never did learn how to get the beef into it. I just wasn't the kind of player that you'd expect to have jerk one out of there.

"The only thing was," Hunter said, "they had a new pitcher in there, and there was only one thing that that kid could do: he could throw aspirins. He didn't have a curve and he didn't have a slider, and all you hoped about his knuckler was that he'd throw it when you got a couple guys on base, because it was automatic passed ball, always in the dirt. But he did have pretty good control, and he wasn't bad in the parks we played in because the lighting wasn't very good, and that fastball of his was a real smoker.

"He got spoiled from that," Hunter said. "The guys who really walloped pitchers just weren't used to anything in those lights that was quite as fast as he was, and they'd try to overpower him and just corkscrew themselves. But I was just a guy that tried to meet the ball, and I had very good eyesight, and a guy like that, guys like that, were just about the only chances I got all year to really park one.

"So Curly Billings told me to bunt," Hunter said. "Curly was a good guy. Had five or six years backing up Clint Courtney in Chicago, and a very bright fellow about strategy. Probably would've gotten a job in the majors if he'd lived long enough. Curly stuttered. Not much, but a little. He had to say something that began with b in order to say anything without stuttering. He said: *But.* 'Buh-but, Hunter,' he said, 'I want you to buh-bunt. Buh-but, go up there and lay it down.'

"I didn't argue with him," Hunter said. "I went up there and I got that bat cocked nice and easy and that pitcher wound up and threw one right in the wheel-house and I got the fat part of it out there, and that kid just supplied all the power, is all. The ball landed six miles away in the coalyard or something. And I just trotted around and went back into the dugout and Curly says to me: 'Buh-but, nice buh-bunt, Hunter.' Then the next three guys struck out, whiff, whiff, whiff, and Curly said: 'Buh-but, Consiglio, play second for Hunter.' And I sat on the bench for the next two weeks. Curly never said a thing to me, and I never said a thing to Curly, and the people in the big office saw those box scores coming in for the next two weeks, and if they were looking for somebody who could play second base pretty well, and maybe do a little utility work at short and third, and they probably were, because they always are, or there's somebody some-where in the majors that is, that you can be traded or waived or sold to, and maybe do a little punch-and-judy hitting so the heavy hitters'll have some runs to drive in ahead of themselves, well, those guys with the big money didn't see my name. They saw somebody else's, somebody who knew enough to buh-bunt when Curly said to buh-bunt.

"Now what you did was nice and flashy, and it worked like a charm," Hunter said. "But if that guy gets around a poke-check, which I understand's the easiest kind of a check to make, and the easiest to get away from, and if your forwards're in, checking like *they're* supposed to, and the guy gets around you, I don't think your goalie's gonna feel very protected, Sam, no matter what you call it. I think he's gonna have to come almost to the blue line and hope to God he can get the guy off the puck without getting faked out himself and giving the guy an empty net."

"Yeah," Sam said.

"What defensemen're supposed to do," Hunter said, "is stay at the point when their team's got the puck, and when the other team's got the puck, pull back in the defensive zone and get set for whatever they're gonna try to do, so you don't leave the poor bastard out there all alone. Isn't that right?"

"Uh huh," Sam said.

"Whaddaya think?" Hunter said. "Is that maybe why you got the idea I said you were up-ice too much?"

"Yeah," Sam said.

"What're you gonna do today?" Hunter said.

"Go back," Sam said, "like I'm supposed to."

"All right," Hunter said, "and I bet if you do that, you won't get caught up-ice anymore."

"I won't score no goals, either." Sam said.

"You wanna play forward?" Hunter said. "You're good enough and you're big enough."

"No," Sam said, "no, I don't."

"Then don't," Hunter said; "play defense. But *play* defense. Don't say you wanna play defense, and then go sneaking around, playing forward too."

"Dad," Sam said, "you gonna be home for supper tonight?"

"If I don't collapse," Hunter said, "and nothing comes up.

We're starting a trial of three or four guys up in Salem today, but, yeah, I expect to be home."

"Michele and Nicky asked me to ask you," Sam said.

"Tell them I said: 'Yes,' " Hunter said.

"I thought you were supposed to do that," Sam said.

"What's the second thing?" Hunter said, grinning.

"Isn't any," Sam said.

Part of Charlie's Report

□ 12

AT 9:15 ON THE MORNING OF NOVEMBER 16, 1973, Horace Carmody asked Hunter if he knew Arthur Collins.

"I don't think so," Hunter said. "Was he one of them guys down the Norfolk DA's Office?"

"The airport," Carmody said. "Over at the airport."

"Oh, yeah," Hunter said. "Big son of a bitch. About two-forty."

"That's the one," Carmody said.

"Made lieutenant, couple years back," Hunter said.

"You know alla guys that make lieutenant, don't you, Deke?" Carmody said.

"I was always fair-to-medium at reading," Hunter said. "They put out that list, and I can handle it. I go right ahead and I read it. See who made lieutenant? Yeah, I can do that."

"It's more, there's more to it'n that," Carmody said. "You know how they make lieutenant?"

"Ah," Hunter said, "it don't matter a bit, I got trial starting today; I'm still not getting away without my morning nagging. Lemme ask you something: did my wife call and tell you I hadda leave the house this morning before she could warm up the pipes, and you should take care of it when I got in here?"

"They're all sergeants on that list," Carmody said. "You study that list of new lieutenants, some time, that's all you're ever gonna see on it. Sergeants."

"You're a sergeant," Hunter said. "Never saw your name on the list."

"And you aren't gonna, either," Carmody said. "You know why?"

89

"You didn't pass the test?" Hunter said.

"I didn't take the test," Carmody said. "You know what I am? I'm a satisfied man. If I want, I can retire right now. As it is, I think I'm gonna give it about four, five more years, and then I retire and go out and get myself a nice job someplace, being chief of police and telling all them little kids about crosswalks, 'and don't go getting in no cars with strangers, the bastards'll pull down your little white panties and then make you blow them.' I'm gonna live to be a hundred, is what I'm gonna do. Go up to New Hampshire, one of those little towns you can spit across, and be chief. I'm not gonna take any shit from anybody, and I'm gonna have one guy working for me, which with luck, he won't show up.

"No thanks," Carmody said. "I took that god-damned exam, with my kind of luck I'd probably pass. Then I got to move, and I got to go someplace, and I got to work my ass off again, 'stead of doing something relaxing and giving you all the complicated stuff and trying to teach you some manners. I did that, if I came in late I'd probably get chewed out. Not me. I like it here."

"Well," Hunter said, "I can see that. I'd watch myself, I was you, you don't get gangrene or something, sleeping with your feet up all the time, but that's your business."

"How old're you?" Carmody said.

"Thirty-two in February," Hunter said.

"What've you got in?" Carmody said.

"With the service credit," Hunter said, "call it almost ten years."

"So," Carmody said, "you got ten, if you want, or twenty, to go. *Corporal*."

"If I stay," Hunter said.

"Lemme ask you this," Carmody said. "You gonna join the Pinkertons, is that what it is?"

"There's guys," Hunter said, "need somebody to go around and investigate things for them."

"Come on," Carmody said, "what's the matter with you? Didn't you hear about it, we got no-fault insurance, now? Those guys're starving to death. Investigate things. Shit. There aren't ten of them left that'll pay you enough to buy your gas."

"There's still divorces and missing persons and that estate work that they do, and the industrial stuff," Hunter said.

"Yeah," Carmody said. "Some weeks you get lucky and catch some asshole with a naked broad, and you might make fifty bucks. Look, you dope, you know what you got here? You got a paycheck. You keep on taking that paycheck for a few more years, and you know something? They'll keep giving you a paycheck, for the rest of your life. When you finally die, they'll give your wife a paycheck. It's not much, maybe, and it's hard to buy many steaks with it, but it's better'n relief.

"You quit now," Carmody said, "yeah, you'll get a paycheck. But you'll freeze your ass off guarding used-car lots at night with a vicious dog that's liable to bite you some fine evening when he gets bored from not finding any kids clipping hubcaps to bite, and you won't get no credit for what you did so far, to get that pension. It's just not as good, is all."

"Okay," Hunter said, "then I'm gonna stay where I am."

"That's dumb," Carmody said.

"Now look," Hunter said, "you're not gonna get away with that. I got up early this morning and my kid won his hockey game and I had my eyes open for several hours, so don't try to pull any of that shit on me. First you tell me I can't leave. Then you tell me I can't stay. I'm afraid of you because you're my superior officer, and everything, and I know you can send me to Leominster without even clearing your throat, and I'll be stupid for anybody that asks me anyway, because I'm naturally stupid. But not that stupid, so no matter what I do, I'm wrong. That's not fair."

"Nobody ever said it was fair," Carmody said. "You get a book some day and look that up and try to find it, where somebody said it was fair. I had an uncle of mine that ran for selectman in every election they had for more'n thirty years. He ran the pool hall, and he did all right off it, but of course everybody else figured the guy ran the pool hall hadda be the devil himself. Until he got to be about seventy. He was still running the pool hall, because I guess he didn't know what the hell else to do. Besides, you don't get no pension from running the pool hall, either. But for some reason he won. You been the devil all your life, when you get old, it's all of a sudden all right. People get used to you being the devil, or something, you keep at it long enough, or maybe you finally get enough of the kids that were your customers, grown up, and they can vote, and they never did think you were the devil anyway. I don't know. But he finally won. And you know what he did?"

"No," Hunter said.

"He had something blow up in his brain about a week before he was gonna get sworn in," Carmody said, "and he dropped dead. Aneurism. I never liked the guy personally very much. What he did was, he had this habit that he had, and he used to chew garlic cloves, and I didn't like the way he smelled when I was a kid. Maybe that's why nobody voted for him, because of that. I dunno. But they didn't, for a long time, and when they did, he dropped dead. That wasn't fair. Probably saved a lot of stomachaches for the other selectmen, but it wasn't fair."

"No," Hunter said.

"You think it was fair?" Carmody said.

"No," Hunter said. "I was agreeing with you. Sometimes that works with my wife, when she gets into one of these moods."

"Okay," Carmody said. "See, sometimes I got trouble with you, because when you say something, I don't always know what you mean. I always think I do, but then sometimes later, I find out that I didn't."

"I can see it's not gonna work with you, though, at least this time," Hunter said.

"See," Carmody said, "and it's the same thing with you. You go around all the time, and then you say something's not fair. Well, so what if it isn't, huh? Shanley's up there, and he's doing all the work today, am I right? He's picking a jury. And you're not even up there with him, helping the guy out the best way you can. Giving him moral support. That isn't fair."

"Not until eleven o'clock," Hunter said. "Judge's gonna put some poor unfortunate bastard away for three hundred years, that Ryan convicted, first."

"Yeah," Carmody said, "well, that doesn't matter. See, and look at poor Teddy Donnelly, sitting there in durance vile, waiting for somebody to try to put him in prison for the rest of his life, and what was he doing, huh? He was driving a car and he had a few drinks and he give some young punk of a cop something like you a whole ration of shit. Is that so bad? That isn't fair. So, what're you gonna do about it, huh? You tell me one thing."

"Well . . . ," Hunter said.

"You can't," Carmody said immediately. "You see what I mean? You can't, I'm just telling you. You're reading that lieutenant list, and you're not paying attention. You got to pay attention, at all fucking times. It's all sergeants on that list, all sergeants. You wanna get on it, first you gotta make sergeant. Simple as that. You read the sergeant list also?"

"Yeah, yeah," Hunter said.

"See?" Carmody said. "Now, that's the difference. Who're the guys that come out with their name on the sergeant list, huh?"

"Corporals," Hunter said.

"Which you are," Carmody said. "Now, but it takes *more'n* just that, doesn't it? More'n being a corporal. That's not enough, is it?"

"Nope," Hunter said.

"Because if it was enough," Carmody said, "then, you being a corporal and everything just as good as all them other corporals, well, if they ran it like the State lottery, then you could just sit there with your fingers crossed and your thumb up your ass and do nothing, and say: 'Okay, either my name comes up or it doesn't.' Maybe that *is* what you're doing. That what you're doing, Deke?"

"No," Hunter said.

"You sure?" Carmody said. "Looks like it to me. Looks to me like you're just sitting around and waiting for God to come up and promote you, you're such a hell of a guy and everything."

"Lemme up, Horace," Hunter said.

"That could be it," Carmody said. "Because if that isn't it you probably would've taken the exam or something. You didn't take the exam, did you?"

"No," Hunter said.

"That's what I thought," Carmody said. "I thought I remembered saying something to you one time, about it, about the test, I mean, and I thought you said you didn't take it. So it's probably the other thing, then. Jesus, I can't get over it. Here I thought I was bringing you up right, and I been letting you walk around with an idea like that in your head all this time.

"I had a cousin," Carmody said, "that, she was in the convent for a while, and then she got out because she didn't like it or something. I forget what it was. She got out, anyway. But she was still very religious, yes indeed, very religious, and she didn't like her smelly old uncle much either, that was her father's brother and he ran the pool hall. She didn't drink and she didn't smoke, which was all right with the rest of us, but what it was, we did drink and smoke and that was not all right with her. And she would just sit there, very straight, hands in her lap, always wore a sweater, a black sweater, didn't matter if it was cold or hot, winter or spring, didn't matter a bit, and she would glare at us. Oh, she was a joy to have around the Christian home."

"What she used to do," Carmody said, "she used to, her idea of getting a good grip on a situation was to go and make a novena about it. That was her cure for everything. My aunt was sick and then my uncle got sick too, and she was up day and night, they had plenty of money but she was up day and night taking care of them because they were all too fuckin' cheap to hire a nurse for at least during the day, and she was always making a novena at the same time. She'd come back and they'd be rolling in shit, they both lost control of their bowels, and she used to tell us how patient and saintly they were. They'd just lie there in the shit until she got back. 'And never once did either of them complain.'

"I quit on that," Carmody said. "The rest of us were helping out on the medical bills, and my wife was doing the grocery shopping for them sometimes, and she would go down there one afternoon a week and the rest of the women would go down there other times, so that Brenda could have a little time off. And do you think she would go to a movie or anything? The library? Take a walk? Have an ice cream cone? Nope. She'd sit there and make tea for everybody, and when either one of them called, she wouldn't let anybody else go near them.

"So then we found out," Carmody said, "the money we're giving them for medicine and things? They're putting it in the bank. They're doing without the medicine that the doctor said they should have, and we're paying for it, because otherwise we knew damned well they wouldn't get it, and goddamnit, they *still* weren't getting it. 'Ma and Pa never had much, you know,' she said. 'Their faith is what sustains them.' Honest to God. So, they died, naturally, and I just hope they got the full benefit of them novenas after it, because they had one shitty time of it before. Even the wakes were lousy. No booze.

"That what you're doing, Deke?" Carmody said. "Saying prayers instead of taking your medicine?"

"Nope," Hunter said.

"Then," Carmody said, "how come you didn't take the exam?"

"I didn't have time," Hunter said. "I haven't been, I haven't been out on the road in about a hundred years. I know what Shanley can get into evidence— well, I know what a good lawyer's supposed to be able to get into evidence—but I don't remember shit about the stuff they ask you about on those exams. What kind of a report you got to make when a goddamned schoolbus gets hit by a steamboat, or something."

"Nobody does," Carmody said. "The difference between you and the other guys is, they go and study it, and they can remember if for that long, at least, to take the test, and those're the guys that make sergeant. And then later on they take another one of those things, and they make sure when they do the exam that they tell the guy that reads the exams what the guy that made up the exams wants him told.

"You know something?" Carmody said. "I used to think it'd be a hell of a lot easier if the guys that wrote the exams just sat down in a room with the guys that correct the exams, and the ones that made them up told the ones that put the marks on them what the right answers were, and then just promote everybody with a certain amount of time in grade. Be much easier."

"I could go for that," Hunter said.

"You obviously think that's the way it actually is," Carmody said. "But, it's not. They still got the middleman in there, and that's you, and you got to write down for the guys that read it what it is that your lad in the Sam Browne belt's got to do when he arrives on a guy driving a screech owl to work in a pickup truck with no taillights.

"I know that it's dogshit," Carmody said. "I agree with you on that. But it's also how they promote guys, and it's those promotions . . . , hey, you do know this, don't you? You weren't thinking, you got promoted, they don't pay you anymore, you weren't thinking that. You didn't think that sergeants have to work for nothing? That all of a sudden, you're working for love?"

"No," Hunter said.

"No," Carmody said, "you'll be just like you are now, Deke. You'd still get your love at home, you'd still work here for money. But there would be a slight difference, Deke, that you oughta perhaps be aware of."

"I know," Hunter said.

"You'd get *more* money," Carmody said. "That's what the difference'd be. And you know something? More money's better'n less money. Much better. I was talking to a guy the other day and he didn't agree with me, but then I was over to the Foxboro Hospital there when I was talking to him, and he was in and I was out, so I don't hesitate to disagree with him. What happens when you get promoted, is, your paycheck's bigger. Not just the next one, like it was a reward or something that you only got once, like when you got promoted from the fourth grade to the fifth and your daddy gave you two bucks. Nope, every single one of them's bigger. And then, you get those for ten or twenty years, same as the smaller ones you would've gotten before, and you know what they do?"

"Yup," Hunter said.

"They give you more money, when you stop doing it, than they would've given you if you'd been doing it for less money when you were still doing it," Carmody said. "Isn't that something? You'd almost want to think maybe they wanted guys bad enough, that can pass the tests and do different kinds of work and all, so bad that they're willing to make that kind of guy better off than the kind of guys they don't want so bad. You think that's it? Probably is.

"Now," Carmody said, "you knock that. You just go ahead, and you take that, and you tell me what there is about it, that's not a better deal'n what you got now."

"I got this thing against money," Hunter said.

"Be careful, now," Carmody said. "I happen to be a police officer in this Commonwealth, and I should tell you, the only other time I heard somebody say something like that was that guy I was telling you about that was in Foxboro, and I think I know why he was in there. I see something that makes me think somebody's a danger to himself or the community, you know, I got an obligation to give you ten days in Bridgewater, during which we will find out if your head's screwed on straight, and if it was when you went in, it's not gonna be when you come out, I can promise you. I dunno know about what you just said. Kind of talk sounds irrational to me. You gonna start eating the rug, I have to go out and leave you alone for a while, I have to go to the bathroom or something?"

"Leave me alone," Hunter said.

"Hey," Carmody said, "I'm not the guy started talking about Collins making the list. You did that."

"I did not," Hunter said.

"You're the one knew he was onna list," Carmody said. "That's what I mean. I didn't ask you if you went bowling with him, for Christ sake. I asked if you knew who he was."

"The big guy that used to be down the airport,"

Hunter said. "That, and he made lieutenant, and that's all I know about him."

"Gonna take the exam?" Carmody said.

"Yeah," Hunter said.

"You said that the last time," Carmody said.

"You *are* worse'n my wife," Hunter said. "You know what I'm gonna do? I'm gonna go down and cuddle up to the Governor and get to drive his car, and the next thing you know, I'll get too fat for anything you got to move around on, and they'll have me over at Ten-ten, shuffling papers around."

"Right," Carmody said, "I can just see you there. I remember George Samuels telling me: 'Stay outa Ten-ten, son. All they got there's the guys that want to milk the golden goose until it's dry.' Besides which, anyway, you'd last about a half an hour with the Governor. Whyn't you be a judge, you want something that's easy and doesn't make you sweat much?"

"I didn't go to law school," Hunter said.

"All them other guys did, though," Carmody said. "If I was a guy, wanted to be a judge, the first thing I'd do'd be go and see the Governor, and I'd go and see him a lot, and when he finally got sick and tired of always having me around to see him all the time, and he really wanted to get rid of me in the worst fucking way, then he would ask me what I wanted. And I would say to him: 'I wanna be a judge.'

"Now I figure," Carmody said, "it'd probably take him a couple of minutes, get over that one. And, when he did, he would say: 'A judge? You go to law school?'

"Then I would spring right in," Carmody said. " 'Your Excellency,' I would say, 'no, I did not, and I don't have any other skeletons in my closet, either. That is exactly what I got going for me, that should make me a judge: I didn't go to law school, and I'm not a member of the bar, and I never committed no other felonies, neither.

" 'You just look at them other guys you got in there now, Your Excellency,' I would say," Carmody said. " 'You just look at them, always hacking around and screwing the thing up and getting you in trouble and letting bad guys out and just doing all kinds of stupid things, huh? Look at them. Can't even agree among themselves, what they oughta be doing. First, one of them says: "Do this, on account of this is what the law says you finally got to do, all right?" So, you're a nice fellow, wanna oblige the guy, you go out and you do it, and you arrest somebody, and you bring him in with his dirty fuckin' pictures or something, and now they got a different judge there. And he looks at you: "The hell you think you're doing, grabbing guys for showing movies? They got the First Amendment. Get the fuck out of here." And then they sue you. Now you see what that means, Your Excellency? First you do what they tell you to do, then they land all over you for doing it, "Can't have you guys doing what the statute says."

" 'Now, Your Excellency,' I would say," Carmody said, " 'and I don't mean any offense from this, but you know why those guys act like that? It's because they all went to law school. That's their idea of a good time. Confusing all the rest of us so sometimes we're supposed to grab the guys at the glory holes, and it's a goddamned outrage all the dirty stuff that's going on, and sometimes we're not supposed to run them in because anybody's got a right to be a fairy if he wants. What you need up there in them black dresses, Your Excellency, is some guys with some common sense.'

"That's what I'd do," Carmody said. "Pay isn't bad, either, twenty-five, thirty thousand a year, you can take a long lunch and all you've got to do's look smart and keep your mouth shut if you're not. Doesn't matter if you really aren't. And you don't even have to remember that more'n two or three times a day. You could manage it easy."

"I'll do it," Hunter said.

"You can't," Carmody said. "I said I was the one that was going to do it. If I did it, the Governor'd probably be convinced. You did it? He'd think about it. He'd probably even buy it for a while. But that's another thing you got to keep in mind: when you want something from a governor, try and get it set up so he hasn't got time to think about it. You did it and he'd say: 'Hey, this guy's a corporal. He's been a corporal ever since Pershing came back. He likes working for twelve grand so much, he doesn't want fourteen. Nope, he's too dumb.'

"You let him think something like that," Carmody said, "he'd end up not even listening to you in the first place. He'd think the real reason was, you're so dumb you couldn't even *be* a lawyer. I dunno if the governor can commit guys or not. He probably can. If I was the governor, I'd commit a guy like that. I wouldn't have him around, a guy so dumb he couldn't even be a lawyer. He'd be likely to give himself a mortal wound, shaving with an electric razor.

"Course," Carmody said, "I suppose you could try that. You could say: 'Hey, Excellency, you see how qualified I am? I'm so stupid I'm not fit to be anything like a cop. Better put me onna bench. You don't and I'm liable to end up at State Police Headquarters for the rest of my life, and that'll screw up something important.' You could do that. It might work."

"You should've been an auctioneer," Hunter said.

"Then on the other hand," Carmody said, "you got Lieutenant Collins. Now there's a smart man. Got his time in at the best wages, and quit. 'Not me,' he said. 'I been living in a rathole long enough. Gimme that pension. From now on, I work fifteen minutes a week and I don't have to wear them goddamned puttees that shut off my circulation, either, and in the meantime, you're gonna keep paying me. I'm gonna make out all right, is what I'm gonna do.'

"And he did," Carmody said. "Got himself a nice fat job with a bank and started going around looking serious at everybody, so they don't take it into their heads, steal any paperclips or anything. Made out like a bandit.

"You know what that guy talks about now?" Carmody said. "You used to see him, Arthur's a pretty good guy, he was down at the airport, there. He always had some pretty good stories, and I understand there was some even better stories that he didn't tell, because he was in them. And he was always talking about what's on the wire, who's going around, who's doing things. Well, not anymore. Now he's always worried. He's got this look on his face. He loves it. 'I don't know what to do. I bought Holiday Inns at twenty-three, and now look at that stock: seventeen.' Oh, he's beautiful. You know what he's gonna do, Deke? He's gonna die rich. And you? You're just gonna die. As cheap as possible, so your wife can buy groceries for the kids next week, maybe."

"Not right off," Hunter said. "I'm getting ready for the sergeants' exam, and it'll take me a while. There's this guy I know, he won't leave me alone. I got to stay around for that. I don't, he'll probably find some way to haunt a dead man."

"Couldn't be bothered," Carmody said. "Not enough money in it. You wanted me to haunt somebody, I'd have to have, oh, say, the pension. And maybe, thirteen. That'd be good. Eight weeks' vacation. Paid by the taxpayers, of course, and on the weekends we'd take out the trusted Auxiliaries and let them direct traffic. Unless there's a softball game.

"That's what I need, you know?" Carmody said. "I like to watch the football, play a little softball, maybe. Never mind all of these drunks that drive cars, always smashing into trees and things, you got to cut them out with a torch and rush 'em to the goddamned hospital at great danger to your own life and limb. Nope, let the other guys do it.

"There's a certain class of guys," Carmody said, "that always wanted to be cops, only their parents or somebody with some sense gave them chemistry sets and they ended up being scientists and distillers and teachers and shit like that, making about a million bucks a year. Hey, more power to them.

"I didn't have any sense," Carmody said. "You didn't have any sense. It's not our fault. We just didn't have any. But the thing of it is, a guy who thinks about things can still get some use out of them. Because, see, they never got over wanting to be cops. So I say: 'Let 'em be cops.' On the weekends. It's better'n if they spent all their spare time in the bathroom, jerking off, and we won't give them guns, or anything, all right? Guns're for cops. But we'll just let them go out there and do all the stuff for nothing that nobody in his right mind'd do for money, and tell them they're cops. They'll be beating down the doors for it.

"Like Collins," Carmody said. "You think that guy was a cop?"

"Sure," Hunter said.

"He was not," Carmody said. "He was a banker. He just started off, he got the wrong blue suit. He's like that little thin guy that's supposed to be inside the big fat guys, trying like a bastard to get out. He was a banker inside of a cop, and he finally got out. He still looks something like a cop, because it's hard to forget. He quit the security business at the bank and went to work for Allied, that business thing that owns everything in sight, and now he's responsible for their security. But he calls his broker, and he really likes it, and by Jesus, when somebody hijacks something off of Allied, they got old Arthur after them, hammer and goddamned fucking tongs. Because Allied owns a lot of companies, and there's always somebody trying to steal something off of one of them, but Arthur owns stock in Allied, and that means those bastards're stealing it off of him. And that my friend, is different. Nobody steals nothing off of old Arthur, boy, no, sir. It's pretty hard to bum a cigarette off the bastard, and that's when he's looking right at you. He's got those quarterly dividends he's got to think about. He doesn't care if the stuff's insured: those insurance premiums come off his profits too. He used to be pretty easygoing, tell a few jokes and have a few beers, but now he's your regular bulldog, gets you by the ankle and starts chewing his way up. But not because he's a cop, used to be a cop, sometimes he forgets he isn't still a cop. Nope, because he was always very shrewd. He was never a cop."

"Okay," Hunter said, "I'll take the exam, then, and when I get there, I'll be like Arthur. Only when I get something hot, I'll call you."

"You don't wanna be a cop, then," Carmody said.

"I am a cop," Hunter said.

"By accident," Carmody said.

"I don't think so," Hunter said.

"You reasonably sure of that?" Carmody said.

"Yeah," Hunter said. "Yeah, I'm sure of it."

"I saw Charlie yesterday afternoon," Carmody said. "After you told me, Donnelly's in, I called Charlie, and I saw him."

"Okay," Hunter said.

"Charlie had quite a lot to say," Carmody said. "For one thing, of course, he's scared shitless of Donnelly."

"I wouldn't think you'd have to go and see a guy that knows Donnelly, to find out that was true," Hunter said.

"Said old Teddy's put at least four guys to sleep, he knows about," Carmody said.

"I believe it," Hunter said. "What interests me is, how'd he get old Teddy out of that quarry where some other guys put him, and into Brattleboro, Vermont, where he was lively enough to steal a car and get himself drunk as a fiddler's bitch?"

"Simple," Carmody said, "According to Charlie, Teddy's branched out into jobs for other guys that don't want certain people around anymore, and he did one in Vermont and put the gentleman in a quarry up there, somewhere around Ludlow or something, and the way Charlie got it was garbled and he sort of assumed it was down here, in Quincy. I guess."

"Pretty thin," Hunter said. "Not that it matters a fuck of a lot, but it sounds pretty thin."

"Well, you know how it is," Carmody said, "isn't anybody I know of, that's always right. Charlie's right a lot of the time, and I tend to trust him."

"What'd he say about Donnelly?" Hunter said.

"Quite a lot," Carmody said, "and some of it sounded pretty interesting, too."

"Let's hear it," Hunter said.

"Let's start with what he said about you," Carmody said. "That was even more interesting."

"Me?" Hunter said.

"Well," Carmody said, "you and that girl you've been fucking, down in Rhode Island, the one with the red hair and the tits? He says maybe there's somebody in the world that's hooked in better with the

Mafia'n that broad is, but offhand, he doesn't know who it might be."

"Horace," Hunter said, "wait a minute."

"I don't think so," Carmody said. "I don't think I really wanna know, what you gotta say, you know? I think I got maybe a pretty big problem with you, and I don't know what the hell to do about it.

"For a long time, Deke," Carmody said, "I kept watching you, and I wondered: how come a guy I know and like, like you, hasn't got any ambition. You got talent. I know that. But you haven't got no ambition, and for a guy with talent, that's kind of unusual. When there's no reason I can see why he hasn't.

"Now," Carmody said, "there's, I start thinking, and the only two reasons I know of, a guy with something on the ball hasn't got no ambition. Guys that didn't start off with any money of their own, at least. One of them's pussy and the other one's money."

"Horace," Hunter said.

"You haven't got any money," Carmody said. "I thought about that. I did. You could've hid it from me. That cottage there, down in Rhode Island, that you're always going to: that could be yours, and you're always just telling me it's her father's, so I won't know. I dunno that much about you. I haven't checked any deeds. It could be. And if you did it right, it wouldn't do me no good to check deeds anyway. But then, I don't think so. Anybody's as dumb as you, he's too dumb to hide money where I can't find it, so I didn't even bother looking.

"That, old pal, leaves pussy," Carmody said. "And I thought about that, and I asked around, and I came up with zilch. But of course I was asking around in Massachusetts, and you were getting laid in Rhode Island, and what I needed, then, was doing time in Massachusetts and not making any deals and exchanging small talk with a lot of guys that steal things in Rhode Island. Which Charlie finished doing lately, as you know.

"Well," Carmody said, "I got thoroughly pissed off at myself. I never even thought of that. There you were down in Rhode Island for a very long trial, that

Rossi thing, which everybody thought you had wired and tied up, and then you lost it, and now you're back here but you're still going down there, and here I am wandering around like a jerk, trying to find out if you're fucking up here. Of course not. You started fucking down there, and I don't even wanna think about, right now, what that means with Rossi getting off, and you're still fucking down there. What an asshole I am. I think I'm getting simple."

"You got to listen to me," Hunter said.

"Nope," Carmody said, "I'm way past that point. With you and everybody else. I'm old enough now so that when I've got something to say, I just go ahead and say it. Let a guy know what I think, where I stand. And I haven't finished with you.

"Money and pussy for a married cop," Carmody said, " 're exactly the same thing. Sooner or later, you're taking either one—and this is only what I think, but then I'm the guy that's doing all the thinking right now, because you sure aren't—sooner or later you're gonna have to do something for it.

"Don't matter to me," Carmody said. "I'm locked in, secure, and it don't matter to me. They get rid of every town in New Hampshire, give up on cops altogether, doesn't matter a fuckin' particle to me. I'll go home, and I'll fish, and every third summer I'll go to Florida and fish some more, and guys'll come up to me and say: 'What happened?' And I'll tell them: 'Made a little miscalculation. Spent my whole life getting to be a cop, and then they did away with cops. Meet my fishing buddies. Here's a guy, made buggy whips. Fella here made near-beer. Got us three pompano yesterday.'

"It'll be all right," Carmody said. "I'll still eat, even if I do have to catch most of it myself. But you, my friend, are something different, and I don't know what the hell to do about you. I got something from a guy that I've gotten a lot of things from, over the years, and you know that, and what I got from him could get somebody else killed, and him with them, and that don't strike me like the kind of gratitude I oughta be showing, you know? But if I tell you, who're you gonna tell? And if I don't tell you, somebody who's a real bad bastard's gonna duck something that he shouldn't duck, and I'm too goddamned old to ought to have to put up with this kind of a problem."

"You, Horace, Jesus," Hunter said. "You gotta let me say something."

"You can say anything you want," Carmody said, "but this is Friday, and I'm not gonna hear it until Monday.

"I don't know this broad," Carmody said. "For all I know, she can suck your spine out. Great. But I don't wanna hear about it. You go up and you sit there with Shanley, and you help him pick this jury, and when he asks you to do something, you do it. But now I'm gonna ask you something, and on Monday you're gonna come in and tell me the answer. *And, Deke, I'm gonna believe it.* No matter what you tell me, I'm gonna believe it, and I'm gonna do what I think I oughta do, believing what you tell me. You tell me then: have they got you or not?"

Barney Locke Was an Expert

□ 13

ON THE EVENING OF NOVEMBER 16, 1973, Deke Hunter and Barney Locke went into the living room of Hunter's house in Canton, Massachusetts, leaving Andrea Hunter and Diane Locke with the dishes soiled by the lasagna. Deke said that he'd been up early to drive Sam to his hockey game, and that he wasn't sure how long he could last. Barney said he had to be up early for a traffic-division detail on a construction project on the Massachusetts Turnpike at Auburn. They sat down.

"You don't look good, Deke," Barney said.

"I been flogging the duck too hard," Hunter said. "I been going day and night, and now we're starting trial on that Danvers National case, and I got to sit with my mouth shut while everlasting-asshole Shanley makes a mess of it. It wears you down."

"Tough case?" Locke said.

"I don't think so," Hunter said. "I think my dog could try this case, and at least get over a directed verdict without worrying very much. But my dog's out of town for the month, and I got Shanley instead. So instead I spent most of the day in the courtroom, watching Shanley waste his peremptory challenges knocking women off the jury."

"Why women?" Locke said.

"I dunno," Hunter said. "I asked him that, after we got through for the day, and he said women do funny things sometimes. Which is true, I guess, but there's two women tellers gonna testify in this case, about how they're scared shitless when the defendants

107

came in, and there's Shanley, knocking women off as fast as he can. Then he let this sneaky-looking bartender stay on. One look at the guy and you know he spends more time booking horses'n he does pouring drinks. I can't figure it out. It always scares the shit out of me when I get Richard Shanley on one of my cases. He's unpredictable."

"What you need," Locke said, "are some tapes." Locke was thirty-two years old. He had reasonably long reddish blond hair, and he wore boots and a gray blazer suit with brass buttons, and a white turtleneck.

"Oh yeah," Hunter said, "what I need is tapes. I had tapes, thank you. It was damned near the end of me. You guys that fuck around, listening in all the time, you think that's the end of the world. You got the tapes and you got the guy frozen stiff and delivered up. Bull*shit*."

"It's broken," Andrea said in the kitchen. Deke could see her through the counter opening of the dining area. She was putting dishes in the sink. "The rinse cycle really doesn't work. You've got to stop it and open it and close it and start it again. Sometimes it doesn't work even then, and you have to do it four or five times.

"I just gave up on it," she said. "It's like everything else. The same thing. Like the refrigerator. They've got . . . , the repairman told me they've got a heater in there for the defrosting, the automatic defrosting? I knew it was there. This's about the tenth time it broke and we hadda pay for a new one. I knew it was in there. He said to me, he said: 'Lady, it's nine years old. You bought it when they were just getting those things developed.' 'What difference does that make?' I said to him. 'Lady,' he says, 'back then, they were practically still inventing that device. Look, lemme tell you something, all right? Don't just, don't assume, refrigerators, *anything,* if they put the thing out, they must have it perfected. Never buy nothing, it first comes out. Cars or anything. Know why? Because they're still working on it.

" 'The trouble is,' he tells me," Andrea said, " 'they can only work on about ten of them at a time. And the guys that work on them, make a lot of money.

And they don't *pay* any money. So, the company brings it out before those guys get through working on it. They got tooling, they got, maybe, subcontractors making new pumps and hardware and plumbing and stuff like that, those guys've got tooling costs too. Plus they gotta stockpile materials.

" 'Now look, lady,' he says to me," Andrea said, " 'I'm gonna tell you something, all right? I shouldn't be telling you this. Somebody hears about it, could cost me my job. Because people like you are my job, that buy things like this. But you really think, they're gonna make a lot of machinery up, spend a lot of money on designing and tooling, hire them ten guys to test things the best way they can, put up a building and plug in about five thousand of these here refrigerators, fill 'em up with all kinds expensive food, and just leave them there for about three or four years which'd be about how long it'd take to find out if the thing worked, just so you don't have to pay forty-eight bucks for me to come around and fix the heater this year? You think they're gonna do that? They are not. It'd cost too much for the thing, after they did it, for you to buy it, and besides, by the time they brought it out for more'n you can afford, somebody else would've brought it out for what you can pay, just like they did with this one, only it don't work very good. Buy a new one. They got real good heaters on them now. They learned a lot from us, only they can't install them new heaters in these old boxes 'cause they'd overload like *that.*'

" 'Look,' I said to him," Andrea said to Diane, " 'what is this stuff, I'm supposed to be feeling sorry for you? Thirty bucks, forty bucks, fifty bucks, get you to come down here and tell me the heater quit the third time in a year, and you haven't got the right parts, and in the meantime, the damned thing's gonna sound like I had an iron lung in the kitchen and all my meat and ice cream and vegetables're gonna melt? Get offa the pot, willya?' I'm telling you, Diane, you got to talk to them like that."

"I know you do," Diane said.

"'I wished I was making thirty dollars every twenty

minutes, go driving around handing out that line of crap like that to people that're losing their food that they hadda work long hours to pay for because the goddamned refrigerator breaks down and everything that's frozen starts melting, thawing, and everything that's regular starts spoiling. You think I paid four hundred bucks for this thing, so I can go next door and borrow ice, and go down to the store and buy bags of it? You son of a bitch. My grandmother had a better one, and she always lived on a farm. It was made of wood, and it had a place on top where you put the ice, and when you needed ice, you expected you were gonna need it, you put a sign in the window and the man stopped with some. And then you had some place to put the ice, so the milk didn't sour.'

" 'Lady,' he says, 'get a new one, then.'

" 'Mister,' I says, 'he won't buy me a new one,' " Andrea said.

"I can't afford one," Deke said.

"I wasn't talking to you," Andrea said, "and I wasn't talking about you, either. I was telling Diane what I said to that robber, and if you want to listen, all right. But don't start getting your two cents' worth in all the time."

"I can't afford two cents, either," Deke said.

" 'It came with the house,' he keeps saying," she said. "I guess I came with the house too. God only knows what'll happen when I break down. I think I'll just have to lie there and do nothing."

"But neither one of us'll be able to tell the difference," Deke said. "I won't, at least."

"They're all the same," Diane Locke said. "The only things he thinks about're his things. In the summer it's the boat. In the winter it's the snowmobile. He hunts in the fall. In the spring I dunno what he does. I think it's fishing. Yeah, he goes fishing. He's never around where he can see anything that goes wrong, or get worried about it, and that kind of thing. He leaves all that kind of thing to me, and personally, I could do without it."

"I'm working, is why," Locke said. "The way you go

through money, it's a wonder I got time enough to sleep."

"You guys," Andrea said, "you just sit in there and drink your beer and relax and let us do the work like always, all right? And leave us alone."

"Isn't that something?" Locke said. "I work my ass off."

"I know it better'n you do, probably," Hunter said. "Every time you go out and buy something, I get to hear about it, in detail. There've been times when I could've killed you. Or else I would've whacked you a good right on the nose, you'd've been handy."

"Rained like a bastard out there last Sunday," Locke said. "Oh, Jesus, did it rain. Got soaked right down to my jock's what I did, out there all day. Got home, I made a big eighty bucks, and what do I get? More of the same, wrapped up different. I work? I get hell for working. I stay home? It turns out I should be working, on account of how we need the money, and if I'm not gonna work, the least I can do is fix all the things that're broken that we haven't got money enough to get somebody to fix because I'm not working. And when I do that, I get hell, because I don't know how to do it right and they don't work after I do it. And besides that, it was broken for a long time before I got around to trying to fix it and it's probably gonna break again, Monday morning, fifteen minutes after I leave for work. I can't figure it out."

"How many're you doing?" Hunter said. "You must be doing five a month, if there's that many weekends in a month."

"Let me tell you something, all right?" Locke said. "The last four weeks, what am I doing?"

"Nothing," Hunter said. "You guys in Boston, you got a great deal. I bet you must work ten, fifteen hours a week. Surveillance, my ass."

"Make it closer, sixty, seventy," Locke said. "I got three locations, and I got three guys that're supposed to be helping me, only they each got a couple machines of their own out. So I only get about half of their time, if I'm lucky. You know Crispino?"

"No," Hunter said.

"Well," Locke said, "write his name down someplace where you won't lose it, and when you find yourself someplace where he is, get the fuck out, all right?"

"Anything you say," Hunter said.

"He's about a hundred and sixty pounds," Locke said, "five feet both ways. And he's a machine gun champion. Old Louville got ahold of him, and the guy can do embroidery with a Thompson.

"Now for some reason or other," Locke said, "he thinks because his arms're like trees and he can hold the muzzle down, this makes him A-Number-One Genius. Which, as a result I got him under me.

"Well," Locke said, "the guy is actually as dumb as rocks. I mean, he is *stupid*. He is spectacularly stupid. When he goes to the head he oughta tie a string around the doorknob and the other end around his dick, so he doesn't forget what he went in there for, and then, after he does it, how to find his way back.

"Now keep in mind," Locke said, "what I've got this guy doing. Not because I think he oughta be doing it. It's the only thing I got for a guy to do, and I got him as one of the guys to do things. I have got this guy taking care of machines, and one of the ones—this is my mistake—I got him taking care of, is one we couldn't get a leased line for. So it's right in the building where the phone actually is. I don't know what the hell it was. No room on the main frame at the phone company or something. But that's where it is.

"Anyway," Locke said, "when I give him this assignment, I didn't know what he was. And I tell him, he's got to go in every forty-eight hours, because that's all the tape we got, and if it's all right with him, I'd just as soon nobody got too good a look at him.

"I got to explain it to him," Locke said. " 'Junior,' I say. He wants everybody to call him *Junior*. Can you imagine that? Here is a guy, thirty years old, looks like a gorilla, he wants everybody to call him *Junior*. Ridiculous. His mummy always called him *Junior*, because he was named after his daddy. 'Junior,' I say, 'you know how these guys are. They are very suspicious. They get the idea that somebody's tapping them, pretty soon they're not gonna be saying so much on that phone anymore, and then we got to go and find the one they switch to, and do a whole lot more surveillance, and get another warrant, and start all over again. And in the meantime, we're probably gonna miss about a month or so of talking that we'd really like to have.

" 'Now that means,' is what I told him," Locke said, " 'I'd just as soon you thought up some way you can get in that basement every day without somebody deciding you're not the meter reader, so he calls the cops or he tells the landlord or something.' Because you know what's gonna happen if he does get grabbed," Locke said, "and so do I. He's gonna say: 'Not me, Officer. I'm Trooper Crispino of the State Police.' And then every hood east of Worcester'll start passing notes to everybody, instead of talking on the phone.

"Now guess what he comes up with," Locke said. "I probably shouldn't criticize this guy, because what I thought of myself instead's not secure either, but his idea is, he's going to tell anybody that asks him that he's from the Building Inspectors, and he's checking every office in the place.

" 'Oh for Christ sake,' I says to him. 'You're not even gonna wait to get captured. You're gonna surrender. You look about as much like a Building Inspector as you do a milkman.' He looks just like a cop."

"So do you," Hunter said. "So do I. I didn't use to look like a cop, I don't think. I wonder how that happens. We all do, though. We all do."

"It's the training," Locke said. "It's the eyes. You look around too much. You go into a place, and the only guys that look around like a cop does're either guys that used to be cops, or are cops, or they're doing something that they don't want cops to know about or see them doing, so when they come in, they look around for cops just like cops look around for them. That's what it is. I think that's what it is. You get used to doing it, so you just keep on doing it all the time or else you don't feel comfortable."

"It's more'n that," Hunter said. "We walk different, too."

"On the balls of your feet," Locke said. "That's

from watching Broderick Crawford too much on television. *Highway Patrol.*"

"Or else we just like to do it," Hunter said, "and we copy it and then we can tell each other, the minute we see somebody else that's in it."

"Well," Locke said, "Crispino doesn't do it. He walks like a fuckin' duck. But otherwise you could put him in a sellout crowd at Fenway Park, and anybody that really needed a cop'd be sitting next to him before the second inning was over, even if he never stood up the whole time. So I said to him: 'Junior, that's not gonna work.' And I've got him, the best I could come up with was to rent a small office and put the machine every day and pretends like he's a cosmetics jobber."
there instead of in the cellar, and Junior goes in there

"Why the hell'd you pick that?" Hunter said.

"Because his mother's an Avon Lady," Locke said. "He can find out something about that business in a hurry, so he doesn't sound like a goddamned idiot if somebody asks him what his business is. 'Look,' I said to him, 'I know you don't like it.' See, what he was gonna say is, he's a second-mortgage investor. What Crispino knows about mortgages you could stick in your ear with a carrot and not feel nothin' but the carrot. 'You don't know anything about mortgages, Guy,' I say to him, and he says: 'Call me *Junior*, okay, Barney?' 'Junior,' I say, 'you still don't know anything about mortgages. It's got to be something you know about, in case somebody asks you. You got to remember that these guys aren't very stupid.' So he did it. Now every time he comes into the office, all the guys say: 'Bing bong, Avon calling,' and he doesn't like it a whole lot, but I figure maybe it'll mean he won't get caught for a month or so, and when he does, maybe by then we'll be able to get a loop on, or a leased line, but at least a loop, and get him across the street. Right now we're running directly off of the terminal box, and sooner or later the guy's gonna check it out and see where we had the alligator clips on it, and then he'll start tracing wires and we'll be out of business. I know it's gonna happen. It's just a matter of time.

"Now," Locke said, "during the week, that's what

I do. Fifty-five, sixty hours a week. I send the guys out, and I go out myself, and I listen to tapes, some of them, at least, and I read the transcripts, and all the time I'm praying to God, one of those dopes I got working under me doesn't get caught and then start explaining things, because you know what one of those nice fellas that's on the take's gonna do with that, when he hears it. I end up blowing everything I've got close to a year invested in, and that takes me all week and the holidays and everything. Then, on the weekends, I'm out on the road."

"You're gonna kill yourself," Hunter said.

"If I was getting someplace," Locke said, "it'd be all right. You take a guy like I know in the Worcester DA's Office, took the real estate agent's exam, he gets his weekends off and he can show a few houses and make a few dollars. You can look at that and say: 'Okay, it's worth it.' You got something to show for it.

"But I haven't," Locke said. "You know what I made? I worked seven out of the last eight paid details that I could've, and I would've worked the other one only I was bushed the day it came in. I got five hundred and fifty bucks out of that, and the government lets me keep four-fifty of it till they can think of a way to come around and get the rest of it in April, and then I'll have to work more details because I will've spent what I got left, now. Hell, it's spent already. I got a cold, I don't have time enough to get a haircut or anything, and it's all supposed to be gravy."

"So you know what I do?" Locke said. "I act like it is, asshole that I am. It's ten-sixteen an hour. And you look at it and you think: if they wanna run them bulldozers and front-end loaders on the weekends, and make me rich asking people to slow down while they back them across the road and everything, fine by me. But the thing of it is, I'm doing it and I'm doing it and I'm still not getting rich. It's very difficult, getting rich, is what I find. I get something, but it looks like lots more'n it really is until you start spending it, and then it doesn't look like much at all. That's what gets you, and then you start minding it and dragging your ass."

"Then quit it, why don't you?" Hunter said.

"Good idea," Locke said. "Trouble is, it's not so fuckin' easy, once you start it. I'm probably gonna go over twenty this year, which is more money in one year'n I ever saw in my whole life. And if I take the exam . . . , I'm really, I dunno. I keep thinking: if I make sergeant, maybe then lieutenant, and then I'll be able to quit the details and not miss it. But, Hell, no way's the money the same.

"It just doesn't work out the way you think it's gonna," Locke said. "I remember, when I started, and this kind of thing first came up, that they would let guys in the DA's offices do them, and you'd've had to tie me down to stop me. I wanted a lot of things. And George Samuels said to me, he was just getting over his accident. Limping like a bastard."

"George Samuels didn't limp," Hunter said.

"He maybe didn't limp when you saw him," Locke said. "He sure-God limped when I saw him. You remember them gypsies down there?"

"No," Hunter said.

"That's why, then," Locke said. "There was a whole group of them, used to walk into stores and take things and they had everybody so buffaloed they wouldn't even call the cops on them. And when you did catch one of them, they had about a hundred different names each, and you never could tell whether you had one of the ones you were looking for or some stray that wandered in from Florida in his goddamned pickup truck and found out there was things most people could get away with.

"They had this racket," Locke said, "which if you had a house with an asphalt driveway, they'd drive up and they'd tell you they'd treat it, you know?"

"Sealant?" Hunter said.

"That's the real stuff," Locke said. "Nobody that needs the stuff and wants somebody else to spread it for him, knows what it looks like, but the King of the Gypsies does."

"Who's the King of the Gypsies?" Hunter said.

"Any male gypsy that gets arrested or gets put in the hospital," Locke said. "They pass that title around like it was the flu bug. Whoever needs it, he's got it, and everybody goes in and raises hell until the people that've got him're so sick and tired of all the yelling that they do what the gypsies want.

"Well," Locke said, "what they'd do, was, you'd go down to Zayre's and you'd look at sealant when your driveway started to crack, and you'd find out it's gonna cost you eighty bucks, say, plus the squeegee to spread it with, plus which you lose a whole day and ruin a pair of shoes putting it on, and it stinks. And then them gypsies come by in the trucks and they'll do the job for thirty bucks. So, what the hell, you go for it, and them gypsies come by and they hop right out of them pickup trucks, and they got all these barrels full of crankcase drippings which they spread on your goddamned driveway, take your money and leave. It's gonna be a year before that stuff gets worn off enough so you can let people walk on your driveway before they walk into your house, and your rugs're gonna be ruined by the oil, but what the hell, where're you gonna find three gypsies that screwed you, huh?

"Well," Locke said, "George hated them gypsies. And there was one of them that was stealing a tractor one night, down in the bogs, there. Got into somebody's shed and knocked over about a hundred and fifty empty cases and drove the thing out through the shallow water and the guy's crop, I guess. And nine or ten people saw there was something going on when the guy got to the road, and called up the barracks, and George heard about it on the radio.

" 'I know who he is, the bastard,' George says," Locke said, "and he got himself dressed.

"George don't wear his pants in the house, you know that?" Locke said. "He's so goddamned cheap he won't wear his pants 'less he's going out. Gets home, the first thing he does, he takes his pants off and puts on his bathrobe, and he sits around in that. I said: 'George, you're just wearing out the bathrobe, 'stead of the pants, you know.' Said he didn't care if he wore out the bathrobe. He could still wear the bathrobe, because nobody was gonna see him in that.

The pants, if he wore them out, people'd see he was wearing worn-out pants. 'You get the seat all shiny.'

" 'My ex-wife,' he said, 'said the same thing.' " Locke said. " 'Used to drive her crazy. I didn't wanna wear my pants out. They warned me about her. They said: "What does she know?" '

"If you wanted to get George upset," Locke said, "all you had to do was play dumb when he got excited. Pissed him off. 'She refused to understand,' he said. He said he spent most of his time convincing people, by doing things, that he was going to do the things he said he was going to do, if they didn't do what he told them to. So the gypsies drove him nuts. He was after those gypsies forever, and everytime he got close to them, the woman that said she was all of their mother'd come in and start screaming, and all of a sudden he wouldn't have any witnesses.

"Which griped him," Locke said. "She was a real jewel, that one. None of her boys ever did anything wrong. And any one of the boys that he arrested was always one of her boys. 'Must've had them in litters, like squirrels,' he said. See, they never get any birth certificates or anything. It's impossible to know for sure who you're dealing with. 'They been around since before Jesus Christ,' he said. 'They're the guys that bought the garments from the soldier that won them in the dice game. They're all over the place.' There were more people scared of the mother'n there were of her boys, and people were scared shitless of her boys.

"So he heard it on the radio, about the tractor," Locke said, "and he put his pants on and went out looking for the guy.

"The guy was drunk," Locke said, "and he was whaling that tractor down Fifty-eight with no lights or anything, and George went out and found him before anybody else did, and ran him off the road. In his own private car, by the way, and this is the guy that saves his pants.

"Now the guy's in the ditch with the tractor," Locke said, "and George gets out of his car and tells him he's under arrest, and up the guy comes out of

the ditch on his tractor, hell-bent for leather and hollering like a banshee, and runs George down.

"George falls in the ditch," Locke said. "It's not a
very deep ditch, but there's water in it, and George's
leg was broken and the bastard slews the tractor onto
the road. He's gonna get away again.

" 'I was so goddamned mad,' he told me," Locke
said, " 'I didn't even think about it.' And he took out
his gun and he shot the bastard, right in the ass.

"Guy loses the tractor," Locke said. "Got hurt
pretty bad, actually, and the bullet was the least of
it. Although George did tell me that he used to notch
his slugs. And George got up and dragged the bum leg
all the way out of the ditch and he got back to the
car and onto the radio, and they said it was really
something. Because in between when he's talking to
them, and giving his position, and telling them they're
gonna need two meat wagons, he's also explaining
certain things by hollering at the prisoner, and he's
not shutting off the mike while he does it.

" 'I'm not riding in nothing with that cocksucker,'
he says. He also, the guy's crawling around and he's
going for the tractor again. 'You bastard, you bastard,' he says, 'you lie still or I'll make you look like
somebody used you to strain spinach.' And he let off
a couple more shots, too, and it didn't matter, you're
hearing it on the radio, he wasn't hitting the guy. It
sounded awful. And the next day a whole bunch of the
guy's relatives went up the Bureau and camped out
there with their goddamned blankets and plastic flow-
ers, waving their arms and screaming the guy's civil
rights've been violated and they want George in jail.

"I went to see George," Locke said. "He was in the
hospital, had his leg up in the air, and he said to me:
'I didn't even think about the leg till the next day. I
got in here, and they got me all stretched out in
traction, a ton of weights hanging off of my foot
and nine hundred pounds of plaster on my leg, and
people're telling me, and all I could think of, was:
"I finally got one of the bastards. I finally got one. I
wish he was dead, the bastard."

"So he says to me, you know?" Locke said. "He

says, well, I was all excited when they finally decided, they're gonna let us take the details, too, even though we're not on the road all the time, and he said to me: 'Don't do it. It's a mistake. It looks like a great deal, but it's a mistake just the same.'

"Somebody started telling me that about something that was honest and'd make me money, then," Locke said, "I wasn't exactly inclined to listen. I was making less'n ten. I was what you called *hungry*.

" 'You're gonna go out there,' George said," Locke said, " 'and you're making a lot of money, doing that. And then the first thing you know, you're gonna start thinking you got a job that pays you a lot of money, and you're gonna start living like that. Only, you haven't. You're a cop. It pays no money. It's not supposed to pay no money, and it doesn't. Pretty soon you'll be working all the time, trying to make it pay money, because then you're gonna think it's supposed to, and it never will.'

"Well," Locke said, "I didn't have any sense, and now I can't live without it. I went right ahead and I did it. I'm not gonna retire. I got several pairs of pants. I never wore a bathrobe in my life since I was ten. I'm too smart for that. 'Way too fine for it. And so now I work my ass off, and I'm no better off'n I was. You got any Bud?"

"For Christ sake," Hunter said, "a classy guy like you, coming in here? If it was somebody else, I would've had Bud, but I figured, you got *standards*. You don't like the Tuborg?"

"When they made the Tuborg in Denmark or Holland or wherever the hell it was they made Tuborg," Locke said, "I used to like it all right. I couldn't afford it, but I liked it, and I only drank a little of it when I could get my hands on it. But now, now they're making it here, and it's just the same old Carling's with a fuckin' lion on the label, and I didn't like that Lake Cochituate water when Mabel was peddling it with the black label, there. Just a different bottle, is what I think."

"I've got some scotch," Hunter said. "I've also got a bottle of Galliano which for some reason or other my father-in-law didn't get his hands on all summer, and I brought it back from the cottage, whole."

"He gave you that Galliano," Andrea said from the kitchen.

"He gave me that Bristol Cream, too," Hunter said, "and then he sat himself down and got comfortable and drank it all. He gave me the Old Forester, and then he drank most of that, and he gave me that nice brandy and when I came back the next weekend there was about enough left of it to give a fly a bath. Your old man likes good booze, but he's too cheap to buy it for himself, so he buys it and calls it presents for me, and then he powers it down. He's gonna get liver trouble if he doesn't stop giving me booze."

"I'll stick with the Tuborg, then," Locke said.

"I really appreciate that," Hunter said. "Most nights, I get home, I'm lucky there's a can of 'Gansett left."

"Only when you had all of them the night before, and that's why," Andrea said. Diane began to laugh. "That's right, Diane," she said. "Did you ever see anything to beat it? One night they come home and get polluted on the beer, and the next night they come home, and the first thing they do is complain. There isn't any beer. Well, who drank it all?"

"You wanna look out," Locke said. "That's grounds for divorce in this state, just like any other conviction for felony that gets you more'n five years. Man comes home from working all day, and there's no cold beer, it says it right in the green books: the abominable and detestable act against nature. It says that. That's what they mean by that. It's against the law for the old lady not to have any cold beer on ice."

"What about," Diane said, "when everything's broken all over the house and the old man won't fix it? What about that?"

"Or get new ones," Andrea said. "That, too, when he won't get new ones."

"We're not getting anyplace here," Hunter said. "Andrea, you think you can stop talking long enough, get us some beer in here?"

She put the bottles on the counter. "You're gonna

have to get up, Your Majesty, I'm afraid, so I can see if you're still sober enough to have it, you don't finally get so drunk you throw up lying down and you choke to death."

"My mother used to talk like that," Locke said, as Hunter fetched the beer. "I used to come home, right after I got out of the service, and I'd decide I was going to have a glass of beer. I used to have to take it out on the porch. The way she talked? Can you curdle beer?"

"I think so," Hunter said, "if you got enough to say about the guy that's drinking it. That's probably what gives you the headache, the next day. I think that's what it is."

"Sour beer," Locke said. "We oughta tell somebody about that. I bet nobody else ever thought of it, that that's what does it."

"Same thing with whiskey," Hunter said. "Wine, anything. I bet that's what it is."

"You know something?" Locke said. "Maybe it's not even just that. Maybe it's everything. The refrigerator, the dishwashers, everything. The disposal? Me and the disposal always got along all right. See, never had a disposal, before. Come home, have supper, I'm a nice fellow, take the garbage out, get my head wet when it's raining just like all the other real people.

"Well," Locke said, "than I find out, there's something wrong with that. It's not dignified. Okay, I was never that crazy about getting wet, and there's a certain number of nights in a year, you get through supper, it's gonna be raining, and I never had any talent for walking around outdoors when it's raining without getting my head wet. So, it's okay with me. I wasn't ever that crazy about washing my hands and looking at that big plastic thing full of fishbones and orange peels in the sink. They got something that'll grind it all up and the chicken bones, fine by me."

"That's another thing that'll make your head ache," Hunter said, "getting it wet too much."

"Course," Locke said. "Now, from that, from getting it wet, I got this thing, when I wake up in the

morning, sounds like somebody warming up a gun-
ship, you know. Sinuses. Well, I bought the thing, the
disposal. And I'm not sure, now, but I figure, that
damned machine's setting me up. It's getting into
ambush, you know? The dishwasher? I feel pretty
good about the dishwasher. So far I didn't do anything,
evidently, to piss it off, and it didn't do anything to
piss me. I'm watching it, but I feel good about it.

"The refrigerator, now," Locke said, "that's a different matter. That refrigerator is a bad bastard. They
all are. The old one made a lot of noise and it was
always groaning and everything, and I figured, well,
that's the way they are. Like George was about the
gypsies. But the new one, well, the old one, every so
often I hadda have a guy come in and feed it about
forty bucks or so, but not so often. But the last time
he comes for the old one, what he tells me is: 'Com-
pressor's going. Better get a new one.' What he meant
was: 'It snuck up on you. Waited until you thought
you had a firm deal with the bastard, and then it
whumped you.'

"The new one's the same way," Locke said. "I
just look at it. All I have to do's look at it, and I
know what it's gonna do. This thing's bigger'n a building, Deke, and I don't trust it. It does things. You
look at the damned thing cross-eyed and it throws ice
at you.

"The old one," Locke said, "didn't have that kind of
fire-power. You hadda practically go over and slip a
disc to get a tray out, and lots of times you'd just think
about it and say the hell with it and have a beer instead. But this new one, what it's doing is softening
us up. I went out there and worked those details in the
rain, nineteen colds and wet feet times two, to buy it
and give it a good home, and you think it appreciates
me? You think it's grateful? It is not. It's just gonna
sit there, and then some day when it figures I got
other things on my mind, like how I am gonna support
all its friends in the goddamned house, it's gonna say to
itself: 'This's the day,' and it's gonna rear back and
break its ice-maker and its coils and that neat little
thing that grinds up the ice for you and pours ice

water, and cold drinks, too. My kids're turning pink, for Christ sake, the way they got that fruit punch pouring out of that door. I think they're gonnna grow up with limp wrists. It's gonna work itself up into a goddamned frenzy and go to hell all at once, and of course I'll call up the guy and tell him to come and see his friend in avocado green, there, and it'll cost me two hundred bucks instead of the old forty I was used to.

"And that," Locke said, "is when I quit. When I got to stay out there in the rain twenty hours instead of four, because the refrigerator's pissed at me, that is when I quit. I know when something's got my by the balls, Deke. I do know that much. I maybe volunteered for Special Forces, but I still got some intelligence. I know when I've been had."

"You know something?" Hunter said. "I hope it does. You can go bleed on somebody else, then. Every time you get something like that, I get to hear about it until I think I'm gonna go out of my mind. Shit."

"That isn't true, Deke," Andrea said. "Just because I mention a few things, is no reason to say that."

"See what I mean?" Hunter said. "She admits it."

"No," Locke said. "I mean, hell, she's got a point there. I happen to think, a guy should take the best care his family, he can."

"Oh, good," Hunter said. "Look, you probably better think about getting going, here. I mean, you got to get up early tomorrow and everything, go out and stand in the rain. I hope it's hail tomorrow, you know that? Great big hailstones, about the size you could go bowling with them. That'd be good. Just for you."

"Nope," Locke said, "I think tomorrow, I'll work inside. I'll just tell them: 'Look, you guys, you wanna work in the rain and everything, see, well, I got this sinus condition. So, I got to go in. You get your ass frozen off, if you want. You're making about eight times what I'm making anyway, watching you make it. You go right ahead. I'll just go up to the HoJo up the road, there, and I'll be having coffee, anybody wants me. Okay? I'll watch the nice cars from there.

You know where you can reach me, you need me for anything.' I'll do it that way."

"Lemme know how you make out on that," Hunter said. "If it works, I'm gonna call Ten-ten and tell them, I got this irresistible urge to work outdoors again. Matter of fact, maybe I got it even if you don't. Maybe I'd rather get wet, than listen to Shanley."

"I don't know the guy," Locke said. "He isn't all right?"

"Look," Hunter said, "he's the type of guy that if you like guys that never in their whole life ever made a mistake, and so they go around all the time and they're giving people that've got the bad luck to work for them hell all the time, and kissing the asses off the guys that they work for, well, in that case you're gonna think he's great."

"In other words," Locke said, "a ball-buster."

"That's the result of it," Hunter said. "He doesn't do anything himself, which means that you gotta haul ass all the time to make up for it. But no, uh, basically what he is is a prick."

"Uh huh," Locke said.

"An overeducated son of a bitch," Hunter said. "Spent all his life in school, and then he comes out and so help me, the bastard knows *every*thing. There's nobody in the whole world that knows anything, next to Shanley, and if you're not careful the bastard'll tell you so.

"The trouble is," Hunter said, "like most guys like that, he really doesn't *know* anything. He's not street-smart. I got this thing going, Donnelly and them?"

"Yeah," Locke said.

"Bad bastards," Hunter said, "the whole lot of them. And Billy Gillis's whacky to boot. They oughta get a lot of time for this, and everybody in the whole world knows it. And they know who brought the bastards in, too.

"Now," Hunter said, "funny enough, that oughta be good for me. If Shanley brings the bacon back, it will be good for me. And I could use some good, about now, you want the truth. But the trouble is, if Shanley don't bring the bacon back, he's gonna say it was my fault. He's that type of guy, like I say, that never made a mistake. If he wins, it's him that won it, and never mind what an asshole I was, he won it anyway. If he loses, it's me that lost it, and how the hell's he supposed to do business if he's only got assholes like me to help him?

"I know, I know," Hunter said. "The people that're gonna do me any good, if we get a not-guilty they're gonna know it was something he did, and if we get guilties, it was me that did it. Okay. Shanley, he can say anything he wants to anybody. He can get his name in the paper a hundred times a week. It'll still be me, where it counts for me.

"Which is okay," Hunter said. "I haven't got any private practice, and he probably shouldn't, seeing the way he shortchanges the Commonwealth to run his, but it's all right. Let him have it. But, if he loses, he's gonna, he isn't gonna be anywhere near as nice about me as I'm being about him. He's gonna say it was me, and I don't care what anybody says then. If you got two guys that want the same thing out of Ten-ten, and one of them's got something in his file like that, that's against him, and the other one doesn't, the prosecutor says he screwed up something big? Well, the guy that's got that in his file is gonna be the one that gets hurt. That's not gonna get what they want."

"You're right," Locke said. "They remember those things."

"They remember those things," Hunter said. "They don't ask anybody about them, because they don't need to ask anybody about them. They know they're not true. And that's what they'd find out, if they did ask. But instead of asking, they just go ahead and they don't take chances, and what they do is, they act like they would if it was true, and they hold it against you."

"What about Horace?" Locke said. "Can't he cover your ass for you? Or, won't he?"

"He's a strange one," Hunter said. "He probably could, but he probably wouldn't. He's . . . , I don't know how to explain the guy. I've been with that guy over seven years now, right? See him in the morning, see him at night. I never had coffee with the guy, unless I bring it in to the office in the morning. I never had lunch with the guy unless we both of us brought sandwiches in. I never went to his house and had dinner. I never had drinks with him. Wait a minute, I did have drinks with him. Once. When I first went up there, we did have a couple of drinks one night. He told me he expected me to take a big load off his back. 'The other guy didn't do a fuckin' thing,' he said. 'I was always making up for him. I'm through with it. You turn out the same way, I'll can ya.' Yeah. Then, I think, he stopped drinking."

"He had to," Locke said.

"I heard that," Hunter said.

"It was gonna kill him if he didn't," Locke said.

"He told me he had diabetes," Hunter said.

"He probably did," Locke said. "He still hadda stop, at least for a while. Maybe he's all right now, I dunno."

"Okay," Hunter said, "cross that one off. I don't blame the guy for not having drinks. But he's not, he's not a very damned friendly guy, you know what I mean? I don't know him any better now'n I did when I started."

"Course," Locke said, "that's probably part of it anyway. You being younger and everything."

"Well, shit," Hunter said, "he's the sergeant. Not me. Hell, he's always after me, make sergeant, but shit, if I did he'd still have twenty years on me, about."

"Yeah," Locke said, "but there's guys like that. They got to be sure all the time. They just keep everybody a little off-balance, every chance they get. I mean, you've done some good things up there. You come around now, you know you got a certain reputation. Guys know who you are. That Rhode Island thing, that didn't do you any harm."

"Didn't do me any good, either," Hunter said. "And I really busted my ass on it, too."

"Would you guys like to hear some music?" Diane said, coming in from the kitchen.

"If it's coming from the stereo, yeah," Hunter said. "I dunno about Barney, but as far as I'm concerned, I had enough of the other kind."

"Don't be too sure of that," Locke said. "That, everybody knows the feds took that thing over as soon as we got a call across the State line. There was nothing wrong with the evidence that you brought in. I think you probably came out of that pretty good. You take a shot at Rossi and that group, everybody knows it's not the same thing as grabbing a kid with a hatful of junk."

"I dunno," Hunter said.

"He's probably afraid of you," Locke said. "And the last thing he wants anybody to do is figure out he's afraid of you. So, consequently, he's gonna keep after you all the time, so you never get a chance to think about it. I had . . . , when I started out with Samuels?"

The Andy Williams record came on the middle of "Precious and Few," preceded by a rough scraping sound.

"And there goes another five bucks for the record," Hunter said, "plus what it's gonna cost me to fix the tone arm. Shit."

"I got there," Locke said, "and, I think it was my first day on the job, and he said to me: 'Now look: I don't like going to court anymore, and I never did anyway. So, you're gonna do everything I do, and I'll do the stuff and you'll do the stuff, and we'll both do the stuff, see? And that way, we're both gonna be doing it. Because they're all just a bunch of old windbags, and I'm sick of them and their laskadaisicalness.' I said: 'What?' He said: 'They talk all the time.' Jesus, he was something. We had to pick up a prisoner at Charles Street Jail one day, and we didn't get out of there until about four, so naturally we got onto the Central Artery and nothing was moving. And George says: 'Quite a lot of conflagration today.'

"Anyway," Locke said, "that was just a bunch of bullshit. He didn't hate going to court. The guy was absolute dynamite on the stand, which I finally found out one time he had to go to court on some case he'd had before I got there. And I started to notice that when I had to go to court, he was always in there, watching, and afterwards he always had a couple things to say to me, that'd help. 'Uh, if I was you, it don't matter to me, you understand, but them shoes oughta be shined.' 'You got to remember, keep your voice up all the time.' 'What you do, you always look at the guy while he's asking the question. Like you're doing. But, when you're giving the answer, you should look at the jury. They're the ones you're supposed to be talking to.'

"We had this wise-ass down from Boston," Locke said. "He had this way of kind of sneering at you when he asked the questions, and I don't think he was awful bright, because he always repeated the answer, and I think he was doing that to get time to think. Whiny voice. So, he pissed me off. He asked me something he'd already asked me, and I answered it the same way again, and I guess the DA was dreaming about getting blown or having a nap or something, because when the guy tells me I changed my answer, I didn't get any protection. And I said: 'No, sir, that's what I said before.' And the judge finally had to have the steno read it back to us, and she read it back, and it was the same, of course. So the guy says to me, he had to say something, make it look like it was still my fault, so he said: 'Well, Trooper, I guess that's probably my second mistake today.' And I said: 'I stopped keeping track, sir.' And everybody had a big laugh and I felt pretty good about it.

"Then I went out," Locke said, "and George comes up to me. 'Give you a little hint. You know what to do when somebody starts pissing on your shoes like that again? You get so polite the whole world can see what a prick he is. People like it a lot better when they get something like that all by themselves. You start telling them, they get so they don't like you, either. 'Smart-ass. Thinks we can't tell the guy's a prick by ourselves.' So I told him, everybody seemed to like it pretty well. And he said: 'This time you probably got away with it. You didn't give away anything that you didn't have a lot of. But I've seen a lot of cases, and a guy just a little smarter'n this one would've asked you if you thought this was some kind of a joke, his client being on trial and everything, and made you look bad. In a close case, you can lose with a fresh remark.'

"Remarkable man," Locke said. "What he wanted to do was make me look good. He always did. I really hated to leave that place. When the transfer came through, and I, he could see it, he told me: "Ahh, go ahead. Go someplace else and learn some other things. I been here too long myself. Make room for the next guy.' That's when I found out, just about everybody that wanted to do investigations, for some reason or the other started out with George Samuels.

"We delivered a guy to the Queens County DA's office one day," Locke said, "drove him down in the company car and everything, and when we were coming back, I guess it was Lake Success or something, I don't know where the hell we were. I didn't know then, either. George was driving and we were lost. Points out the window, just as calm as he could be. 'Lake Superior,' he says. Then he starts telling me what I got to do when I get where I'm going, when the rookies come in to the Attorney General's Office, and of course everything he told me to do for them was something he'd already done for me. And that's what I tried to do."

"Horace isn't like that," Hunter said. "He's always undermining me."

Andrea came into the living room from the kitchen. Diane came in from the bathroom. They sat down, "Well, fellas," Diane said, "what kind of police work we gonna talk about tonight?"

"Gee," Locke said, "didn't bother you last week?"

"It's all you guys can talk about," Andrea said. "It's your whole life. You haven't got anything else to talk about at all."

"Last Saturday," Locke said, "that tape I was telling you about? I brought the thing home. You know what my wife has got? She has got a very dirty mind."

"I have not," Diane said.

"Right in the middle of it," Locke said, "Crispino brought the thing back and played it, and he couldn't fuckin' believe his ears. They're talking about some very mean thing they're gonna do to this Mickey, because he's been doing something they don't like, and right in the middle of how they're gonna cut off his right ear and make him eat it without no salt, Romeo starts talking about his girlfriend. The kid that's gonna prosecute it in court, Walsh, he hears it. And here is a kid with a certain amount of good sense. When Walshie first heard it, I thought he was gonna go out of his goddamned tree. 'We play this in court,' he says, 'well, I bet you we never have to play this in court, because if Romeo doesn't file every single discovery motion in the book and get his own copy of what we got here, I'm gonna make him a present of it. If his wife ever hears this, prison'll look like a vacation for him.' So, we give them the tapes, they asked for them, and on Wednesday Romeo comes in looking kind of white around the gills, and says he's gonna plead. I dunno if it was the tape, or what it was, but the stuff's all filed in court, now, and the case's over and everything, so I brought it home. I was gonna take it down the club and play it for the guys. It's public record."

"I thought they could stop that," Hunter said.

"They can," Locke said. "But they gotta ask to stop it, and Romeo's dumb-shit lawyer didn't have enough brains. He didn't ask to impound it."

"So," Locke said, "we had dinner, we're having a few drinks, and this one spots it and wants to know what it is. And her brother and his wife and this other couple're over. And, anyway, I wound up playing it.

"Well," Locke said, "like I say, right in the middle of it, something got into Romeo and he started complaining. His wife won't blow him, and in addition to which, there's some things he always wanted to do to her, that she won't let him. So, it got to be too much for him, and he got himself this hot-to-trot bimbo, and it turns out—he was talking about it, in detail—there wasn't anything she couldn't do, wouldn't do or didn't want done. Including some things he never thought of.

"Well anyway," Locke said, "what happened, was, she blew his brains right out of his head. Took him for about a million bucks, and then she meets this other guy that's doing better'n he is, and he gave her a Thunderbird, and now she's not giving Romeo any more lube jobs and front-end alignments, and he's going nuts. 'I can't help it,' he says. 'I got this taste for it now. I thought I was bad off when I didn't know what it was like.' And then he starts describing it. I should've brought it tonight."

"Not in my house," Andrea said.

"Well," Locke said, "that's really what I expected from this one, that kind of reaction."

"I thought it was awful, Andrea," Diane said.

"You thought it was so awful," Locke said, "I wasn't sure if I was gonna last the night."

"Barney," Diane said.

"Yeah," Locke said, " 'Barney.' I was worn down to a frazzle. I called up my brother-in-law the next day, when I finally regain consciousness, and I say: 'Hey, how's it going, Ralphie?' And he says: 'If I live, I'm not sure I'm gonna, but if I do, is there any chance you could maybe get me a copy, that tape?' On second thought, I'm glad I didn't bring it. I do have to get up early tomorrow."

"You can bring it next time," Hunter said.

"Not if I'm here," Andrea said.

The Rest of Charlie's Report

ON THE MORNING OF NOVEMBER 19, 1973, Sergeant Carmody sat in his office chair with his hands clasped across his fly. He had a frown on his face. He said to Deke Hunter: "Well, have a nice weekend?"

Hunter took some time before he answered. "Wasn't bad," he said. "Took the two oldest the Pats game, so naturally Nicky's all mad at me and the wife's on his side. But I figure, before the end of the month I'll scrounge up a couple Celtics tickets and take him, and it'll be all right. There's always somebody griping about something, anyway. It's a little easier when it's one of the kids."

"Pats played pretty good, I thought," Carmody said.

"Very good," Hunter said. "I thought when the Packers come out there and started running it up right away, I thought: 'Boy, I did it again. Come out here, and it's a nice day, everything, cold in the wind but otherwise all right, and I still booted it.' But they came back real good. You wait around some, they're gonna have a club there, before they're through."

"Okay," Carmody said. "Now, what about that other thing, there?"

"The other thing, there," Hunter said.

"I asked you, Friday," Carmody said, "do something, this weekend. Some thinking."

"Goddamnit," Hunter said, "you're right. I was supposed to do some thinking."

"You didn't do any thinking," Carmody said.

"Oh, wrong as hell, Horace," Hunter said. "I was thinking the whole time. Yes, sir."

"And what'd you decide?" Carmody said.

"Well, Sergeant," Hunter said, "I decided. What I decided, you're definitely right. No question about it."

"I am," Carmody said.

"Yes indeed, you are," Hunter said. "I decided: I am definitely taking the sergeant's exam, and this time I am really gonna study for it. You got it absolutely right. A guy wants something, what he's got to do is get out there and go after it. It's the only way."

"Then there's the other thing," Carmody said.

"Doesn't do to think about too many things at once," Hunter said. "Must be I left the other thing out or something. What was it?"

"The broad in Rhode Island," Carmody said.

"There's no broad in Rhode Island," Hunter said.

"Deke," Carmody said, "I like to think I'm a friend of yours. Remember, I said, whatever you tell me, I'm gonna believe you? Remember that?"

"Horace," Hunter said, "I got a memory like things're written down on paper. But I mean it, Horace, there's no broad in Rhode Island. They had a whole investigation down there. I guess you didn't hear about it. There is no broads in that whole state. Just guys. A bunch of lying bastards and Mafia types and stuff like that, and some guys that like to pretend. But no broads at all. You go down there, and you see something, looks to you like a broad, you better look out, is all I can tell you. Because that's a lying bastard that just likes to dress up and put rice bags in his bra and all of that, so guys'll make passes at him, and get all embarrassed when they find out.

"Now you know me, Horace," Hunter said. "I spent a lot of time down there on that Rossi case, and I'm not your regular out-of-state jerk that'll fall for that routine they got down there. I wouldn't go for, I wouldn't have nothing to do with no guys. I wouldn't care what they were wearing."

"No," Carmody said.

"I mean," Hunter said, "you just got to look at things, you know? I got this big case going. There's this friend of mine, knows something about it. It's probably pretty hot stuff. If I was putting it in the satchel with some guy, no matter if he was wearing something, this friend of mine'd probably start to wonder: well, what happens, somebody tells my wife, huh? So, you see what I mean."

"Yeah," Carmody said.

"I was even saying to my kids," Hunter said. "You know, Pats come back in the second half, well, the reason was, they started playing together. Nobody ever got anyplace in a goddamned football game, keeping secrets from the other guys."

"No," Carmody said.

"Same with me and Shanley and the rest of the people in this office," Hunter said. "I mean, if there's something in this case, that I don't know about, if Shanley don't know about it either, it's not only gonna wreck me. Shit. It's also gonna wreck him. He'll probably be mad as hell. I know I would be."

"Probably," Carmody said.

"Guy'd be entitled to an explanation," Hunter said. "And I'd have to give him one. 'Didn't you know about this?' 'Well, yeah, I heard something. I mean, uh, Horace told me,' what you said, and all, 'and, and I, well, uh . . . ,' and what do I tell him, huh? I haven't done nothing. I haven't done anything because I don't know what the hell to do about something that I don't know about. 'Horace wouldn't tell me. Said he had something, but he doesn't trust me.'

" 'Well, for Christ sake, why not?' he's gonna say," Hunter said. "And that's when I say: 'Well, Horace thinks I been getting laid, and he don't like it. You know who he's a lot like? He's a lot like Ryan.'

" 'No shit,' Shanley's gonna say," Hunter said. "And I'm gonna say: 'No shit. I really mean it.' You see what I mean, Horace? Guy's gonna think he lost a big sure thing 'cause I had my knickers off. Not gonna like that."

"No," Carmody said.

"Shit, I mean," Hunter said. "That's not gonna do it. Everybody's got problems. You got guys, haven't got enough dough. You got guys that're out getting laid. You got guys that gamble, and there's probably one or two guys or so that even had some trouble with the sauce, you know? Can't drink. And any one of those guys, there's probably no reason he can't do his job or anything.

"Now," Hunter said, "what I figure, that's the important thing, that the guy can do his job. So, when somebody comes up to him and says: 'I hear you can't eat no sugar,' he can just say to them: 'Fuck you. I'm not here to eat sugar. I ain't no fuckin' horse. I'm here to put your friend in jail, is what I'm here for. You wanna tell people, I got diabetes, go ahead. Maybe they'll make me take a disability retirement. Maybe not. But I can still work, and while you're going around spreading things, I'm gonna see to it, your friend goes to jail.'"

"This is a guy," Carmody said, "that Charlie knows from the can. And I know him from Arthur Collins, that I already talked to about him, and he verifies.

"Arthur goes out one night on a medium grab," Carmody said. "The guy's basically a little piece of shit, doesn't amount to a pisshole in the snow, he's been in before, of course. And Arthur figures, what the hell, it's not like it was something new for the guy, he'll behave himself. So he goes in there alone, which he's not supposed to do. It's the guy's girlfriend's apartment. And the guy's in the closet.

"'I go in there,' Arthur says, 'in the closet. I open the door and there's shoes all over the floor. Must've been twenty pairs of shoes in there, except one pair's got feet in them and they're not girl's shoes and they're not girl's feet, either. Easy enough. I got careless. I said: "Come on out, I blow your fuckin' brains out." Only, of course, I haven't got my weapon out and I haven't cleaned it in about a hundred years and it's probably all full of rust and wouldn't fire anyway.' You know what a guy oughta carry?" Carmody said.

"A fuckin' howitzer," Hunter said.

"A stainless steel Smith," Carmody said. "I thought a lot about that, and I decided that. There's only one thing you can do to one of those things and that's stick a piece of wood or something down the barrel, you don't want it to work right. You don't have to clean it, so you get oil all over your clothes the next day when you put it on. You don't have to do anything with it. It doesn't care if you sweat; it still won't rust. And your wife can have her period and still happen to touch it, and it wouldn't turn green. You take a cloth, and maybe once every ten years or so you put a little oil on it, and it's your friend for life."

"Not mine," Hunter said. "You know how many times I used that thing? When I'm on the range, and that's all. I'm a thinker. I don't go for that shit where they start shooting at you. That starts to happen, where I'm gonna go is home, I think. They can call me up when they finish. Let me know how it came out. Guys can get hurt doing that."

"Yeah," Carmody said, "and generally the ones that get hurt're the ones that think like that. Take the thing the day it's issued to them and put it on and just leave it there, and start thinking to themselves: 'I'm never gonna get into a spot where I'm gonna have to use it.' Because they're the ones that always do, and then it doesn't work. No, the thing you got to do, you got to get one of them stainless, and then you can think anything you want, because it's not gonna matter. Because if you do need that thing, and you pull it out, by Jesus, it'll do what it's supposed to do. It will fuckin' *work*."

"I don't see you with one of them," Hunter said. "You still got the old issue."

"They don't issue them," Carmody said.

"Okay," Hunter said, "but if they're that good, they should."

"There's guys that decide things like that," Carmody said, "and they think it builds character or something if you keep on using something that's not as good anymore, because somebody made something better. Treasury issues them. Three-fifty-seven mags. Nice weapon but a little kicky."

"I'll go to work for Treasury, then," Hunter said.

"Can if you want," Carmody said. "Me, I wouldn't."

"Means you got to buy your own, then," Hunter said.

"Nah," Carmody said, "not me. I only got a little while to go. I've done all right with what I got, and I'll use it till I quit. But a young guy? If I had ten years to go, I would. You get a rate on that item, you could probably take it home for eighty-five bucks. And it'd be worth it. It's the best security there is."

"Brains're better," Hunter said.

"I wouldn't know," Carmody said. "I never had any. That's why I decided, I was gonna be a cop. If I was any dumber I would've been eligible for law school."

"You should've gone anyway," Hunter said. "Had that operation where they take part of your brain out and fill up the empty part with cottage cheese. With your disposition, you would've done great."

"I'm doing all right, some of the time," Carmody said. "I got an honorable discharge from the service. I finally found a woman stupid enough to marry me, and our kids turned out pretty good. We almost got the mortgage paid off, and as far as I know, she never stepped out on me and I never gave her no reason to complain about me, on anything that'd count, anyway. I haven't had much excitement for the past thirty years or so, and that's the way I like it. Some guys're different. I'm not. I don't understand things," Carmody said, "I think about . . . , there's some things I don't understand."

"There's a lot of things I don't understand," Hunter said.

"There's . . . ," Carmody said, "Charlie said, he's about my age. I've known him a long time, on and off. When he wasn't in the can for some asshole stunt he decided to pull. You know what Charlie told me? He told me Shanley's pumping Dottie Deininger, down at Queen of Angels."

"No shit," Hunter said. "No fuckin' *shit*."

"That's what he told me," Carmody said.

"She is built like a brick shithouse," Hunter said.

"She is," Carmody said. "Fine-looking woman. Of course, there might be some other things to think about, besides how big her tits are."

"Yeah," Hunter said. "That case still on appeal?"

"Of course," Carmody said. "The guy's got about a million dollars, and I imagine he probably doesn't really want to do his ten to fifteen. Course it's on appeal. And I betcha if he loses the appeal, he screws, too, down to Panama with Vesco, or wherever it is that they go where we can't get at them."

"But they might have to retry it," Hunter said.

"Yup," Carmody said. He got up slowly from his chair and put his hands in his pockets and walked over to the window and looked out onto the paved frontage of the courthouse, where the grass had been removed to add parking spaces near the door for judges. He took his hands out of his pockets and rested his forearms on the wooden frame of the slanted glass wind deflector at the bottom of the window. There was strong morning sunlight, and his face and his gray crewcut took it and reflected it like old, silvered boards.

"You'd like that, wouldn't you," Hunter said.

"Yup," Carmody said. "Next to an enema with a firehose, I'd like that best of all. That goddamned thing took over six weeks to try, and that was almost three years ago. The jury was out three days. If they knock out some evidence and then send it back for retrial, we're gonna have all the same people marching around outside the courthouse with their goddamned signs again, all the old crazies and all the young crazies screaming about mercy killing and murder, and maybe this time we lose."

Carmody turned around and rested his elbows on the sill and stared at Hunter. "And then we got the interesting question of what happens when the defense finds out that there's a prosecutor banging the principal prosecution witness. They could even put Shanley on the stand, I suppose, and if Ryan tries the case again, let him try to save what he can out of that."

"Can I cross-examine?" Hunter said. "I haven't got a ticket to do it, but I sure know a lot about Shanley. Can I, please, huh, huh?"

Carmody expelled breath noisily through his nostrils. "You and the rest of the world," he said. "Shanley can explain he didn't start dashing her till after the first trial, when they convicted the guy. Might even get somebody to believe him. 'Doesn't have anything to do with her testifying about the good doctor stepping on the victim's oxygen hose. Just a personal thing, between her and me. Nothing to do with this case. It's just fuckin', Your Honor, good old-fashioned fucking.' "

"Jesus," Hunter said.

Carmody turned back and looked out the window again. "I knew the kid was having trouble," he said. "You hear things."

"I know she got all riled up down at the Charthouse and heaved a glass of wine in his face," Hunter said.

"That was just one of the public things," Carmody said. "Jesus Christ, when that kid came in here, the sky was the limit for that kid. Two and a half years ago? Not much more'n that. He looked good, he had a job that was gonna give him a lot of visibility, there was talk, *serious* talk, they were getting ready to run him for Congress. You remember what you told me, he told you? Attorney General? It wasn't out of the picture. Not by any means. The boss told me that one day. Said he was damned glad people were saying Shanley oughta run for Congress, and then statewide, because it meant he wasn't sitting here giving a lot of exposure to somebody that could maybe take him out in a couple years when he ran for reelection as DA. And since then, if we haven't hadda ask people eight or nine times not to make a whole lot of noise about some idiot trick that he's pulled with his wife, it's been more'n that.

"Last Christmas," Carmody said, "he bought her the fur coat. I don't know what it was. Mink, probably. So they had a fine time for themselves one night, and she was giving him hell about something, and then she went and took a bath. And she was still yelling at him, and he took out this electric razor that she gave him for Christmas and he says: 'Well, that's all right,' and he went downstairs and got the coat out and shaved it. Shaved about nine stripes in it. Absolutely ruined it."

"Son of a bitch," Hunter said. "I wouldn't've thought the guy'd have it in him."

"It gets worse," Carmody said. "He's too quiet to suit her. She's sitting there in the tub and she figures he must be up to something. So she comes out of the tub and he's standing there at the bottom of the stairs and he shows her the coat. Down she comes, bare-ass, shrieking, and he just opened the door and he either pushed her out or else she couldn't stop and she ran out by herself, jaybird-naked, into the snow."

"Jesus," Hunter said.

"Then he shut the door," Carmody said. "Left her out there for a while, so she could bang on the door and holler and yell in case some of the neighbors might've missed it when she came out in the first place."

"I wished I'd seen it," Hunter said. "I never saw anything like that before, and she's not a bad-looking woman, either. Nice ass."

"This is the promising young Assistant District Attorney and his lovely wife that've got such a great future in politics, that're doing this," Carmody said. "Not to mention how it's gonna improve all the cases he tries, with people laughing at him all the time. The boss called me up, and I had a talk with the local police that had to come around before he'd let her in, and there was all kinds of times keeping it off the blotter and out of the paper. I mean, Jesus. He's making a goddamned fool of himself. And now Charlie tells me this, and I just can't understand you guys. Doctor Kincaid's seventy, now, and he looks about ninety, all stooped over and there's dandruff all over his suit, and if we got to bring in the kindly old doctor and try him again on an old mercy killing that the principal witness is banging the prosecutor, it'd make your hair stand on end. I can't understand you guys."

Carmody turned again and walked back to his desk and sat down. "If it's not one of you, it's the other," he said. " 'You know what it is?' Charlie said to me. 'The whole world's gone nuts, is what it is.' I think Charlie's right."

"You gonna tell me what else he said?" Hunter said.

"I might as well," Carmody said. "I talked to Ar-

thur, like I say, and this was the guy that bit him.
'He was hiding in the closet,' Arthur said, 'and when
I saw his feet he must've remembered he had them
down there, and hoisted himself up on the clothes
bar, and the feet in the shoes went right out of sight
behind the bathrobes and the stuff.' So Arthur naturally got pissed off. Guy thinks he's stupid, can't see
the clothes moving or something. So Arthur reaches
in there, and he calls him a silly bastard or something,
and the guy bit him on the arm."

" 'Right through my shirtsleeve, for Christ sake,'
Arthur says. 'I was afraid I was gonna get lockjaw
or something.' So he snakes the guy out of there. You
ever hear of Dominic Tessio?"

"No," Hunter said. "Wait a minute. Is he the guy
that's the undertaker down in Boston, there?"

"Cousins," Carmody said. "The guy that's got the
funeral parlor's Dominic's cousin. Dominic's Donnie
Doyle."

"Ah," Hunter said, "that fucker. He's into everything that ever happened."

"He used to be," Carmody said. "That's what I
said, when Charlie mentioned his name. But evidently
he got started on pills. Arthur said that guy came out
of the closet and you could've gone ice-skating on his
eyeballs. 'I beat the shit out of him, naturally,' Arthur
says. 'I told him: "I get through with you, I'm gonna
put down on the sheet you fell *down* the stairs three
times and *up* the stairs twice, you little prick." '

"He's only about, I dunno, five-seven, I guess,"
Carmody said, "around one-forty, and he's close to
fifty years old, then. So Arthur gets through with him,
and he takes the guy down the hospital, and of course
the guy was stoned. Absolutely blind out of his fuckin'
mind. I was talking to Arthur. 'The guy was flying,'
he said. 'I was actually sorry I did it. I wasn't sorry
I did it while I was doing it, but I was sorry afterwards.

" 'I mean, I know the guy,' Arthur says. 'He's a
thief, but he's not a bad bastard. He never hurt anybody, at least until he bit me. He just didn't know

what he was doing. He was 'way out there, someplace I never been. Just a dumb shit. But he was all right about it. I went in to see him, after. Said he was sorry he acted like that.'

"Well," Carmody said, "Donnie's your witness."

"He's not my witness," Hunter said. "I wouldn't know the guy if he bit *me*."

"You're gonna," Carmody said. "Donnie was in the can when they did that number. Donnelly and them."

"That oughta take care of him, then," Hunter said. "Very few guys I know of, in the can for biting cops, hanging around banks."

"How about saloons?" Carmody said. "How about a guy that's supposed to be working in a tire store, he's on work-release and all, and among other things he happens to be a drunk. So he's hanging around a bar and getting stiff as usual, and it was Donnelly, was the guy that was buying him drinks?"

"Donnelly never bought a guy a drink in his life," Hunter said.

"How about," Carmody said, "try this: Donnelly's buying the guy drinks in Worcester right about the same time you and Shanley say Donnelly's robbing the bank in Danvers? How about that? Think that'd help Donnelly?"

"That might help Donnelly some," Hunter said. "Of course, the guy's lying. He's a goddamned liar. I got Donnelly's picture in the bank."

"Must've been somebody else, looks like Donnelly," Carmody said. "This guy's gonna swear, Donnelly was in Worcester, standing drinks at the Good Time in Kelly Square. There's no way Donnelly could've made it to Danvers and back, and so forth, in time enough."

"He's lying," Hunter said.

"That's what Charlie told me," Carmody said.

"Well," Hunter said, "I don't care what Charlie told you. He's lying."

"*That's* what Charlie told me," Carmody said. "He says Donnie says he's gonna lie. That's what Donnie told him."

"Well," Hunter said, "that's pretty."

"He's got damned good reason for it," Carmody said. "At least, he thinks he does, according to Charlie. When Donnelly was on the loose, he went around and he saw Donnie, and he told Donnie he's gonna lie, and if he doesn't lie, Donnelly's gonna have somebody kill him. If he's too busy himself, that weekend."

"You know," Hunter said, "if the guy was ever on them pills you said he was on, he got off them. That's a very good reason. If Donnelly said he was gonna have somebody kill me, I'd even clean the damned gun. I'd believe Donnelly, if he said that."

"According to Charlie," Carmody said, "you and Donnie think a lot the same way. So, he's gonna get up there, very firm and natural and all, sincere, and his hands'll be shaking, but if anybody notices they're gonna think it's booze, which part of it is, and he's gonna tell everybody that Donnelly was in Worcester. It'll sound very good. What do you think they're gonna call that?"

"Lemme think a minute," Hunter said. "I think I got it. A reasonable doubt?"

"A reasonable doubt," Carmody said. "That's exactly it. I think that's exactly what Donnelly's after."

"Uh huh," Hunter said. "And, if Donnelly wasn't there, when we got a picture of him there, then maybe Donovan and Marr and Gillis also weren't there, am I right?"

"I wouldn't be surprised if that's what they had in mind," Carmody said. "Put it this way: if it was to turn out that the jury thought that, they wouldn't be mad."

"All right," Hunter said. "Lemme think of something to do to the bastard."

"How about this?" Carmody said. "How about, after he tries to blow Donnelly out, we get him on cross and he turns right around and he has to admit he doesn't know if Donnelly was anyplace near Worcester that day, because he, personally, himself, wasn't in Worcester that day. He was in Dedham."

"Was he?" Hunter said.

"Yup," Carmody said. "He was in the Norfolk House. They had him in Concord, and he, the guy he was working for, before he bit Arthur, he said he'd take Donnie back in the tire store if Donnie could get work-release. So, he really wanted it, and they asked Arthur, and Arthur said, nah, he didn't care, it was just something the guy did when he was stoned. So they put him in Billerica. And he was working in Shrewsbury, days, and coming back to the can every night, and it was a hell of a thing.

"So," Carmody said, "they moved him to Worcester, which he didn't want to go to, for some reason, and then he got sick. So, on March the nineteenth, he had the flu, and they wanted to put him in Norfolk Hospital. But there was some kind of foul-up, and when he got there, there wasn't any room for him. So they put him in Dedham, to wait until there was, and that's where he was on the twenty-second of March, when Donnelly robbed the bank. He was in Dedham, and we can prove it."

"I am never gonna get used to that," Hunter said. "Guys in jail. They're having drinks, they're going out, they're working, they're coming back, they're making telephone calls and every so often they go out and bitch to the newspapers. You know they're bringing stuff back and forth."

"Look," Carmody said, "this guy? You wanna bitch? All right, bitch. But this guy, by the time we get through with him helping Donnelly, Donnelly can stand up and plead guilty, or else he can stay sitting down and let the jury find him guilty, it's not gonna matter. The guy's a lush, all right? Some of them, I agree with you. But this guy, you wanna keep him quiet and out of trouble? Forget jail. Give him two gallons of whiskey a week and let him run a tab at the bar down the corner. He won't bother a single solitary soul. There's nothing wrong with him. He's just a drunk."

"I don't care," Hunter said. "I heard all that shit. And I heard it and heard it, and I don't care. Used to be . . . Look at those guys. Used to be, you put a guy in jail, before, where he naturally belongs anyway because he robs a bank or something everytime he gets out, and somebody just has to go and catch him and put him in again, if you put him in before, he *went* in, by Jesus, and he made license plates and he ate what they put in front of him, or else he went hungry. If he got out of line, you blew the pepper-fogger at him, and if he really got out of line, he got hit on the head till he stopped it, and he kept his mouth shut and beat his meat and learned some respect and things like that.

"Now," Hunter said, "now you take him down there he's out before you can get the car started. He's on the phone. He wants season's tickets, the Bruins, and he's planning a fuckin' vacation or something, and if there's something he doesn't like, well, he just calls the *Globe* or something and they send some starry-eyed broad out to talk to him, about how jail's a bad thing and he doesn't like it at all. 'My wife comes to see me, three times a week, and I got this girl, comes in here Fridays, and the only thing they got for us's twin beds. I'm all cramped up.' Then he bangs the reporter on the twin bed, so she'll know.

"I think it's crazy," Hunter said. "Being in jail's better'n being a cop, for Christ sake. I dunno why I even bother. I put up with Shanley. . . . This's gonna make Shanley look awful good, isn't it?"

"Yup," Carmody said.

"I just thought of that," Hunter said.

"Like a fucking magician," Carmody said.

"Sure," Hunter said. "Another rabbit out of the famous goddamned hat. Shanley's gonna get this dink on cross and stand up and holler and yell something fierce and put on a great act. He'll probably run against Kennedy after this one. Well, okay, when do I see the guy?"

"I dunno," Carmody said. "I'm supposed to see Charlie tonight, after I talk to you. You wanna tell Shanley?"

"Not yet, at least," Hunter said.

"That's what I thought, too," Carmody said. "First,

we get it all set up and everything, and find out the fuck where we stand. Then . . ."

"Then," Hunter said, "when we get this guy handled, we start thinking about how to handle Shanley."

PART FOUR

Andrea's Expectations

The Importance of Things

□ 15

OUTSIDE THE CINEMA in the South Shore Shopping Plaza in Braintree, Massachusetts, Andrea at ten-fifteen on the evening of November 19, 1973, walked slowly, so that Deke put his hands in his raincoat pockets and hunched his shoulders and took small steps, very deliberately. "I don't want you to think I didn't enjoy it," she said.

"I don't," he said.

"Because I did," she said. "We don't get out by ourselves often enough. There never seems to be enough time."

"We've got too many other things to do," he said.

"We shouldn't have," she said. "We should do what we want. We should stop doing what everybody else wants, and start doing what we want. Don't you think that?"

"Sure," he said.

"I wanted to come out tonight," she said.

"That's what I thought you meant when you said you did," he said.

"In spite of the fact that I've got a wash to do and there's a lot of mending," she said.

"You want to have a drink?" he said. "We could go over the Plantation House."

"That's just a pickup joint," she said.

"I wouldn't know," he said, "I've never been there."

"Deke," she said, "you were there with me."

"When was I in there with you?" he said.

There was a very fine mist that softened the lights on the Christmas decorations in the Plaza.

150

"You forget pretty fast," she said. "We went in there once when it was, when we were dating. We went in there then. We went in with the Driscolls. It was something else, then. Charterhouse? I don't know. We had steaks and you were drinking too much and you said something to her. I don't know what it was. We never saw them again. I never saw them again."

"Stevie Driscoll," he said. "Stevie Driscoll, and, what in hell was his wife's name? He called her something and it wasn't her name, but that was what he called her."

"Maybe you saw them again," she said. "I know I didn't. Maybe it was me they didn't like."

"Kivvie," he said. "Kivvie Driscoll. She had buck teeth."

"She did not," Andrea said.

"Well," he said. "you can call it what you want. She had front teeth and they stuck out. Like a woodchuck or a fuckin' beaver. Maybe you got to make a certain measurement before they qualify for buck, I dunno. She had big teeth in front. What'd we do that night?"

"What do you mean?" she said. " 'What did we do that night?' "

"I mean, what'd we do that night?" he said. "I haven't seen Stevie . . . , he was in my Reserve outfit, for Christ sake. I been out of Reserves, well, Christ, we've been married ten years. He was the guy who used to write down who was there and who wasn't. A fucking campus soldier. That's why I was friendly with him, for Christ sake. I was always late for drills. The only reason I was going to drills was that the parent club had this crazy idea I could go to my right and hit the curve ball, and they got me in a unit so I wouldn't get drafted and go get my ass shot off in Viet Nam. I couldn't stand the guy, but I was always late for drills, and he was the guy that marked you absent if you showed up late. He was going to Bridgewater State Teachers' College, and he, I wonder what the hell ever happened to him. Nothing good, I hope."

"It's the brutality that gets me in those things," she said. "I used to like going to movies, but when I see that, something like that, it's the brutality that gets me. I don't see how people can stand to go to see those X-rated ones."

"You've never seen one, that I know about," he said.

"I still don't know," she said.

"They go to see them because they're dirty," he said.

"I'd have dreams about them," she said. "Nightmares. I don't think they should allow people to make pictures like that."

"There's nobody," he said, "made you go there, you know. Matter of fact, I think I hadda pay the guy about six bucks, I think it was, before he'd let either one of us in."

"What worries me," she said, "is the kids. What if they see something like that?"

"You got to be," he said, "I dunno, seventeen or eighteen or something like that. I know I'm eligible. Nobody's asked me for an ID lately."

"Even then," she said. "What's it gonna do to them, if it makes me feel like that? All kind of sick and everything. Watching people shoot people."

"Well," he said, "you're not actually watching people shoot people. You're watching people pretend to shoot people who pretend to get shot. They can make it very realistic, and all, but it's still ketchup. The kids know that. They grew up on television, practically."

"They showed her breasts," Andrea said.

"They didn't show them very long," he said. "All you really got was a glimpse of one of them."

"You knew what it was, though," she said. "And her rear end, too."

"Well," he said, "everybody's got one of them. All you got to do is back up to a mirror, you want to see one of them."

"I don't have to go to a movie, though," she said.

"Of course, you don't have to," he said. "You go to a movie because you want to."

"I don't see why they have to do that," she said. "The next thing you know, they'll be showing you people going to the bathroom."

"They won't be showing me," he said. "I'll be having a drink someplace."

"You didn't want to come," she said.

"I was perfectly willing to come," he said. "I just got, I meant: if they make a movie about somebody taking a shit, I won't go to it. I don't care if somebody else goes to it, but I'm not gonna go to it. I agree with you. What do I wanna watch that for? I don't. So where's the beef?"

"What we could do," she said, "Child World's still open. We could go over and see if they've got what Nicky wants."

"I don't want to do that," he said.

"If you don't," she said, "it just means, I'm going to have to."

"Well," he said, "that's all right. I still don't. I want to have a drink. We can either go over the Plantation, or we can get in the car and go to the Sheraton thing, or we can go up the Red Coach. Now, whaddaya wanna do?"

"You were gone early this morning," she said.

"I'll be gone early tomorrow morning, too," he said. "I forgot to tell you: I got this case that's being tried, and it's a fairly long way from home, and I have to be there. Every day."

"I know that," she said.

"In which case," he said, "there is no need saying what you just said."

"I just don't see," she said, "why you never have any time for your family."

"I do the best I can," he said.

"The best you can do," she said, "the thing you do best, I mean, is duck out.

"All right," she said, "let's have a drink. And then we'll go home, and that'll be just one more thing I have to do on my own, because you're not around. And it won't mean a damned thing to you."

"What won't?" he said.

"Where we go," she said. "You won't remember it."

"Remember what?" he said.

"It'll be just like the Plantation House," she said. "Or whatever it was. It won't mean anything to you.

And tomorrow or the next day I'll come down here and get something for Nicky, and it'll probably be the wrong thing. Because you're the one that knows what kind of hockey game he wants, I'm not. And then, on Christmas, he'll be disappointed. They can call off Christmas from now on, if they want. As far as I'm concerned."

"I wasn't sure they didn't," he said.

"He wants to play hockey, like Sam," she said.

"He's not big enough," he said. "When he's big enough, he can play. He's gonna have to wait. There's no way I can make him bigger."

"And then," she said, "I suppose I'll have to get up when it's still dark, and take him to play. Because you'll be too busy. Either you won't've gotten home, or else you'll've left early."

"Okay," he said.

"I had a nice time tonight," she said. "You didn't, did you."

"I was doing all right, as I recall," he said. "Until I came out of the movies, at least."

"You don't want me to talk to you," she said.

"Well," he said, "since you ask, all right. I'll tell you. Now I'm not wishing for anything, understand? But if I had a hearing aid, right now, I think I would turn it off."

The Jury Selection Continued

16

THE FIRST CRIMINAL SESSION of the October, 1973, sitting of the Superior Court of Massachusetts, for the County of Essex, at the shiretown of Salem, was conducted in the courtroom on the second floor, at the front of the building.

That courtroom, like the rest of the interior of the old courthouse, was painted putrescent green. The walls had not been scraped between successive applications of paint; the people who applied the paint did not bother to thin it, the contract calling for apportionment of costs between labor and materials and the contractor being a man who sold paint, in each instance, as well as a man who hired painters. The painters did not, in any instance, make any serious effort to smooth out brush strokes, or make the surfaces even. Over radiators the paint bubbled, and then it cracked. Under the sills of windows, imperfectly glazed, water got behind the thick paint and eroded the plaster. Always somewhere on the floor, and on the threadbare rug of indeterminate pattern in the bar enclosure, there was the white dust of disintegrated plaster.

On the easterly side of the courtroom, there was an old brown metal water cooler, between the side rail of the jury box and the schoolmasterly desk provided for the bailiff. Its contents afforded some relief to nervous witnesses, who accepted the paper cups—the kind, favored by dentists, which are made up of many folds, and become soggy unless the water is consumed promptly—with shaking hands. More often, the water cooler was a place for a trial lawyer to go when he got an unexpected answer, or forgot his next question, and wanted to think about the whole matter.

The jury box had hard wooden chairs on two tiers, eight crowded into each row, because while the box was built to hold twelve good men and true, the law was changed to provide for the impaneling of as many as four alternate jurors, in order to permit verdicts to be reached if one of the first twelve was taken ill, or died, during the course of a protracted trial. From the front rail of the jury box hung brass rings, and from the rings was suspended a curtain the color of an old pool table surface, by order of a judge in the mid-1960s who remarked that female jurors had taken to wearing miniskirts, and that clerks, lawyers and litigants had occasionally become distracted.

The woodwork in the courtroom was ornate, and made of oak. It was varnished, and quite well maintained. The floors needed repair. The acoustics were dreadful. In the summer the courtroom was hot, and the church and the Registry of Deeds, on either side of the courthouse, blocked the breeze. In the winter the courtroom was drafty.

On November 21, 1973, Deke Hunter entered the main courtroom at 9:55 A.M., and was momentarily concerned when he did not see Richard J. Shanley in there. Judge Peter Macarthur was already on the bench. Deputy Clerk Peter Mishawa called a case: *Commonwealth v. Francis*. Assistant District Attorney John Ryan stood up and declared that the Commonwealth understood a change of plea was contemplated.

Between 9:55 and 10:40, Deke Hunter, more relaxed after Mishawa signaled "half an hour" by mouthing the words in his direction, observed without interest that Dalton M. Francis, "of Newburyport in the County aforesaid, did, upon the 17th day of February, in the year of Our Lord One thousand, nine hundred and seventy-three, assault and beat, by means of a dangerous weapon, to wit: an automobile, one Harold M. Murphy," and that Mr. Francis admitted it. Harold M. Murphy, counsel for the defendant asserted, was the constant companion of Hilda Francis, the defendant's estranged wife, and upon seeing Mr. Murphy at the intersection of Bow and Whittenden streets in Newburyport, crossing against the light, Mr. Francis had run him down, "thereby causing him great bodily harm."

Mr. Francis acknowledged that this was his third offense in seven years. In 1966, he had been convicted, by a jury, of unarmed robbery of a small grocery store. He had received a sentence of two and one-half years in the House of Correction, suspended for two years, and he was placed on probation for that time. In 1969, he was convicted, upon his plea, of unlicensed possession of a firearm, and two charges of assault and battery by means of a dangerous weapon were dismissed, but remained on his rap sheet as having been brought. His probationary period having been exhausted, he was sentenced to two and one-half years in the House of Correction, to be served. It was in May of 1972, while he was still confined of his liberty, that Hilda had taken up with Mr. Murphy, who was unemployed and without visible means of support.

Having read the probation report, Judge Macarthur received the recommendation of the District Attorney's Office (Assistant District Attorney John Ryan suggested a term of ten years, to be served. When he finished, he permitted himself his usual small smile), and heard a plea for lenience from James J. Makarius, counsel for the defense, who urged that the defendant be placed on probation, because he had committed the assault without premeditation, being overcome with jealousy and rage when he saw his rival carrying two shopping bags and jaywalking. Judge Macarthur said that permanent disability of the left leg and arm seemed to him to be punishment for jaywalking in excess of the statutory penalty, and that he disapproved, in any event, of Mr. Francis's willingness to take the law into his own hands. The Judge further observed that the defendant, who stood in a frayed corduroy sport jacket, with his eyes downcast, must sooner or later learn to control his impulses.

Deputy Clerk Mishawa then instructed the defendant to "consider your sentence as the court has awarded it." Mr. Francis received a term in the Massachusetts Correctional Institution at Concord, not to exceed five years, and was manacled and led away, his eyes still downcast, his expression one of discouragement.

The clerk conferred briefly with Judge Macarthur. "Jurors called in the *Donnelly* case," the clerk said. "Counsel, defendants." Richard J. Shanley was missing. John Killilea and Sam Wyman and Tommy Hart were out in the corridor, shifting from foot to foot on the marble tile floor and watching while the handcuffs were removed from their clients' wrists. The clerk conferred with Judge Macarthur. Then he turned to the courtroom and said: "The Court will take a brief recess." The prisoners were brought in two minutes after the Judge left the bench, and seventeen minutes before he finished his third cup of coffee of the morning.

Teddy Donnelly wore a dark gray double-breasted suit, a white shirt, no necktie. He was slope-shouldered and he slouched when he walked, and the scar on his cheek was white against his tan. His black eyes were set deep in his face, and he had heavy black eyebrows. He extended his arms in front of him as he sat down, as though verifying that the handcuffs had been removed in the corridor outside the courtroom, so that prospective jurors in the courtroom, presumably unmindful of eight corrections officers watching him and Andy Marr and Leaper Donovan, would not conclude that he was a dangerous man, and therefore a guilty one. Teddy Donnelly stared at Deke Hunter, thirty feet away at the prosecution table, as he had stared at him on November 20, 1973. Deke, as he had done the previous day, nodded. Teddy did not.

Edward M. Donnelly, born New Bedford, Massachusetts, February 15, 1924, was the fifth of seven children born to Etta and Joseph Donnelly. His brother Timothy, firstborn, died of influenza in the epidemic. His sister Katherine, the third child born to his parents, successfully completed her novitiate as a Maryknoll nun in the autumn of 1938, and went to Africa. His father worked in the lumber business until his death, at fifty-six, from what Etta Donnelly said was plain cussedness. One brother became a realtor. One brother became a lawyer, by going to school nights, and spent much of his career as a District Court defense attorney assuring various cops that he had nothing to do with Teddy, and didn't know where the hell he was, and didn't wish to. Another brother was killed at Kwajalein. A sister, Mary Louise, married a member of the Teamsters' Union who worked for Coca-Cola, and chiefly ignored the rest of the family.

Teddy Donnelly was arrested for the first time on the tenth of October, 1938, on charges of burglarizing a variety store. He was placed on probation, and remanded to the custody of his parents. On the thirteenth of November, 1939, he was arrested for the second time, having been caught in the act of burglarizing a residence in Fairhaven, Massachusetts. In consequence of that, he was adjudged a delinquent, by reason of having committed a breaking and entering in the nighttime, with intent to commit larceny of more than one hundred dollars, and committed to the Shirley Reformatory. He had been engaged in stealing a sizable coin collection from a summer house; the collection was valued at ten thousand dollars, and that was conservative.

In April of 1942, Donnelly was conditionally accepted for service with the Seabees. That acceptance was in turn a condition of his release from Shirley. In June of 1942, while assigned to the Great Lakes Naval Training Center, he was court-martialed for striking a noncommissioned officer. In September of 1942, he was court-martialed for disrespect to a superior officer, and given ten days in the brig. In May of 1942, on liberty in San Francisco for one week before shipping out to the Pacific Theater, he became involved in a fight in a bar and was arrested by the Shore Patrol after he stabbed another sailor in the left eye. He was court-martialed again, and sentenced to five years at hard labor and a dishonorable discharge.

In 1947, having forfeited all pay and allowances, Donnelly was released from the navy prison at Portsmouth, New Hampshire. He went to Boston, where he found work as a forklift truck operator in a junkyard in Brighton. In 1948, he met and married Judith

Griffin, who lived with him for slightly more than three months until she became convinced that her weekly beatings were likely to continue for the rest of his life, and left him. On December first, 1948, he held up the A & P store in Rockland, Massachusetts. He and three accomplices were arrested three hours after the robbery, in Chelsea, Massachusetts. Convicted in February of 1949 of robbery while armed, he was sentenced to fifteen years in the Charlestown State Prison. There he met Andrew Marr.

Paroled in August of 1959, Donnelly was arrested on May 15, 1963, on charges of robbery of the Granite City Trust Company in Quincy, Massachusetts. While he was held in lieu of bail, at the Charles Street Jail, he was served with a warrant issued by the federal court for his arrest on charges of robbing the Worcester County National Bank. He was acquitted on the State charges, brought on the Granite City robbery, because the witness, developed by the State Police, disappeared. The federal charges were dropped; the same witness was required to prove them. Donnelly was released from custody on April 29, 1964.

On July 8, 1971, Donnelly was arrested on a federal complaint alleging that he and two other men, Michael Donovan and Andrew Marr, robbed the Hampden County Trust Company in Springfield of $14,585 on July 1, 1971. The FBI arranged for a lineup to be held at the Charles Street Jail. The lineup was legally defective, under a court decision handed down before the case came to trial, and the United States Attorney dismissed the indictment. Donnelly was released from custody on November 4, 1971.

Michael Donovan, on the morning of November 21, 1973, wore a dark blue doubleknit suit with brass buttons. He wore a pale blue shirt and a blue-and-white polka-dot tie and highly polished Johnston & Murphy black loafters. He was bald. He wore black-framed glasses. He had a very light complexion. He weighed one hundred and seventy pounds. He was five feet, ten inches tall. He was thirty-eight years old.

Michael Donovan was the only child of William and Theresa Donovan of Swampscott, Massachusetts.

He was an excellent athlete at Swampscott High, graduating with the class of 1953 (having missed a year of school, while in junior high, because he had contracted scarlet fever) as an All-Scholastic in track (broadjumping, pole-vaulting, and the 100-yard dash), basketball (forward, averaging 23.5 points per game) and football (defensive end). He was a B student, which somewhat diminished William Donovan's satisfaction in his son; William Donovan was an attorney in Boston, and believed Michael should excel in everything (as, in fact, he believed he had excelled).

In 1957, Michael Donovan graduated with honors from Stonehill College. His degree was in physical education. His interest was in playing poker, which had brought him around one hundred dollars a week during the academic year, for no more than twenty hours a week in the Student Lounge. He did not report that skill to William Donovan, who in his ignorance therefore continued Michael's weekly allowance of twenty dollars, and paid his room, board and tuition.

Upon graduation, Michael received his lieutenant's commission in the Army Reserve, in successful completion of his studies in ROTC. He was assigned to Fort Gordon, Georgia, where he played indifferently well as a running back for the base football team, and quite well indeed as a cardplayer. After two years of active duty, he was returned to Reserve status. He came back to Massachusetts, where he got an apartment on Beacon Street, in Boston, played a little football in the Park League, and got a job as an independent insurance agent in the Goldsboro office. He did not sell very much insurance. He did attend a regular poker gathering, meeting three nights a week in a room on the fifth floor of the Statler Hilton, where he seldom lost very much, was careful never to win very big, and was permitted to take out about $350 a week because most people didn't pay very much attention to Michael.

Andrew Marr did.

Andy Marr was born on February 9, 1930, at Springfield, Massachusetts. He was the third child of three born to Francis and Frances Marr. Francis was a truckdriver for Valley Industries, a firm dealing primarily in bottled propane gas and well-drilling. He had an average of 104.6 in the Pioneer Valley Candlepin Bowling League. In July of each year, he and his wife took the children to Lake Sunapee, New Hampshire, for two weeks in a rented cottage. They visited Mount Washington and Lake Winnipesaukee and Salisbury Beach, and bought decals in bright colors at those places and stuck them on the windows of their maroon DeSoto sedan. Andrew's sister Kathleen went to Springfield Business School and got a job as a secretary in the offices of the Massachusetts Mutual Life Insurance Company right after World War II. She also was a member of the company's ladies' bowling team. Geraldine, the brightest of the children, worked her way through her first year at the University of Massachusetts at Amherst, and then won a scholarship for her next three years. After graduating, in 1950, she went to work as a junior high mathematics teacher in Agawam, Massachusetts. Mr. Marr died of a heart attack on January 3, 1968; each year after that, Geraldine and Kathleen accompanied their mother to Lake Sunapee, New Hampshire, for two weeks, where they rented the same cottage they had used for almost forty years. In the evenings they went out for dinner to inexpensive restaurants, and they did not ever mention Andy.

Andy Marr finished his junior year at Cathedral High School in Springfield in June of 1946, and he did not return in the fall when school reopened. He did not return because he was held in lieu of fifty thousand dollars bail in the Hampshire County House of Correction, on charges that he was one of three young men who attempted to rob the Tobacco Valley Cooperative Bank in Granby on the last Friday in July; a teller was shot and badly wounded during the attempt. The court and the District Attorney's Office elected to try Andrew as an adult; on February 18, 1947, he was convicted, and sentenced to twenty years in the Charlestown State Prison. His co-defendants, each of whom was over twenty-one and had a record of prior convictions, were sentenced to terms of life imprisonment; the judge admonished Andrew to make good use of the merciful second chance that was being extended to him, and to learn a trade that would keep him out of trouble when he was released. He was nine days over seventeen years old. He weighed one hundred and thirty-two pounds, was five feet, five inches tall, and had large blue eyes and blond hair.

During his first three weeks in Charlestown State Prison, Andy Marr was buggered twenty times, and forced to commit sodomy sixteen times. He was compelled to submit to fellatio eleven times. Finding Teddy Donnelly the least brutal of those who used him, and the best equipped to protect him, he became Donnelly's doll, which saved him from further beatings, afforded time for his sprained wrist and hyperextended shoulder—wrenched by a car thief who was holding him while an arsonist pulled his pants down to get at his penis—to heal and reduced his homosexual experiences to one a day. He grew to like Teddy Donnelly, who was satisfied with blow jobs and did not cause Andy any rectal pain.

With credit for time served while awaiting trial, Andrew Marr was granted parole on September 12, 1960. He was thirty years old. He had earned his high school equivalency diploma while in prison. He knew how to make cabinets and license plates. He had never been in bed with a woman. He knew how to drive a car, but he did not have a valid operator's license. He had received no correspondence from any member of his family since his arrest in the summer of 1946; the Red Cross, in Springfield, never received any acknowledgment for the cartons of Pall Mall cigarettes that the Marrs had had delivered to him each year at Christmas and on his birthday. He had twenty dollars and a suit and shoes that did not fit him, and an introduction to one Artie Ferry, who ran the Arliss Trucking Company and would give a guy a job if he was hard up. Andy got a furnished room in a tenement in Somerville and waited almost a month before he called Teddy Donnelly and asked him if there was anything going on that would get a fellow enough money to do something besides drink dimies at

the Ocean Tap in the Square. That was how he got
the money to be admitted to the poker game at the
Statler Hilton, where he met Michael Donovan, com-
plimented him on his skill as a cardplayer, and found
a companion with whom to do seventy-five push-ups,
and an hour of roadwork, each day. Early in 1965,
when Michael Donovan complained that the insurance
business was boring, and the poker game did not yield
the kind of money that he wanted for trips to the
Bahamas, Andy introduced him to Donnelly.

On the morning of November 21, 1973, Andy Marr
wore a green blazer and a blue shirt and a red tie and
a bored expression. He sat down in the courtroom
and massaged his wrists.

Richard J. Shanley, wearing a blue suit and a blue
and maroon striped tie, came into the courtroom at
10:45, and talked in murmurs with John Killilea, Sam
Wyman and Tommy Hart. The judge came in at
10:59. "Court," the bailiff said, stretching out the syl-
lable and finishing on a rising inflection, "all rise."

Until 1:00 P.M., when the court recessed for lunch,
female members of religious orders and mothers of
children under sixteen, at home, were automatically
excused, by statute, from service on the jury. Sam Wyman, in a currency-green vested suit and with a very
formal manner, protested that virtually every other
prospective juror should be excused for cause, because
Judge Macarthur refused to ask them whether they
had ever had any close personal friends employed
by any law enforcement agency. John Killilea, in a
gray flannel vested suit, complained that the entire
panel was legally unacceptable, because not enough
women and blacks had been called for service.
Tommy Hart exercised three peremptory challenges,
knocking off what he privately described to Shanley as
"fat ladies over fifty," because "the old fuckers have
all got Christmas Clubs in those goddamned banks
and they think if the joint's tipped over, they'll never
get their fifty bucks at Thanksgiving." Hart wore a
dark brown suit, and there was a trace of scotch on
his breath when he said: "Good morning."

During the morning session, Deke Hunter got up

three times from his chair at the prosecutor's table, and took a drink of water from the cooler near the bailiff's chair. From 2:00 P.M. until 4:00, when Judge Macarthur with evident relief adjourned the court until 9:30 A.M on the twenty-second (with instructions to avoid discussions of the case), Hunter sat still, and fought off the urges to sleep (because that would make the judge angry) and to drink more water (because he had had two beers with his lunch, and had all he could do to retain that much fluid without unbearable pain).

In his office on the first floor of the courthouse, in the remains of the late November afternoon sunlight, Deke Hunter talked to Carmody about the case, and about Andy Marr.

"He is one fresh bastard," Hunter said. "He's getting his usual escort out of the courthouse today, and this is a guy's in deep shit, all right? He says to me: 'How's it going, Corporal?'

"I told him right to his face," Hunter said. "I said: 'Andy, I'm not the one that's going. You're the one that's going. Pretty long time, too, I miss my guess.'

"He looked at me," Hunter said. " 'Don't be too sure, Corporal,' he says. 'Things got a way of happening.'

" 'Yeah,' I says, 'well, maybe. But not this time.'

" 'Me?' he says. 'Yeah, you could be right. But just the same, you wanna look out. Don't eat yellow snow, Corporal.'

" 'Keep the ball low and away, Andy,' I says," Hunter said. " 'Make 'em hit into the ground.' "

"He's talking about Doyle," Carmody said.

"Of course he is," Hunter said. "He's being all smug about it, too. He thinks he's got the fuckin' thing wired, if Donnelly gets off, the son of a bitch.

"Those jurors?" Hunter said. "Those jurors're dying. There's eleven of them, and they're dying already. Can't believe what's happening to them. Get yanked out of the civil session? Oh, boy, something interesting for a change.

"Well," Hunter said, "they've been at this almost a

week, now, and there's still not enough of them around to start anything. They're never gonna *see* a gun. Around Easter, for that. And wait'll they hear the alibi. They'll die of suffocation."

"Gillis's getting jumpy," Carmody said. "Tobin called in this morning from where they're keeping him, see if you thought you're gonna need the guy today, and he said he's climbing the walls. Very jumpy guy."

"I'm sure he is," Hunter said. "If I was in Shanley's hands, I'd be jumpy. Hell, if I was in my hands, with all the clout I've got with Shanley, I'd be jumpy."

"He's double jumpy," Carmody said. "Somebody with a lot of brains told him about that Rossi case, and he knew about that, but not that you were on it."

"And you know something?" Hunter said. "When I got that case, I thought it was gonna be the greatest thing ever happened to me."

"There's a lot of guys around," Carmody said, "and not all of them're on our side, either, lots of them, that thought there was no way in the world that Rossi case could get lost."

"Me too," Hunter said. "I was one of them. There was nobody more surprised'n I was."

"Yes there was," Carmody said. "You gonna see Doyle tonight, make sure nobody gets surprised again?"

"Yup," Hunter said. "Sure's I can, at least."

Madeleine Was More Contented

17

IN ROOM 221 of the Caravan Motel in Woonsocket, Rhode Island, after 11:00 P.M. on November 21, 1973, Hunter lay naked in bed with Madeleine St. Anne.

"A pleasure, I must say," she said. Another semi-trailer went by, its lights coursing across the drawn shade. "It's warm in here and everything. Even got sheets on the bed, so you don't scrape all the skin off your elbows and stuff. Kind of a *sleazy* joint, maybe, but a pleasure all the same. An unexpected pleasure, too. They're the best kind."

"There was a guy I knew, I was in the service," Hunter said, "used to be a Recon Marine. Career. He didn't know *any*thing. Actually, he did. I just thought he didn't know anything. He was on Saipan, apparently, and his idea of a good breakfast was Japs, fresh or cooked. Perfect bastard with a flamethrower. I guess. Guy had more medals'n Carter had pills. Everybody used to say: 'Take it easy.' Guys used to remind each other: 'Don't say that.' And then somebody'd forget, and say it, and he'd be sitting there in that NCO Club like he was part of the stool. The longer he sat there, the likelier it was somebody'd say it, and it didn't matter whether they were talking to him or not. Say that, he always said the same thing. Talked 'way down in his throat, like he'd been chewing on a piece of meat and swallowed it and decided he wanted to say something while it was still on the way down. When he talked, what he said was all wet, you know?

167

'Take it any way you can get it.' Then he'd say: 'Keep your thumb on it.'

"Guys hated him," Hunter said. "Llewellyn Rainey. Sergeant Rain, they called him. 'And he don't know enough to come in out of it, either.'

"Now," Hunter said, "I don't know. Maybe he wasn't stupid after all. Maybe he was smart. He knew what he could do. There was only one thing he could do. Two things. When he was young, he could figure out ways to kill people faster'n they could figure out ways to kill him. When he was older, he could teach people to kill people faster'n the people they were up against could do the job against them. He had a thing he could do, and maybe it was the only thing, but he knew where it was and he found the place where he could sell it, and that was all. You can't be dumb if you can do that, and that's what's the best kind."

"You did have the ten bucks, though," she said. "See, I knew you did. You didn't know you did. See how much better this is?"

"Hey," Hunter said, "twelve-seventy-five. This's no cheap joint, you come in and the pillows're still hot, they got to take a towel count in the morning, see what the traffic was. This is a classy place. They got running water and everything."

"You wanna take a shower together, is that it?" she said.

"Sugar," he said, "that's dirty talk. Besides, we're not dirty. That'd be wasting water. What's the matter with you?"

"There's nothing the matter with me, except I'm horny," she said. "Why else would I wind up in a motel with a guy that calls me practically when I'm right ready to leave and go home for supper? You know any other reason? You know my weakness."

"You like to get laid," Hunter said.

"It's not that kind of a thing," she said. "There's not only a few people that've got that kind of weakness, you know? I keep telling myself that, anyway."

"What about Freddie?" Hunter said.

"You know something?" she said. "Freddie's doing great. Called me, the morning recess, he's got to see a guy. 'Oh, great.' I say. 'We got any batteries for the vibrator?' "

"For Christ sake, Mad," Hunter said.

"Well, it pissed me off," she said. "What're you complaining about? Wasn't for that, I wouldn't be here. You would've hadda go without."

"I could've stood it," he said.

"You didn't come down here to see me?" she said.

"I hadda see a maggot," he said.

"What'd you tell your wife?" she said.

"That I hadda see a maggot," he said. "That's what I had to do."

"This was something else," she said.

"This was something else," he said. "This was a bonus. But I did have to see a maggot."

"Where was the maggot?" she said.

"He was in a place," he said, "and I went and I saw him. And I talked to him. And then I came down here, and pretty soon, I'm gonna go home."

"I may still need the batteries, then," she said.

"Well," Hunter said, "you got your car. Whaddaya need, a buck for Ray-O-Vacs?"

"I got a buck," she said. "I make more'n you do."

"Okay," Hunter said, "then you can pay for the room."

"I didn't see any luggage," she said. "You got to pay for the room in advance, I understand, you haven't got any luggage. I want something to eat."

"You came to the right place, lady," Hunter said. "I got a snack right here for you."

"That's not what I meant," she said. "Room service."

"Good thing for you," he said, "they haven't got any, here. Cockroach'd bring it, carry the tray and come in on roller skates."

"Then take me out," she said.

"No way," he said. "We'll go someplace, and you'll get custard pie, and then you'll lift the damned thing up and pour vinegar on the plate and let it all soak through the crust. I know you herring-chokers."

"You're not the one that's eating it," she said.

"I was," he said. "It was less'n half an hour ago. I didn't hear no complaints then."

"You would've had trouble hearing anything," she said.

"Okay," he said, "you said it. I didn't. You have been getting a little hippy lately, I notice. Having a few doughnuts with the coffee, mornings? Couple frappes or something?"

There was some silence. "Deke," she said, after a while, "I don't know how to put this, okay?"

"I'm about to clear waivers, I think," he said.

"What's that?" she said.

"It's what I used to do, all the time," he said. "Wait for the coach that you got along with the best, tell you the manager wants to see you in his office. Outright release. Traded. Sold. They're giving up on you. I used to worry about it. Now, I don't anymore."

"You," she said, "you've changed some, you know?"

"Gee," he said, "no, actually I don't. I think I'm the same great guy I was the last time you saw me. Except, I will admit, it's warmer in here and they have got sheets and stuff."

"Where's your car?" she said.

"At home," he said.

"How'd you get here?" she said.

"Took a cab," he said.

"Come on," she said.

"Okay," he said, "I'll do the best I can. Woman like you'd wear a man out."

"That's not what I mean," she said. "How'd you get here?"

"You gonna tell?" he said.

"Of course not," she said.

"A miniature sleigh, and eight tiny reindeer," Hunter said. "I came in through the chimney. You didn't know that was your chimney, did you, Mad?"

She began to laugh. "Where's your car, Deke?"

"Sold it," he said. "Fuckin' thing took too much gas. I sat there and I listened to the President, and then I sold it. Fuckin' crook."

"The last time," she said, "you were so worried, somebody might see your car. I just wondered."

"I done my bit for democracy," he said. "That's what I did. I tell you, it's a public obligation. Sell your car. Stop burning up gas. Stay home. Cheat on your taxes. That's what you got to do."

"Cheat on your wife," she said.

"Cheat on your wife," he said, nodding. "Cheat on your husband. That's another thing. Equal rights. Everybody gets an equal right, cheat on everybody else. Damned right. Take care of everybody, and conserve the other kind of energy like a bastard."

"What'd the maggot say?" she said.

"Said he was a maggot, of course," Hunter said. "Those guys're all right as long's you know what they are, and they know that you know. You can tell right off. Just throw out a piece of rotten meat, and they'll land right on it and start munching away. Now all I got to do is prove it with about two hundred guys that saw it with their own eyes, and they're all deacons in their church or something, and I'll have myself a nice tight case that'll probably take Rossi about, oh, say, a couple hours to beat, before he walks off from it."

"You after him again?" she said.

"Not again," he said. "Still."

"You oughta give up," she said.

"I don't like giving up," he said. "I had to do it a few times, and I did it, but I never got to like it. It sucks, is what it does. It's the one thing I used to agree with Sergeant Rain about. He used to get us out there, he was teaching us to drive tanks, and he used to tell us: I'll tell you when a tank's dead. It's when the guys in the tank think the tank's dead. Never till then. But then, when they think that, it's dead then, all right. A tank's a great thing. It'll never be dead if you think it's not. As long as it'll move, it's not dead. I don't care how slow. You got a tank, you take care of the tank, the tank'll take care of you. This's serious business. There's more metal onna tank'n there is on you.' "

"Where's your tank, now?" she said.

"Sold it to the guy that bought the car," Hunter said. "He's a perfect pigeon, that guy. He'll buy anything. You think a car uses gas, boy, you oughta see a tank. Added to which, the treads tear up the road, and parking the thing's a bitch."

"You're never gonna get him, you know," she said. "He's too smart for people."

"Not for me," Hunter said. "Nobody's too smart for me. The ones that're too smart for me, they go to bed early. But consequently nobody's too smart for me, because I stay up late, and I get up early too."

"Makes your eyes red," she said.

"Not mine," he said. "My eyes never get red. They get bags under them, yeah, but they never get red. I just tell people: 'I been putting on some weight.' Them guys don't know anything. Besides," he said, "I got a secret from them, now, I didn't used to have."

"You don't give them enough credit," she said. "That was your problem, the last time."

"But that was the last time," he said. "This is this time. The hell do I need credit for? Credit's for guys haven't got the ten bucks. I got something else, and it's better'n credit."

"The ten bucks," she said.

"Nah," he said. "What I got, you don't even need the ten bucks. What I got . . . , with what I got, you don't need anything."

She raised herself on her left elbow. "What's that?" she said.

He moved his head on the pillow and clasped his hands behind his head. He smiled. "I'm not telling," he said.

Things as They Became

□ 18

IN THE LIVING ROOM of the Hunter house, on the night of November 22, 1973, the late news flickered without sound or attention on the television, and the pale bluish light from the tube lay on their faces while they talked in low voices so as not to disturb the children.

"Where were you last night?" Andrea said.

"When's last night?" Deke said.

"Where were you last night?" she said. "Where were you?"

"I was lots of places last night," he said. "That's what I mean. You mean: when it got dark, where was I?"

"Just tell me where you were," she said.

"Where were you?" he said.

"I was here," she said. "Waiting for you. I had the television on and they were having something about President Kennedy, and then, when you didn't come home, I shut it off and I went to bed."

"It doesn't seem like ten years," he said. "It doesn't seem like ten years at all. You know that?"

"It doesn't," she said.

"I was in Boston a couple, three weeks ago," he said. "I was going up past Cambridge Street, and the guy that was with me said he hadda see a guy in the Kennedy Center, and I let him off, and that's when it hit me: those buildings've been there ever since I can remember. But they haven't been. They named those buildings after him, and they built them after he was

173

dead, and it's ten years now, ten years ago that he got killed. It doesn't seem like it."

"I didn't watch it," she said. "I was waiting for you."

"To do what?" he said.

"To talk to you," she said. "I thought you'd be home before ten-thirty, the way you said you would be, and I waited up for you. It was after eleven before I went to bed."

"It's after eleven now," he said.

"I need my sleep, Deke," she said.

"So do I," he said, "especially since I got the hockey detail again tomorrow morning."

"I don't see how you can do it," she said. "It must've been after two when you got home this morning."

"Two-fifteen or so, I guess," he said.

"Two-thirty, at least," she said. "I was up at two-fifteen. Michele was crying, and then I hadda go to the bathroom. You weren't here."

"I said it was around two-fifteen," he said. "I dunno."

"Well," she said, "where were you?"

"When court got over?" he said. "Is that where you want me to start?"

"I want you to tell me where you were," she said. "I think I want you to tell me where you were. Maybe I don't."

"Make up your mind," he said. "I've got to get to bed. The longer we sit here, the later it's gonna be when I do, and that makes it that much sooner I got to get up with Sam."

"If it's too much for you," she said, "I suppose I can do it."

"When you signed me up for this," Hunter said, "you said it was because you couldn't do it."

"It's too hard for me," she said. "I can't go without sleep the way you apparently can."

"Well," he said, "it's no picnic for me, either."

"Then don't do it," she said. "Tell him, since you know how important it is to him, you can stay out till all hours of the day and night, doing whatever it is that you won't tell me about, but . . . , and that it makes you too tired to take him to play hockey. Tell him that."

"Andrea," he said, "four-thirty in the morning's just crazy. It's a crazy time, it's a crazy thing to do. Those rinks, they build them and pay them off on crazy people. You gotta be nuts, get up in the middle of the night and get your kid up, to go and play hockey."

"There must be a lot of crazy people, then," she said.

"There is," he said. "There's lots more of us'n there is of them. You know how hard it is to find a parking place near the door at five o'clock in the morning? Sometimes I have to park so far away, I have to let the kid off at the door. It's too far for him to walk on the skate-guards. There must be, I dunno, sixty, seventy, maybe a hundred and twenty-five cars around that place. They got four rinks, and they're building two more, and they're all full. At five o'clock in the morning. Where'd it all come from? Who decided, if a kid can't get somebody to drive him to play hockey before the goddamned sun's up, so he can fall asleep in school all day, he's gonna have a dee-prived childhood and grow up to be a rapist or something?"

"I don't know," she said.

"I don't know either," he said.

"Where were you, Deke?" she said. "If you don't want to tell me, all right, don't tell me. But you have to tell me, you don't want to tell me."

"After court," he said, "I hadda fight with Shanley. No, that's today. After court yesterday, I hadda talk with Horace."

"How long did that take?" she said.

"I dunno," he said. "Maybe I spent an hour with him. He's a pretty good guy. He knows a lot. You wanna write it down someplace, so you can keep track of things?"

"I just want to know," she said. "You're my husband, and I think I've got a right to know what you're doing. My mother always knew where my father was, and what he was doing. He wasn't out all the time, like you are."

"There a difference, you know," Hunter said, "between being a cop and being a guy that sells real estate and stuff."

"That's what he told me," she said, "a long time ago, and I told him: it didn't matter. I was still in love with you, and you were in love with me, and that was what mattered. That we loved each other. That's what you told me, Deke, and I believed you."

"I wasn't a cop then," he said.

"Deke," she said, "you weren't anything, then."

"I was Hearst High School All American," he said.

"For New England," she said.

"In three sports, I might add," he said.

"Right," she said. "And then it turned out, you're too small for football in college, and your marks aren't good enough to get you a baseball scholarship, and you're not tall enough for college basketball. There were hundreds like you. So what good did it do you?"

"It got me the prettiest cheerleader," he said.

"Yeah," she said, "but cheerleading was just something I did. I wasn't going to be a cheerleader all my life. Maybe I should've been. I was good at that. I was happy, then. But I was in college, and I thought . . . , I don't know. If I'd've stayed in, if I hadn't quit to marry you . . . I don't know."

"You didn't quit to marry me," he said.

"I didn't know anything," she said. "I don't know anything. Except the things I do, I don't know how to do anything. Sometimes, when I wake up in the morning, I don't know why I'm doing it. You're right. I didn't quit college to marry you. I just went there, and then I stopped going there. It was the same thing."

"I was going away," he said. "I didn't know if I was gonna come back or not. It was your idea just as much as it was mine. You knew what it was. You knew what you were getting into."

"I didn't," she said. "I really did not. I thought I did. I told my father I did. But I didn't. I didn't know what it was all about. Who was there, to tell me? Nobody. I wouldn't've asked them if there had been. I wouldn't've even known what to ask them. That night you played in Fenway Park?"

"Yeah," he said.

"That's what I thought it was going to be all about," she said. "I thought it was going to be my being there, and being so proud of you, that I was your girl. That's what I thought I was getting into. When I went to college, it was . . . , I wasn't really *going* there. It was just something to do while you did whatever it was that you were going to do, until you were ready for me. That you had to do. I would wait. All I ever was, was your girl. And it stinks."

"I'm sorry," he said.

"It's not you," she said. "It's not your fault. It's not even me. It's not my fault. I shouldn't've said that. But there's nothing it'll do any good to be sorry about, and that means there isn't anything to be sorry about, because it won't do any good, no good at all. It wasn't anything you did. It probably wasn't even anything that I did. Nobody did anything. Nobody knew anything. Nobody even said anything. Nobody who *knew* anything, anyway. If there was anybody around that knew anything, they didn't open their goddamned fucking mouth."

"Are you drunk?" he said.

"I had a couple drinks," she said. "I thought you were gonna be home by seven. Then you didn't call. And I started thinking. My father, he was late too, sometimes, but he always called. And I started to worry. 'Why doesn't he call?' And then I thought. 'The hell with him. I'll wait. I'll wait like I always do.' "

"Oh," he said.

"Well, Deke," she said, "there really isn't anything that I can do about it. If you know what I mean. I can't make you call me. I can't even make you want to call me, so at least you would feel bad if you wanted to call me and you couldn't. Or if you're someplace where you could call me but you just don't think of it until afterwards, when you're someplace else that you can't. Does that make sense? I can't make you sorry you're not with me, or wish that you could be, or anything. What the hell *can* I do, anyway? I can't do anything."

"Andrea," he said.

"When you were going down there for tryouts," she said, "I didn't know anything. That was all I could think about. I would get asked, was I going to the proms and everything? Was I going away, college week in Bermuda, Fort Lauderdale, maybe? I was never going. I never even really thought about going. My parents used to ask me if I was going, if I wanted to go someplace for spring vacation, when they called me up, and I never even thought about it until they asked me, and I didn't think about it afterwards, either. 'My boyfriend's got a tryout with the Yankees. He's not around.' The Tigers. The Cubs. I never went to anything in the spring. It was like I wasn't even there. I wasn't part of anything, because I was part of you, and you weren't there, so I wasn't, either. That was all I could think about."

"Most guys," he said, "can't hit a major-league curve. Turned out, I was one of them. Also a major-league fastball. And I had a little trouble, going to my right. I wished I didn't, but as a matter of fact, I did."

"It isn't that," she said. "That isn't what I'm talking about at all. I don't know what it is. Things just didn't turn out like I thought they would."

"How'd you think they'd turn out?" he said.

"When you thought you were gonna get drafted," she said, "and we talked it over, and you decided to enlist instead, I don't know what I thought. After it turned out, I wasn't pregnant, after all, even though everything we did was because of that, I was still glad. Because there was never any doubt in my mind. It was, it would've been, just a matter of doing something sooner'n we'd planned. But I knew it'd work out. I knew a girl in college who thought she was pregnant for a while, and it really upset her. But not me. All I could think about was that when you got back, you'd do something, and we'd do something, and I really didn't care what it was, you know? All I wanted was for you to come back, and not to get hurt, and then we'd be all right. The way I used to think about it was that we'd get a house and have kids and you'd have a job that you would go to in the morning and at night you'd come home from it. And we'd be happy.

I'd be happy. Because I was living with you, and it was all right because we were married, and I was your girl. That's what I thought. It was nice to think about, that way."

"Okay," he said.

"I didn't know a goddamned fucking thing," she said.

"Andrea," he said.

"I didn't," she said. "You came back, and you were so handsome in your uniform, and I remember my father saying: 'What's he going to do now?'

"I never really thought about it," she said. "I was so happy. Anything you wanted. It was all right with me. I just wanted to be with you. Just wanted to be with you. And he told me: 'It does matter.' And I didn't think it did."

"I shouldn't've gone into police work," he said. "You've said it so many times. The hours and everything."

"It's not the work," she said. "It's not what you do. My father was wrong. He's been wrong. Lots. But he was right sometimes, too."

"Like about me," he said.

"Sometimes he was," she said. "Maybe he was. If you'd've told me, fifteen years ago, that those words'd ever come out of my mouth, I would've said you were crazy. I didn't used to think like this. I just started. But maybe he was."

"What'd he say?" Hunter said. "I'd like to know."

"*Oh*, no," she said. "You two get along lousy now. I have to listen to you about him, and then I have to listen to him about you, and then I get from my mother what he said to her and forgot when he's talking to me."

"Oh," he said.

"He never really said anything," she said. "It was just . . . , I could tell."

"That he didn't like me," Hunter said.

"He did like you," she said.

"For a while, he didn't," she said.

"When was that?" Hunter said. "Was it, by any chance, when I hadda even admit it to myself, that I wasn't gonna make the majors and I might as well quit, and that meant he couldn't ever get the chance to go around bragging about how he could get tickets to any goddamned dogfight that anybody ever threw? Or was it, until I started doing his goddamned donkey work, taking care of his property while he gets a nice tan and rubs it in because he's listening to the ball-game."

"He does like you," she said. "He told me that. 'It's not that I don't like him. What matters is whether you like him. I'm not gonna have to live with him. And whether he likes you. That's what's important. You can marry the garbageman if you want, and he'll make you happy. But be sure you do like him, and he likes you, and it's not ...' "

"Not what?" he said.

"Nothing," she said.

"Not nothing?" he said.

"No," she said, "not: nothing. 'Not just some high-school romance that went on too long and then ended, but you went and got yourselves married to each other just before that, when you should've waited until it was all over and then married somebody else.' "

"You could've fooled me," Hunter said. "You did fool me, as a matter of fact. I didn't think it was that, and that it was getting over."

"Neither did I," she said, "and it wasn't. I didn't mean that."

"You said it," he said.

"Because you asked me," she said. "You're the one that wanted to know. It didn't mean anything to me. It never meant anything to me. When you were going to school, and working in Western Auto," she said, "that was all right with me. Because I knew it was just temporary, and we wouldn't always be living in an apartment. I knew that. It didn't bother me. I even wished you stayed in school."

"Hard to do that," he said, "on two bucks an hour, with a baby coming."

"Did it bother you?" she said. "It didn't bother me at all."

"Once I was out of it, it didn't," he said. "I was

glad as hell to get out of that. I was too old. I saw too much. I didn't like sitting around all the time without a goddamned dime to do anything with. You remember that red car."

"Yes," she said. "I liked that better, I guess."

"I sure did," he said.

"I'm sorry you had to get rid of it," she said.

"I didn't *like* getting rid of it," he said. "No, I didn't. But it was all right, if you know what I mean. It was just something I had to do. It was the same with the other things."

"If you'd've gotten your barber license, like you were talking about doing for a while, there," she said. "Anything would've been all right with me, so long as you were happy."

"I'd probably have varicose veins," he said. "Besides, I doubt if there's many barbers around today that're coming out of the year with the same pay I get."

"It doesn't matter if there are," she said. "I'm glad you're a cop. You love being a cop. It's what you should be. It doesn't bother me at all."

"I don't love it," he said. "And it's not what I should be at all. I'll tell you what I should be now: I should be talking to reporters about how I figure I've got three, maybe four years left, and then I'd like to stay in the game. I should be going out of the dressing room and into the parking lot and getting into a brand new red Cadillac convertible that's all paid for, which would even make me forget that little red Eighty-eight that never did get paid for.

"It's a job, Andrea," he said. "It's just a job. Last year it was nowhere near as good a job as being a pilot. Except when I was in the service, I wasn't learning to fly. I was supposed to be learning to kill people quietly, and I don't even think I learned that very well. A year ago, pilots made about forty. This year there's no kerosene, and they're laying pilots off, and I hope they saved their money because there's not gonna be any forty thousand when you're sitting around at home. So this year, I got a better job'n one of those pilots've got.

"It's still just a job," he said. "It's not bad. Sometimes it's kind of fun. Sometimes. Not all the time. Sometimes it's a big pain in the ass. Like today. But not all the time for that, either. It's better'n being a barber because it doesn't matter how long guys decide to let their hair grow. Or if they got any kerosene. It's steady. But it's nothing to love."

"You work awful hard at it," she said. "You care how things come out."

"I'm supposed to care how things come out," he said. "And because: I'd better. That's why I work hard. Sometimes in the middle of the night I wake up, and you're asleep, and I start thinking: Well, maybe if I'd worked at it harder. Maybe I would've made it. I don't see how I could've worked at it harder, but when I wake up in the middle of the night, that's what I think. And then I think: I better work as hard as I can at this.

"There's always gonna be crooks," he said. "A guy in my position'll always have something to do. You do it the best way you can. You fight with Shanley a couple of hours, you get through work and you go out to Uxbridge and you find a ratty old bar with an old rat in it, and you talk to the rat awhile and then you come home. And the next morning you get up and you take the kid to hockey and you go to work and come home again, when you're finished.

"Your old man, Andrea," he said, "he obviously knows something I missed and I wished he didn't keep it to himself so long. What it is, I don't know. I don't think Horace knows, and I'm pretty sure Shanley doesn't. Although he's such a prick that if he did, he'd pretend that he didn't, just so he could fool people. What is it? I don't even know what you ask a guy, that knows, so he will tell you.

"I'm doing something," he said. "For doing it, I get the chance to do it again tomorrow, some pay, and not much else. It's hard, you know? Of course you know. It's hard on me and it's hard on you, and it's probably not doing the kids much good either. But it does feed us, and when it rains we don't get too wet, and in the winter we can keep the place warm enough so nobody dies of exposure while they're sleeping. But you don't make any progress. You never make any progress."

"To what?" she said.

"I don't know," he said. "To the end of it, and the beginning of the next thing. When we got here I figured: boy, our own house. And I used to go out in the morning, to work, and it was nice, and then three days later I came home, and I used to look forward to everything that I had to do. The next thing and the thing after that. This Christmas was good. I used to think. Next Christmas, we'll have shrimp or something. And then we had them. And then next Christmas. Next Thanksgiving. The next birthday, the presents'll be a little bit nicer'n they were this year, and this year they were better'n last year, and you know something?"

"No," she said.

"When I was a kid," he said, "what I wanted was a twenty-two. When I was nine years old, what I wanted was a Marlin lever-action twenty-two, with the straight grip that wouldn't catch on the saddle scabbard. Now what the hell I thought I was gonna do with a cowboy rifle, I do not know. A shotgun would've been sensible, I guess, because I could've gotten a duck or a rabbit or a pheasant or a deer with it. But the only thing I could've done with a twenty-two was shoot rats or squirrels, or maybe snakes, and I never had any desire to eat any one of them things. But that was what I wanted. Now, my old man did not make good money."

"He was a good guy, though," she said.

"He was a very good guy," he said. "He worked his ass off, and he got us from Brighton to Malden to East Bridgewater, where there was trees and grass and pretty girls to chase. He used to get up as early as I do now, to take Sam skating, only he did it every day, so he could work two shifts instead of one down at the abattoir, to get things for us. The only thing when I was playing sports that bothered him was that in the football season, he had to give up a day's, a half a day's pay which he wanted for us, so he could come and see me play. And he still wouldn't've missed it for anything, you know? He, that was just the way he was.

"So," he said, "the one thing in the world I want is the Marlin. They used to have pictures of them on matchbooks. He smoked a pipe and he used those matchbooks. He didn't smoke cigarettes because they were too expensive. Fat lot of good it did him. And when the matchbook was empty, he would just leave it around, and they all had rifles on them. Some of them had pictures of razor blades. Well, it was the ones with the rifles that bothered me. That was the one thing in the world that I wanted, then, and I think it cost sixty-nine dollars and ninety-five cents.

"So I remember," he said, "there was Christmas, and I was nine, and I got a Lionel train. The Santa Fe diesels, double diesels, red and silver. And there was this cattle car, that there was this thing that went with it, and you got the cattle car up to this particular platform on this particular piece of track, and you pushed a button and these little black plastic cows came out of the car and walked around the platform and went back in the car and came out again. There were gates on the platform. You could make the cows come out, and make the train go around again, and then pull the train up again at the platform and stop the car there and open up the gates and let the cows back in again. The doors went up on the car when you pushed the button. I think he bought it for me because those little black plastic cows mostly did what they were supposed to, and the cows they got over at the abattoir were always getting out into the street and tearing around through people's backyards, knocking down clotheslines and scaring the hell out of everybody.

"Then there was a milk car," he said. "It was white. The cattle car was orange, sort of, but the milk car was white. And there was another platform, and a particular piece of track that went with it, and that platform was green and white. And what you did there was, you pulled the milk car up, and you pushed the button, and this little man in a white uniform come out and put these silver milk cans on it, on the platform. And then when you wanted him to do it again, you put the cans through this hatch in the roof, and made the train go around again, and then push the button and out he would come with them. See, it wasn't the kind of thing where they had it so he would take them back in, if you pushed the button. All it could do was put them out, and then it was empty, and you had to do something if you wanted it to work again. But it worked better'n the cattle car. The cows worked on vibration. They moved from vibration. The platform vibrated. They had these little rubber feelers on the bottoms of them, and sometimes they would hit a flat spot and they wouldn't move. Like the players on the electric football game that Sam's got, that don't always go where you want them to."

"Nicky wants one of those too," she said.

"Nicky's not old enough for it yet," he said, "and he doesn't need one anyway. One of those things to a house is enough.

"I was nine then, like I said," he said, "and I was just like every other nine-year-old kid then, and every kid now. I knew there wasn't any Santa Claus, but it was a good con job to put on the grown-ups, because they hadda deliver if they didn't want you to think there wasn't any Santa Claus. But I knew who hadda pay for all that stuff that you got under the tree when you woke up. I knew he gave it to me. He knew I knew. He had to pay for it, and I also knew that. It probably cost him over a hundred bucks for that train, and he didn't have it. And he certainly didn't go out and spend that much on my mother, or my sisters, either. And he got up with me, that morning, and I saw the train, and he was so proud of it. It was all set up, and he was probably up all night doing that, too, on the rug. And he wants to know, he's showing me how all the things work, and the cattle come out and the milk cans, too, and the whistle blows. Everything. 'It came from Eric Fuchs,' he says. So I said to him: 'I wanted a rifle.'

"I did want a rifle," he said. "It was true. I was counting on a rifle. The rifle was the only thing in the world that I wanted. I was nine years old. Maybe I was eight years old. I dunno. I didn't know anything. I just wanted a rifle.

"He got this look on his face," Hunter said, "like I kicked him in the balls. It wrecked everything for him, my saying that. And the only thing that made me, the only reason I wrecked everything for him like that, was that he was wrecking everything for me. Which, of course, I couldn't tell him. He didn't want to give me something I wanted. He wanted to give me something that he wanted me to want. He was probably right. I was too young to have a rifle, maybe.

"That's what he told me, anyway," he said. "I didn't know how to handle a rifle. So I asked him: 'How'm I supposed to learn to handle a rifle if I haven't got a rifle?' And this and that, which only made him madder. He was really mad at me. I was really mad at him, too. Only now, if I was him, I would agree with him instead of me. But this's now, and that's then, and then I didn't know that. And then the next year, he gave me the rifle."

"Too late?" she said. "You didn't want it anymore?"

"Yes, I did," he said. "If it was anything, I wanted it more. That was all I thought about for the whole next year, it seemed like, was having that rifle. He gave it to me and he said: 'I hope you're satisfied,' and I opened up that box and it was just what I wanted. And I told him it was, and that didn't make him happy either. Because I had won and he lost, I guess. I went out with it, I couldn't have any shells for it unless he was with me, and when I went out with it, to show the guys, I dunno, I think that was the first thing I ever got, that I ever really wanted, and I thought that gun was what was gonna make all the difference in the world to me.

"It didn't," he said.

"That's what I said, and you disagreed with me," she said. "You got it too late."

"That wasn't it," he said. "I'm telling you, I did want it, and I got it, and it didn't make any difference, is all. I was so glad to have that damned thing it's a wonder I didn't ruin it just dry-snapping it. There were these two friends of mine. That same Christmas one of them got a regular Daisy air rifle, and the other one got a Red Ryder carbine, and they could have BBs, and actually shoot at bottles and stuff, and break them. Cats. Birds. And I couldn't do anything with what I had. Windows. But it was a real gun, and that was enough for me. Only, it wasn't."

"Why not?" she said.

"I don't know," he said. "It's the same kind of thing we've got now. When we got here, it's our house, like I was saying. I'm doing something that's not bad, at least, and I like it and everything. I can stand it. And there isn't really gonna be anybody that can throw me out of it, unless I fuck something up so bad it's a new record. They're always gonna need guys that can do what I can do. And I was happy. Just like you. Am I right?"

"I still am," she said. "I was happy and I still am."

"No," he said, "no, you're not. You got things on your mind."

"I've got you on my mind," she said. "I wonder where you are. I wonder what you're doing. I wonder why you don't come home, and stuff. Those things. I think about those things a lot. Why you don't call. But I wouldn't want, I wouldn't want anything else."

"You want other things," he said.

"I want things to work," she said. "When I talk about, I need those appliances. I'm used to them. And when they don't work," she said softly, "and I tell you, that it makes my life harder, you don't seem to care."

"Andrea," he said, "on my salary, there's only so many things you can fix. You can only fix things so many times, and there's nothing in what I make, extra, for getting new things. You're always telling me how prices're going up. I know that. I can't do anything about it. If we're gonna blow ninety bucks on the hockey stuff for Sam, and the basketball camps and the swimming and all the other stuff, well, if you start hunting around for that ninety bucks when you need something new in the kitchen, you're not gonna find it anywhere, because it'll be gone. It is gone. The only reason we got two cars is that the State owns one of them and I hope to God they can afford the gas for it, because I sure can't. And then you don't want to drive the other one."

"I'm afraid of it," she said. "I think it's worn out."

"It's got a lot of miles on it," he said. "I'd like to have a new one, myself. I'd like a new convertible, like I said, with white leather seats and a white top. I'd like that very much. And I'd have about as much chance of being able to pay for it this time as I did when I bought that Olds in nineteen-sixty-one. But it's no closer to being worn out when I'm driving it and you're riding in it'n it is if you're driving it all by yourself.

"That's what I mean," he said. "I didn't know anything. I got here and everything was new. The car, too. It never occurred to me, some day it'd wear out, most of it all at the same time because we bought it all at the same time, and that I wouldn't have the ready cash to replace it. The bank gave me thirty years to pay for this stuff when it was new, and two for the car, and I paid off the car but I'm still paying the mortgage. There's no way I can get thirty years more to keep paying on the old stuff that's broken and doesn't work anymore.

"Now nobody told me that," he said. "You would've thought, if I had brains enough to get myself dressed in the morning, I would've thought of that, that refrigerators and that kind of thing don't last thirty years. But I didn't."

"You make as much," she said, "you make more than my father did, lots of years, when he was working."

"It was twenty years ago, when he was doing that," he said. "That's another thing I got trouble getting used to: I can personally remember things that happened twenty years ago. Not everything, but enough things. And then years from now, I'll be able to remember things that happened thirty years ago. Money was worth more, then. It's not the same thing, now. It looks like the same thing, it's the same size and the same color and they still've got all those serial numbers on it, but it's not the same thing that your father was making.

Besides that, we're trying to do for three kids on what I make that your father only hadda do for one kid, on it.

"It's not like I don't know what you mean," he said. "I do know that. I get to thinking that way myself, sometimes. A lot. I have to catch myself. In the morning, when I go out, at first everything looks the same's it did when we moved in here. Some of it could use a little paint, maybe, but otherwise, pretty much the same.

"I come into the driveway at night," he said. "Still the same. Looks the same. But, it's not the same. It's like what sixteen, seventeen thousand dollars a year looked like when he was making it, and he was making that a year and putting five of it away, and that's why he could send you to college for, oh, probably it cost him sixteen, sixteen hundred dollars a year or so. But, I was talking to Wally Beach there, and he told me, he's busting ass day and night because his kid's in BU and it's costing him almost five grand a year, by the time he gets through, and we got three of them.

"I'm making pretty good money," Hunter said. "But I'll never get no shopping-center year like your old man had, because they're not available to cops, and they're not selling high-test like they used to, over four gallons for a buck, like they were when your father was working. Looks the same, but it's different.

"It's the same on the job," he said. "I got this guy Shanley, and I'll have his motor going pretty soon, I think, regular bear in a man's suit, and I get up early and it's late at night when I get home, and I'm doing the best I can. So everything oughta be all right, I think. Sometimes I even think it is.

"But I really know it's not," he said. "You sit there, and you tell me things, and I know exactly how you feel, and that's the way that I feel, too. Something's missing, and I don't even know what the hell it is, or why it's missing, and anyway, goddamnit, it shouldn't be. I did everything the way I was supposed to. *What the hell happened?*

"The trouble is," he said, "the trouble is that I don't know. You and Shanley, I like you a lot better, but you've still got something in common. I don't know what the hell happened. I don't know how come. You want me to tell you I'll change things, and I can't. I can't even tell you how things got the way they are, or that I'll go out and find out and come back and tell you. I can't even do that, because I don't know where to start."

"Do what?" she said. "I don't know what you're talking about."

"I know it," he said. "That's my fault, I guess. It's not the way that things were supposed to be. I could stay out forever, and then come back, late, and spend all my time looking, and you'd be mad at me and I still couldn't tell you."

PART FIVE

□

The Verdict

Horace Carmody Had Been Out Sick

19

ON NOVEMBER 26, 1973, in the office at the court-house, Hunter filled Carmody in: "We got the rest of the jury Thursday afternoon. Lucky for Richard J., the people's lawyer, it was almost three-thirty, and the Judge quit early without having him make his open-ing. Because I don't think he was ready. No reason why he would be, of course; he's only known for four days he was gonna have to do it sooner or later. What'd you have, anyway?"

"Trots," Carmody said. "One of the kids in the neighborhood thinks my wife's his mother or some-thing, so he's over the house all the time after school, and it's the same as it was when we had kids in the house: whatever goes through the school, goes through us also. I'll be lucky if I haven't got whooping cough before the year's over. Rougher now, too, now that I'm older. Don't bounce back like you used to, I find."

"You're all over it now, I hope," Hunter said.

"Oh, yeah," Carmody said. "I've been all right, really, since Saturday. It's really that twenty-four-hour virus that keeps you up all night, so that when you get over it, you didn't get any sleep, either, and you're as weak as a kitten. But I'm okay now. You see Doyle?"

"Saw him Thursday night," Hunter said. "Met him in a tavern up in Uxbridge."

"He's an awful piece of shit, isn't he?" Carmody said.

"Awful," Hunter said.

"You notice how he smells?" Carmody said.

192

"Notice?" Hunter said. "Notice? Five minutes into the mission I was looking around for my gas mask. He's . . . , wow."

"I bet the guy," Carmody said, "I'd be willing to bet, the guy hasn't had a bath in five years. Well, they probably hosed him down the last time he went in for something. But good Christ does he stink. I couldn't stand myself if I smelled like that all the time. Smells like he's rotting. Decay, you know?"

"In a way," Hunter said, "I guess he is. He told me he's got some kind of trouble with his skin. I guess I didn't keep a straight face when the wind shifted my way or something. Said he's got this medicine he has to put on, and he admits it, that it does make him smell terrible. 'But if I don't,' he said, 'then I got to scratch all the time. I scratch so much sometimes, it makes me bleed, you know? Then I get it between my legs, and I can't even walk."

"Yeah," Carmody said, "well, okay. Maybe he can't help it. But I'd advise you, you get him in before your jury, here, you better make sure the wind's blowing from them to him, because they get a whiff of that guy and they're not gonna hear one word he says."

"He's actually kind of a sad case," Hunter said. "He's scared absolutely shitless of Donnelly."

"He oughta be," Carmody said. "Goat-ass was Teddy's satchel when they were in the can for a while. He knows the guy."

"He told me," Hunter said, "that he went to see Charlie Thomas on his own, and asked him what he should do. Said Charlie said he could trust us. And that if he didn't come to us, and we found out, afterwards, that he came in and lied, he'd go to jail again for perjury.

"'I can't do that,' he told me. 'I can't do another bit. It'll kill me, the next time. I just can't do it. I'm working some, now. And all I want for people to do for me is leave me alone, and that's all, and I'll leave them alone, and that's all I want to do. Only, they won't. They got in the habit of doing things to me, I guess, and they won't cut it out.'

"He told me," Hunter said, "that Charlie told him

that we really want these guys, and we really got them, and they're going and they know it. You must've done a little missionary work there, Horace."

"I chipped in a little something," Carmody said. "Charlie's an awful frontrunner. He's trading all the time. He only deals with people that he thinks're gonna be able to do something for him if he needs it. Charlie likes you lots better if you're tough, and deliver, 'n he does if he thinks you're soft. You don't get nothing off of Charlie if he thinks you're in trouble."

"Said Charlie gave us a real recommendation," Hunter said. " 'Treat a man like a man. So, I'm gonna do like Charlie says. I always trusted Charlie Thomas and I haven't never been disappointed. Charlie says you guys're all right, so I trust you, too. But there's only one reason I'm doing this,' he says, 'and I'm not saying it's anything else. It's to save my ass.'

"I said I understood that," Hunter said. "Then he said: 'And I know what they call me, too.' I felt sorry for the guy."

"It's not a life I'd choose," Carmody said.

"What was bothering him," Hunter said, "was something he heard about Shanley."

"That's another thing about Charlie," Carmody said. "You never really do get all of him. You think you've got him on your side, and he says he's on your side, but he's always got a little something left over that he's saving for somebody else. Charlie's awful cute. Couple, three times, he went to jail for it."

"Well," Hunter said, "that was what was on Doyle's mind. Shanley. Because if one of us, including Shanley, boots this thing, Doyle's gonna be D-E-A-D. Which is awful final. And Doyle knows it. So I hadda tell the little rat a few things."

"Nothing you can't back up, I hope," Carmody said.

"At the time," Hunter said, "I didn't expect any trouble."

"Oh, oh," Carmody said.

"Well," Hunter said, "I did have a little fight with the learned prosecutor before I went up there, and I would've had a bigger fight if he'd had time for one.

But he kept saying: 'Go see the guy. I'm in a hurry.' So I never did get any promises out of the bastard, and I more or less had to fly with what I thought'd work."

"What time was that?" Carmody said.

"Four-thirty or so," Hunter said. "Right after court."

"Going to see Dottie, I bet," Carmody said. "Quick roll in the hay. She goes in to work about five-thirty, I think."

"Well, it was a quickie Thursday, then," Hunter said. "I held him up for a good half hour, even though I didn't get anything out of him. 'Tell him whatever he wants to hear,' Shanley says. 'I don't care how you do it. Do whatever you have to do, and stop bothering me about it?"

"That is the kind of blank check," Carmody said, "which in my experience, the guy that gives it to you's usually very pissed off when you try to cash it."

"It was the only one I had," Hunter said. "Friday morning I come in here, I'm looking for Shanley, of course. Shanley's also looking for me. Doesn't want the details, I got out of Doyle. He's got about six lines of notes even he can't read, and he's gonna go up there and wing his opening to the jury. I wished I had his confidence. Then, he says, I'm the first witness.

"Now I'd just as soon be the first witness," Hunter said. "I know the damned case better'n anybody else in the courtroom 'cept Teddy and Leaper and Andy, and they're not in the mood to discuss it where anybody can see them. Somebody's got to start the thing off, and I'm gonna have to testify sooner or later anyway, so fine, let's get my performance over with right off, and then bring in the amateurs. Gives me more time to get things lined up.

"What pisses me off, about being first witness," Hunter said, "is *wh*y I'm first witness. It's not because it's easier for the jury, or better for the case, or anything silly like that. It's because Mister Shanley's been fucking around for several weeks instead of getting himself ready to try this goddamned case, and he knows he can buy another couple hours of time by putting me on first, so he can read the file while I'm talking."

"You do all right?" Carmody said.

"I think so," Hunter said. "I told them all about arresting Billy and how he was 'way out over the bay when I did it, and what he told us, and how he went there and looked and we got Andy Marr and Leaper in the motel room where he said they were, doing what he said they'd be doing. And then about how, yes, I had occasion at some time during that day to examine certain surveillance cameras, and to remove something from them, and it looked like film to me, and I took it to the guy to have it developed. And that was about it."

"How was the cross?" Carmody said.

"Funny thing," Hunter said. "Fat John started off, and he was fairly gentle. I think even his client was kind of surprised."

"He'll usually come at you like a man falling out of a tree," Carmody said.

"I think that's what Leaper expected," Hunter said. "I know it's what I expected. Leaper was a little disappointed, I think. I wasn't. Maybe he's slipping."

"Maybe you're slipping, if you think that," Carmody said.

"Whaddaya mean?" Hunter said.

"Fat John Killilea is the original cagey bastard," Carmody said. "You think those guys sometimes fool around with the evidence, don't you."

"I suspected it, sometimes," Hunter said.

"Sure, and you were right, too," Carmody said. "But the reason you suspected it was because you happened to get a guy that was touching things up and he wasn't very good at it.

"When a good one of them does it," Carmody said, "it's like a painting when he gets through, it's so good. And Fat John's one of the best. When he fools around with evidence, it's a masterpiece when he gets through. I had a case with him once, and I didn't know who the hell he was, so I called up this guy that used to be in here, and I asked him. 'You better watch out for that guy,' he says. 'He's been around a long time. He knows every trick in the book. Some of them he invented.'

"Remember the Crime Commission?" Carmody said. "Fat John had three of them guys, one Councillor and two others, and you know how many of the ones he had that got hooked? One. And that was the one, wouldn't listen to Fat John, and he took the stand, and the Assistant AG murdered him, of course. Just like John said he would, when he told his client not to get up there in the first place.

"Some time," Carmody said, "you take yourself a look at some of those half-assed sideshows that the Bar Association or something's always running, for lawyers that don't know what they're doing. Which, if all of them went, you could fill Fenway Park. And you count how many times Fat John's up there on the platform, strutting around and making a whole lot of noise so the hayseeds from the woods'll think of him the next time one of their clients that owns the hardware store whacks his wife with a claw hammer out of stock, and needs a high-powered criminal lawyer, fast.

"I'll save you the trouble," Carmody said. "Every time, is how many. That guy makes nothing but money, and it's been my experience, the guys that're making lots of money in his line of work are not stupid. They grab some guy tomorrow night in Swansea for fucking a cow, if he's got the right kind of money, Fat John'll be there in the morning, filing motions and making a big pain in the ass of himself. And then he'll try the case, and if he can't drive the DA nuts with all the papers he throws at him, he'll make the cow confess she put the guy up to it. And if that doesn't work," Carmody said, "and the guy gets a guilty, when it's all over, the guy'll be in a private hospital someplace with a cow of his own. I knew a guy once, that had him," Carmody said, "and he beat a good case that I made. Check case. And I come up to him afterwards, because I never did have any real dislike for the guy, and I congratulated him. He was from Tennessee. And he says to me, that he didn't expect to beat it. Then he points to Fat John. 'Down my way,' he says, 'we got a saying about a lawyer, that he's so good he could get buggery reduced to a charge of following too close, and that's how good he is.' What'd he ask you?"

"Mostly about Billy Gillis," Hunter said. "How drunk he was, whether he understood his rights, things like that. I couldn't understand it. Fat John represents Leaper Donovan. That's not gonna do Leaper any good, Gillis was too drunk to understand his rights."

"You guys get a warrant before you went into that motel room?" Carmody said.

"Nope," Hunter said. "Didn't need one."

"You sure?" Carmody said.

"The judge that heard the motion to suppress the evidence, he was," Hunter said. "Judge Macarthur wouldn't let him reopen it the other day, so I think that's settled, at least for now."

"It's something else, then," Carmody said. " 'Been around a long time,' this guy I knew a long time told me. 'Made a lot of money, made a lot of friends. Knows how the game's played. Look out for him. Assume nothing. He's got this sign on his desk in his office. One of those little brass plaques: *Assume Nothing.*' When Fat John runs a cross-examination and you can't see the point of it, you probably got problems. Better start thinking about it. Why would he waste his time like that? Is he just putting on a show? How about Wyman? What'd he do?"

"Wyman talked about the same things," Hunter said. "Whether Andy got his rights and understood them. 'Who opened the door?' It was Andy. Stuff like that."

"What about Tommy Hart?" Carmody said.

"No questions on cross," Hunter said.

"Saving up the alibi defense," Carmody said. "Gonna try to make the jury think he's so confident he doesn't have to bother with the preliminary stuff. Then what?"

"That took care of Friday," Hunter said. "Friday in court, anyway. Down here, I had a little lash-up with Mister Shanley."

"What set him off?" Carmody said. "You did so

well, and everything, he's got the whole weekend to prepare for the civilians, what's the problem?"

"It was partly me," Hunter said. "I was pissed at him, putting the case in bass-ackwards because that way he can start with me, and I frankly didn't have the balls to tell him I was pissed. Then I was pissed because he didn't at least say: 'Thank you' to me for bailing him out like that."

"Of course not," Carmody said. "He didn't put you up there because he wanted you to be his friend for life, you asshole. He put you up there because he needed somebody to deliver, and you got just as much invested in this as he has."

"Yeah," Hunter said.

"Guys don't get thanked for being useful," Carmody said. "Not by the guys that use them, at least. That's what useful guys're for. There's another guy you're misjudging, Corporal: Mister Shanley. You think he's lazy and stupid. Well, he's maybe lazy, but when there's two guys, and one of those guys is using the other guy very good to cover his own ass, and the guy that's getting used isn't getting anything he wouldn't've gotten if he didn't let the first guy use him, well, if there's one of those guys that's stupid, I think I know which one it is, and it's not the one that's getting what he wants, either. You think when he gets out of his car in the morning when he gets to work, he thanks the car?"

"That cocksucker," Hunter said.

"You call him that?" Carmody said.

"Horace," Hunter said, "for all I know, I may have. I dunno."

"Tell me what happened this time," Carmody said.

"I started telling him about Doyle," Hunter said. "I told him Goat-ass wanted to talk to him personally.

" 'About what?' he says.

" 'About the case,' I said. 'He wants to be sure everything's understood.'

" 'I'm not wasting my time like that,' he says. 'Tell the little bastard to come in here, do his number and get the fuck out. I'm telling him nothing.' "

"Oh, Jesus," Carmody said. "He really is stupid, isn't he?"

"It's hard to get his attention," Hunter said. "My father used to work at the Brighton Abattoir, and what he did was whack the cow on the head with a sixteen-pound maul when they were getting ready to turn the beast into steaks, and when I'm working with Shanley, I wished to God I had that maul.

"I said to him: 'Richard, my friend, here are some facts that maybe you oughta have. This guy is not cuddling up to us because he loves Donnelly. He hates Donnelly. He is scared fuckin' blind of Donnelly.

"'The thing of it is, Mister Prosecutor,' I said, 'he is also scared of me. Not because I'm a cop. He's not that crazy about cops, but he's not scared of them right now because he's gotten old, and besides, he's not doing anything. He's scared of me because he thinks I can get him killed, if I'm careless, and he's right. Not *probably* right, Richard. *Right*.

"'Now,' I says, 'he is also in no mood to go steady with you, either. Because he's scared of you, just like he's scared of me, and you know something? For the same reason. You, if you're not careful, can get him killed. You got to go make very nice with this fellow, and not give anything away, like you knew he was a ringer when he came in because he told a cop he was. Because if you do, they will put out his light for him. And, knowing this, he would like some reassurance.'

"'I'm not making no deals,' Shanley says. 'I already know what he's gonna say, and I can destroy him without ever seeing him before he takes the stand. You're the guys that make the deals.' And he gets this disgusted look on his face. Then he says: 'And lemme tell *you* something, Deke old sport,' and he jabs me on the chest with his finger.

"Now we were right in his little old office," Hunter said, "and we didn't have the door closed, either. And I went right through the roof. 'You do that again, you little prick,' I says, 'and I knock you on your ass so fast when you wake up you won't be able to remember if you were ever standing up.' "

"Good, good," Carmody said. "Just what we all need in the smooth-running office."

"I could've killed him," Hunter said. "You know what that dumb shit says to me? He says: 'And furthermore, you guys're keeping things back, the way you always do when you get a case and fall in love with some little scumbag that isn't worth a hill of shit. You think you're fooling me? You think I'm dumb enough to believe this is all you know, that the guy's just a volunteer that decided to come in because he was afraid of a perjury rap? You think that? Well, you better not think that, because I know, just as well as you do, that one of those cocksuckers up there had a hand in this, and then he got scared and fed you something, and now you're protecting him.' "

"He's right," Carmody said.

"That son of a bitch," Hunter said. " 'Of course one of them did,' I said, 'it was goddamned Donnelly, only we got a break for ourselves because this guy Horace knows tipped him off that Doyle was worried.'

" 'Not him,' Shanley said, 'one of those goddamned lawyers.' Can you imagine that?" Hunter said.

"Deke," Carmody said, "he's right."

"He's right?" Hunter said.

"He's right," Carmody said.

"It is one of the lawyers?" Hunter said.

"That's where it started, us finding out about it," Carmody said.

Hunter sat down at his desk. "Oh, Jesus," he said. "Which one of them did it?"

"Did it, or told?" Carmody said.

"Did it, I suppose, was Tommy Hart," Hunter said. "He's Donnelly's lawyer, and there wasn't anything like this in the case until we caught that fucker."

"Tommy didn't do it," Carmody said. "Tommy knew about it, but he didn't tell. He can't, under the privilege, or at least he thinks he can't, even though there're some that think he has to."

"Told, then," Hunter said. "Shanley thinks it's Killilea that's behind the whole thing."

"Right again, as far as telling's concerned," Carmody said.

"Two in one day," Hunter said. "For Shanley, that retires the trophy. What'd Fat John do?"

"Basically what he did was answer the phone," Carmody said. "Look, you remember I told you, Charlie always saves something? Well, the principal thing he saves is his own ass. And Charlie gets the call from Goat-ass, and the first thing he does is get fairly scared himself. So he calls up Fat John, and Charlie said: 'I'm only telling you this in case you need it to protect the guy, all right? Nothing else. Because he is all right.' And he asked Fat John if maybe Goat-ass was finally around the bend. And Fat John told him, he kind of didn't think so, because him and Tommy Hart were trying a case together in Middlesex County, and this is just before Donnelly come charging out of the woods, there, and got grabbed, and Tommy Hart meets him one night in the Esquire Lounge, and Fat John was there. And Donnelly told Hart what he did to Goat-ass, in case he got caught.

"Now Fat John's not Donnelly's lawyer," Carmody said. "Teddy, whatever Teddy says in front of him, Fat John can repeat as much as he likes. Except, of course, he can maybe get shot in his big fat belly for doing it, which is inclined to make a man stop and think for a while. So Charlie asked Fat John what he thought Charlie should do, and Fat John accused him of looking for free legal advice as usual, and then he told Charlie to get in touch with me."

"You know what Shanley said," Hunter said.

"I can guess," Carmody said.

" 'Guys like Killilea?' he says. 'They're not much better'n guys like Doyle. I know he's behind it, and you know he's behind it, and if it's not him, it's Hart or it's Wyman. They're all the same. They're always screwing around with things behind everybody's back. They've been doing it for centuries. But lemme tell you something: someday, someone's gonna tuck it to one of those bastards, and you do it and the rest of them'll sit up and take notice. You put Fat John in the laundry for this one, and it's gonna stop a whole lot of shit that's always going on and everybody knows it, and nobody ever had the common balls to do anything about it.'

"And he says," Hunter said, "he said: 'You take, if it's Killilea you get for doing it, boy, then you are going to get some results, and then maybe these guys that're officers of the court, and're supposed to be making sure their clients aren't running around all over the place, getting guys to tell lies for them, that anybody that's got anything to do with the case knows're lies, but can't prove it, maybe then they'll start acting like they're supposed to be acting, and telling the judges they've got guys that're getting perjury committed and obstructing justice and what do we want to do about it.

"'And I'm telling you this, Deke,' he says to me, 'I feel strongly about this.' Then he goes into this new courtroom voice he's got, that he speaks from 'way down in his chest. First day, Fat John comes out at the recess and congratulated him, his voice was finally changing. 'If it takes one of those goddamned liars, if we've got to sacrifice one of them to do that, well, let me tell you something: I can stand it. I can take the loss. This isn't a club we're running here, where people can just come in and sneak off by themselves and make deals, make any kind of deals they want and just give each other hand-jobs all the time. This is supposed to be the *law* we're enforcing here, and I shouldn't have to tell you that.' "

"Oh for Christ sake," Carmody said. "Why doesn't he save that shit for all those speeches he gives the Kiwanis and the Rotary and the crime-fighting Ladies Auxiliary? Shit."

"'I've never even seen this guy Tessio, Doyle, whatever his name is,' he says to me," Hunter said. "'I don't need to. I know he's stupid and his brains're fried and he don't know his ass from his elbow, and you give me five minutes of cross with that guy and I'll have it out of him, who the lawyer was that was present when Donnelly put him up to it. And that'll be the end of that son of a bitch.' "

"Right for the third time," Carmody said.

"Righter'n he thinks, in fact," Hunter said. "Maybe not, though. Maybe he'd just as soon, Fat John got whacked for doing what Shanley says he should be doing, only more in public."

"Can lead to a nasty exit wound, though," Carmody said.

"I think we've got to think of something," Hunter said. "Several things, in fact, and damned fast, too."

"Not me, white man," Carmody said, getting up. "This jewel is your problem. I'm off the clock, and I'm going home."

"Thanks a lot," Hunter said.

"Almost twenty years ago," Carmody said, "I was in a situation something like this, a DA's office, and I was just like you; if I didn't have my tail in a crack all the time, I thought I did, and I had this bitch of a goddamned thing I was working on, that now I can't even remember. I guess it was a murder case, but I'm not really sure. So, I was busting ass over it, and it was late, and I was still in the office, and consequently when they decided to haul in every trooper they could find, because all the cons in the Cherry Hill section'd gone nuts, they found me right off.

"Now I spent what seemed like a year in that prison yard," Carmody said. "I was there in full pack when General Whitney pulled the tank in, and he's gonna blast his way in, and I was there when Teddy Green finally decided to quit it. And there's two things I remember. One is that it was colder'n a plastic toilet seat in that yard. That wind just caromed around in there like it was something the devil sent personal. And the other is the thing, the only thing that I contributed, to the entire clambake, was when I saw this fellow with a bazooka, an item that I knew something about. And he was gonna knock a big hole in the wall and then we're all going in after them. 'Like hell we are,' I said, and when they asked me if I was refusing an order, I told them: 'Hell, no. There's not gonna be anybody left to go in there, because when the fire comes out the back of that thing, while the rocket's going out the front, it's gonna blast right off that wall and cook us all. I'm not refusing anything. I'm making a prediction.' So they didn't do it.

"You see what I mean," Carmody said. "Somebody, sometimes, not always but sometimes, can persuade a guy with a weapon not to use it and take out himself and all his friends. If he sounds like he knows what he's talking about."

A Clean, Well-lighted Joint

20

IN THE PLEASANT CAFE on Washington Street in Roslindale, Massachusetts, on the evening of November 26, 1973, Andrea Hunter said she supposed it was all right. There were men around the other tables, in tanker jackets, discussing the Celtics and Bruins and drinking Bud out of the bottle.

"I dunno," Hunter said. "The beer's in an actual glass. The veal was good. It was nice and fresh and it wasn't one of those things that comes out square on your plate because they put it together out of scraps they had around. The ziti was good. It was hot when it came, and the sauce was good. I could've used a little more bread, maybe, but what the hell, I'm starting to get a gut on me as it is. I think it's all right. Pretty damned good, in fact."

"What else would they serve you beer in?" she said.

"All kinds of things," Hunter said. "There's all kinds of places around, got tricky things to serve you flat beer in, and then dare you to say, you don't like it. It's nice to get something real for a change."

"They don't even have tablecloths," she said. "Just paper placemats."

"That's all right," he said, "I didn't wanna eat a tablecloth anyway. Look, it's the Pleasant, all right? It's not the Hilton, and I didn't say it was. You and them nice friends you're always talking about, that we haven't got, well, if we ever get them, then we'll go to the Hilton and see if you can get a real meatball sandwich for a buck-fifteen.

"I'll save you the trouble," he said. "Forget it. You

can't do it. All those places with the timber on the outside and you're supposed to be in a castle or something. A fort. The only reason they give you a knife with the bread is because it's not bread. It, I don't know what the hell it is, really, but it isn't bread. It just looks like a little loaf of bread. I think they must make it out of something. Old Styrofoam cups, probably. They oughta give you a hatchet to cut it with, a goddamned battle-axe, and you eat it and it goes down and it just lies there, and when you get through, you have to give the man thirty bucks. For roast beef which, if you were eating it and somebody came around and told you it was red tunafish with meat juice poured over it, you wouldn't be able to argue with him.

"I like this place," he said. "I used to come here a lot. I used to come here when the sandwich was sixty-five cents and they still had dimies."

"I don't get to go out that much," she said. "When I do, I like to go someplace nice."

"I asked you," he said. "You remember, I asked you. And you said it was all right."

"You told me we were coming out here to get a dishwasher," she said.

"And we did," he said. "You get a better price from this guy, and I swear, that thing I just give the man a hundred and ninety bucks for's a dishwasher. I know it is."

"But we still haven't got it," she said. "Tomorrow, after supper, I'm still gonna have to do the dishes by hand. God only knows when they'll deliver it. Jordan's delivers the next day, practically. And then we've got to get a man to come and put it in."

"For the next day," he said, "you pay another thirty-five bucks, Andrea. Thirty-five bucks that I haven't got. I'm a little thin on the one-ninety, if it's the truth you want.

"Second thing," he said. "There's no way I can get a dishwasher in the car, and get it out if I could. And it'd wreck the springs if I did, and the shocks, and I just put a new muffler in that thing. Then, when I got it home, with the car all beaten to shit, I couldn't connect it.

"Look," he said, "you know something? There's a certain number of things I don't know shit about, and connecting up plumbing's only one of them. Stan Musial was the Donora Greyhound because he came from Donora, Pennsylvania, and he could run fast. Ned Garver was the diminutive righthander and he won twenty games or something for the Saint Louis Browns and he came from Ney, Ohio. Mel Parnell was the stylish southpaw. There was a guy named Miranda, got arrested in Arizona one time and I guess the cops didn't treat him right, and the rest of us've hadda pay for it ever since.

"That's the kind of things I know, Andrea," he said. "You wanted a master plumber on twenty-four-hour call, you should've married one."

"Christmas is coming," she said.

"No shit," he said.

"You don't have to talk that way to me," she said. "What'd you get me for Christmas?"

"It's a surprise," he said. "You're worse'n the kids."

"You haven't got me anything," she said. "You haven't even thought about it yet, I bet."

"Andrea," he said, "it's a month until Christmas."

"Well," she said, "do you suppose you could think about it before Christmas Eve, this year? Get me something nice, Deke."

"I'll get you something nice," he said.

"And if you can't think of anything," she said, "you could always ask me, you know. There might be something I would really like to have, for myself. Instead of you coming home late, the day before Christmas, lugging some nightgown or perfume that I know you just bought because you knew you had to buy something and you didn't get to it and so that was what you did."

"Okay," he said, "I'm asking: what should I get you?"

"Can't think of anything, can you?" she said.

"You never should've gotten married," he said.

"You should've been a cop. You'd've been great if you were a cop."

"Can you?" she said.

"Look," he said, "I thought, I was under the impression, you just told me to ask you."

"I did," she said, "and you couldn't come up with anything."

"I just came up with something," he said.

"Deke," she said, "that dishwasher is not gonna be my Christmas present. Period. That's exactly what I was afraid of, was gonna happen, that you'd do that. When I was talking to you about it for so long, and you weren't doing anything about it, I knew you were just stalling. So when it came Christmas, you'd get it, and then give me some little thing for a present. I know you pretty well."

"I *was* stalling," he said. "I didn't have the money for it. I hadda wait for my expense check to come. In the second place, if we went to some place where they let you charge things, you're not gonna get a good price on it. But I swear to God, Andrea . . . , I mean, for Christ sake. Let me tell you something, all right? I haven't got it to throw around. You want something, you just stop at the closest place that sells it, and you buy it. I think that'd be nice. But it's not the way it is."

"You're always telling me something," she said. "You've got this lousy job and everything."

"Andrea," he said, "I could've sworn, didn't you tell me, just the other night, it's what I should be doing and it's all right with you?"

"It is what you should be doing," she said. "It's that, all right. It must be that. Even if all it does for you is make you so tired and cranky all that time that it's just about impossible to get along with you, and you don't have time for anything else."

"I took the kids the Celtics game, didn't I?" he said.

"Who paid for that?" she said.

"Your father," he said.

"Sure," she said, "when did you ever pay for anything they really wanted to do?"

"The Patriots game," he said.

"Three tickets," she said. "Not four, so they could all go. Not five, so maybe I could do something once in a while. Three tickets."

"That's all the guy had," he said.

"Nicky could've sat in your lap," she said. "You could've squeezed in, or something."

"Andrea," he said, "big or little, you got to have a ticket, get into the stadium. Whaddaya want me to do? Boost the littlest over the fence when the cops aren't watching?"

"Never," she said. "That's when. When something comes along that's a real treat for all of them, it's always because my father had to shell out for it. All it costs you is your time."

"Anything your goddamned fucking goddamned father gives those kids," he said, "*or* you, I fucking goddamned right well earned it. I spend more time worrying about the goddamned cottage, and working on the goddamned cottage, 'n I do sleeping."

"You begrudge him everything you do for him," she said. "You don't show me any consideration. You don't give me any of your time. You come home drunk and I never know when to expect you. What time're you gonna be home tomorrow night?"

"I don't know," he said. "We're still on the Commonwealth's case in chief. If nothing happens, the regular time."

"The regular time," she said. "What time's that, Deke, around sunrise?"

"For supper," he said.

"And if something happens?" she said.

"I don't know," he said.

"I knew it," she said.

"Andrea," he said, "I haven't got any control over the way things happen in cases. If I did, I would've got guilties in the Rossi thing."

"I'm sick of hearing about that," she said. "A bunch of wop bookmakers. And you've been talking about it for years. Who *cares?*"

"I do," he said. "I cared a lot. I worked hard on

that case, and so did the guys from the Bureau, and we lost it anyway. I cared about it."

"But not about when you come in," she said. "Except you always make sure that it's late. What've you got planned, to do with your family, now that it's going to be Thanksgiving weekend?"

"Well," he said, "I figured to have dinner."

"Are you going back down to the cottage?" she said.

"Why don't you tell me?" he said.

"Are you going back down there?" she said.

"I don't want to," he said. "But it more or less looks like I'd better, doesn't it?"

"Are you going to ask us if we want to come along?" she said.

"All right," he said. "Andrea, would you and the kids like to come down to Weekapaug Friday with me, since I got the day off from court, and see what the fuckin' vandals did to the fuckin' cottage, and if I can fix it?"

"What would we do down there?" she said.

"Well," he said, "I don't know as you'd have much of anything to do. You could take a walk on the beach. You could sit around a cold cottage. You could sit in the car and gripe. I don't know."

"How long're you going to be there?" she said.

"I don't know," he said. "All I know is what you told me, he told you. The cops down there said. That somebody evidently tore the boards off some of the windows. Now that's all I know because that's all you told me. I don't know if they then smashed the glass and went in. If they went in, I dunno if they did any damage. If they did any damage, I don't know if I can fix what they did. I don't know if they took the boards they ripped off of them windows and made a fire on the beach with them, or if they just broke them in half for more laughs. Or if they just took them off and threw them on the ground. So consequently I don't know whether I got to go someplace and get more lumber, or what.

"Now," he said, "you tell me. It's a two-hour drive down, and a two-hour drive back, and I don't

know how to tell you how long it's gonna take me to
do what I've gotta do, because I don't know what
I've got to do. So, you tell me: how long's it gonna
take me, okay?"

"I thought so," she said. "Midnight, two in the
morning again. Just like always. I'm not going to keep
the kids up that late. I'm the one that has to put up
with them the next day, when you do something like
that.

"Deke," she said, "if you don't like us so much
that you don't want to spend any of your time with
us, why don't you stop getting our hopes up all the
time and just go away and leave us and get it all
over with. Why don't you just go ahead and do it?
Haven't you got the guts?"

"Andrea," he said, "I had a long day and I'm tired.
Since I'm tired, I'm going to do something stupid and
answer your question. If we split up, one of us'd have
to live in a tree, and I've got a pretty good idea who
that'd be. What's more, you'd complain when I came
to see the kids, I had leaves on my feet, I was track-
ing in, and that wouldn't help my bursitis any. I don't
want to do it, is why," he said. "This is more'n bad
enough to suit me, but it's nowhere near as bad as
what I can get instead."

"Deke," she said, after a while, "you know something? I'm going to tell you something: you stink."

Special Treatment

□ 21

ON NOVEMBER 27, 1973, Assistant District Attorney Shanley commenced direct examination of William F. Gillis. Gillis, wearing a powder blue doubleknit suit and a black shirt, no necktie, ran his right hand through his blond hair after he answered each question. He did not look at the defendants until he was asked to identify them by pointing them out in the courtroom. Then he did not look at them again.

The defendants stared at Gillis every minute that he was on the stand.

Gillis said he was forty years old. He said he had completed eighth grade at the Sacred Heart School in Roslindale, Massachusetts, and two years at the Don Bosco Vocational High School in Boston. He said he was trained as a sheet-metal worker. He said he was a veteran of the United States Army, and that he had served in Korea, and had been honorably discharged. He said he was married. He admitted to prior convictions for bank robbery in 1958, for which he was sentenced to an indeterminate term, not to exceed five years, in the Concord Reformatory, and in 1964, when he was sentenced to ten years in the Massachusetts Correctional Institution at Walpole. He said he had been paroled, on the second offense, in May of 1970, and had returned to his trade as a sheet-metal worker at a plant in Braintree, Massachusetts. He said he was introduced to Andrew Marr by a mutual friend, whose name he did not recall, at a place he did not recall, "sometime in nineteen-seventy-one, I think. Maybe it was in the spring. I think it was at a wedding. I met

213

him at a wedding." He did not recall whether he and Marr had any conversation at the wedding.

Several months after he met Marr, Gillis said, he encountered him by chance one evening in a bar near Boston Garden, where he had stopped for a beer before attending a Celtics game. "Me and this guy I know, he had three tickets. Only the other guy that was gonna come with us, couldn't make it. So we stop off for a beer, and Mister Marr is in there with some guys, and he recognized me, we recognized each other. And he come over, and this and that, and this guy I know says: 'Hey, whyn'tcha come with us, see the game? Ticket's, nobody's gonna use it, I'm just gonna wind up giving it away, some kid on the ramp.' So, and he did. He come with us to the game. And when we're coming out, you know, he says: 'Thanks,' and that he really enjoyed it."

Gillis coughed often during his testimony. After the morning recess, on the twenty-seventh, there was a small brown carafe of water on the clerk's bench near the witness stand, and a glass, and Gillis took frequent sips after he resumed the stand.

Gillis said that his friend often had Celtics tickets in the autumn of 1971. "And this other guy that we both know," Gillis said, "that we would usually invite, he was having some kind of trouble at home, I guess, some kind of sickness and there would be a lot of times on which he couldn't make it. Only, see, he would usually think he was gonna be able to make it, and then he wouldn't be able to, and he would tell us on the afternoon when we were going to the game that something came up and he couldn't make it. So, my friend liked Andy pretty well, and if there was nobody else in the shop that we wanted to come along, we, I would go and call Andy."

"And, Mister Gillis," Shanley said, "that was only partly because Mister Marr was good company, wasn't it?"

"Well," Gillis said, "yeah. Yeah, he was good company. I thought he was an all-right guy."

"But there was another reason why you and your

friend thought of Mister Marr so frequently, wasn't there?" Shanley said.

After a bench conference on the first day of trial, the Judge had ruled that it would be sufficient for one of the three defense attorneys to enter objections, and ask for notation of exceptions to rulings denying objections. Judge Macarthur said the record would reflect that an objection by any defendant would be understood to be an objection by each of the defendants, so that if he committed reversible error in the course of the trial, each of the defendants would be able to appeal on any issue raised. Sam Wyman, who believed himself better versed in the law than Hart or Killilea, but believed them to be superior in questioning witnesses, made most of the objections after that. Killilea and Hart made objections only when the interests of Donovan and Donnelly were different from those of the defendant Marr.

"Objection," Wyman said, complaining that Shanley's last question was "leading." The objection was sustained.

"Did you, Mister Gillis," Shanley said, "just yes or no, did you have another reason for inviting Mister Marr?"

Wyman objected again. The objection was overruled.

"Yes," Gillis said.

"What was it?" Shanley said.

"He always gave us the late lines on the point spreads," Gillis said. "We bet the way he said, and we won some money." Gillis said he and his friend continued to follow Marr's advice on basketball betting through the 1971–1972 season, and "did pretty well. We did take a bath on the playoffs, kind of, though." He said he occasionally went with Marr to play cards at the Statler, where he met Michael Donovan, and that they usually had a couple drinks afterwards "at this place we went to where they didn't close at the regular time." He said he liked Leaper okay, but did not become as friendly with him as he was with Marr.

In the autumn of 1972, Gillis said, he and Marr obtained season's tickets to the Celtics games, "be-

cause this other friend of mine wasn't around anymore." Shanley asked him where his other friend went.
"He went to prison," Gillis said. "No, he went to jail.
His wife was bugging him, that he wasn't doing something right or something, so he stopped sending her
the money, and then she had the cops come and get
him and he still wouldn't pay so the judge put him in
jail, and he said he was gonna rot there before he gave
her a dime."

Gillis said he was working some overtime in the late
autumn of 1972, and couldn't always use his ticket.
He said it was his practice to call Marr, so that Marr
could give the ticket to somebody else. He said he was
still betting, "but not doing so good then." He said that
the man who used his ticket, when he couldn't, had
access to tickets to the Bruins games. "And so, when
he couldn't go to them games, Mister Marr would get
ahold of me, and sometimes if I could go, I would
use that guy's tickets."

Gillis said that he continued to visit the poker
games, "even though what I usually did was, I lost."

"What was your income during this period?" Shanley said.

"I was, you mean from working?" Gillis said.

"Working, and any other source of income you
might have had," Shanley said.

"From working, I was taking home usually about
two-eighty-five, three hundred a week. It depended,
see, on if I was getting overtime. And then, well, like
I said, I was losing at the poker games, because, well,
I was losing."

"How much, on the average?" Shanley said.

Gillis frowned. "It was a long time ago," he said.
"I, and it wasn't always the same. Sometimes I would
win. Sometimes I would win a few bucks. Maybe
thirty, thirty-five, forty dollars. If I lost, about the
same. I usually lost. One night I lost a hundred and
eighty bucks, and I remember that because I only, I
had made two-eighty that week because they took out
for health insurance or something, I dunno, and I only
had a hundred bucks left for the week when I got
through, and I hadda go down the credit union and

take out a loan for three hundred on account I had some bills to pay."

"Three hundred when you lost one-eighty?" Shanley said.

"Well, and also," Gillis said, "my wife was after me, that I was gambling too much, and I wanted her to think, I won. So I did that."

Gillis said that he won enough on the Super Bowl to pay off the credit union, but that he continued losing steadily at cards. "So, in February, I think it was, I'm not so good on dates, if you know what I mean like I said, I was saying something to Mister Marr about this, and he said, and we were both doing lousy on the Celtics" (he pronounced it *sell-ticks*) "and also on the Bruins, there, and he said he was also tap city, and did I want to do something that him and Mister Donovan was talking to a guy about. And I said I was, and they took me, they made arrangements that we would meet this fellow that they were talking to."

"And who was that?" Shanley said.

"Mister Donnelly," Gillis said. He said he had never met Donnelly before, or seen him.

"Had you heard of him?" Shanley said.

"Objection," Wyman said, "rank hearsay."

"Sustained," Judge Macarthur said, "and don't do that again, Mister Shanley."

Gillis said that on "the night in question," he met Marr and Donovan at the Green Moon on the Lynnway in Lynn, "about nine o'clock. I think it was about nine o'clock. We went in and we went back and there was this guy sitting all by himself in a booth at the back, and that was Mister Donnelly."

"All right," Shanley said, "now, Mister Gillis, would you give us your best recollection of what was said that evening by you, Mister Marr, Mister Donovan and Mister Donnelly, what they said, what you said, as best you remember it."

"We said: 'Hello.' They said that this other guy was Teddy Donnelly."

"Objection," Wyman said.

"Mister Witness," Judge Macarthur said, "please don't give conclusions about what other people said.

Tell us what they said, and who said it. Who said: 'This other guy is Teddy Donnelly'? if anyone did."

"I think it was Mister Marr," Gillis said. "I didn't know Leaper as good's I knew Andy. Leaper don't talk very much anyway, except when he's picking up a girl or something."

"Objection, and ask that that go out," Wyman said. "Nonresponsive."

"Sustained," Judge Macarthur said. "Members of the jury, you are instructed to disregard everything that Mister Gillis just said, after he said that Mister Marr was the man who introduced him to Mister Donnelly."

"Objection." Wyman said. "He said he *thinks* it was Mister Marr."

"And I," Shanley said, "object to Mister Wyman's characterization of what the witness said. That's for the jury to decide."

Killilea objected to Shanley's remarks being made in the presence of the jury, and Hart talked at the same time, saying: "This is one of that fellow's favorite tricks, and I move that he be reprimanded for it, Your Honor, and instructed not to do it again."

Shanley opened his mouth. Judge Macarthur spoke first. "We will proceed here, Counsel, without any further of these interruptions. Mister Shanley, put your next question."

"What if anything happened after the introductions were performed?" Shanley said.

"We sat down," Gillis said. "We ordered a drink. And we started to talk."

"What did you talk about?" Shanley said. "Once again, now, your best recollection of the conversation, what was said and who said it."

"They said they were going to rob the Danvers National, and was I interested in coming in on it," Gillis said.

By 1:00 P.M. when the court took the luncheon recess, Judge Macarthur, Killilea, Hart and Wyman were satisfied that Shanley could not invent or devise any question that would bring a completely responsive

answer from William Gillis. The Judge asked the lawyers to remain after the jury and the witness and the
defendants and the spectators had left the courtroom.
"And this will be off the record," he said. "Now," he
said, "I have some plans to go to Florida in February
of next year, and I'm beginning to think they're probably in jeopardy if this witness, if Mister Shanley here
is not allowed to lead this witness a little."

"I think I've made my point with the jury," Wyman
said. "I don't contemplate repeated objections after
lunch, unless the fellow becomes completely outra-
geous."

"Mister Killilea?" Judge Macarthur said.

"I think the guy's fairly dim," Killilea said. "He's
killing my guy, of course. . . ."

"By saying that he picks up girls, John?" The Judge
said.

"If that kills a guy anymore," Killilea said. "No,
let him go. He can answer any way he wants. I do
think cross's gonna be kind of interesting, though."

"Tommy?" the Judge said.

"Me too," Hart said. "Shanley, where the hell do
you guys dig up these morons?"

The Judge began to laugh.

"It's true, Judge," Hart said. "I tried one in the
federal court about a month ago, and the guy got so
nervous on the stand he wet his pants. You could see
it. And this dope, if he was driving the getaway car,
I know one thing: it hadda be an automatic transmis-
sion, because there's no way in the world that Billy
Gillis could handle three pedals. Two's probably over
his limit."

"We recruit 'em, Tommy," Shanley said. "We get
a list of your old clients, and we check it against the
prison rosters, and then we just wait for your guys to
hit the street and go looking for them as soon as
something happens."

"I never represented Gillis," Hart said.

"Okay," the Judge said. "Whaddaya think, Dick?
Can you finish your direct this afternoon?"

"Probably," Shanley said, "unless I ask him something about robbing the bank and he starts in telling me about his friends that don't pay their alimony."

On the afternoon of the twenty-seventh, Gillis testified that after about an hour of conversation, on the February evening at the Green Moon, they had agreed to rob the Danvers National on the soonest convenient Thursday, "on account of how, Mister Donnelly said, that was when the Brink's guys brought in the dough for the construction guys at the Missile Research Labs there, that was working on it. And he said his guess was, there was about fifty thousand in cash more in the bank on Thursdays'n there was any other day.

"Mister Marr was gonna get the cars," Gillis said. "The one we would drive to the bank, and the getaway, and the switch car, the one that we would get into after. And Mister Donnelly was gonna get the guns, and Mister Donovan was gonna see this guy he knew, that he thought'd probably change the money for us, and see what it'd cost us, and I didn't have to do nothing. Except, of course, I wasn't only gonna get but half of one of their shares. I was gonna get half of what Leaper was gonna get. You follow me? Him and Teddy and Mister Marr was each gonna get twenny-five percent of what we got, and then there was gonna be the other twenny-five percent, and I was gonna get half of that, and then them guys're gonna split the other half that I didn't get. You follow me?"

Shanley said he did. Gillis testified that the twenty-second was chosen because there was some difficulty in obtaining the weapons. He said there were three more meetings, all at the Green Moon. He said Michael Donovan had been ill with the flu, and had missed one, and John Killilea successfully objected to introduction of evidence about the conversation at that meeting, against Donovan. Judge Macarthur instructed the jury that they could not consider that evidence against Donovan unless "you should first find that by that time, there existed a joint concert of action among the four defendants and Mister Gillis, and, having made that finding, beyond a reasonable doubt, that what was done at that meeting by the other three participants, in the absence of defendant Donovan, was done for the purpose of advancing a joint purpose with which he had already associated himself." The jury looked puzzled.

During the afternoon recess, from 3:05 P.M. to 3:20 P.M., Killilea said to Shanley, Wyman and Hart that he didn't know why the fuck he bothered making that kind of objection, "because it doesn't mean shit, and all it gets you's an instruction that nobody pays any attention to anyway."

Hart said: "You do it so your goddamned client doesn't have that to scream about when he gets in the can and starts thinking about how there must be some way he can prove you were incompetent, and get himself a new trial, and incidentally sue the ass off you, personally. That's why you do it."

"That's why I do it," Killilea said. "Tommy, you have got a real instinct for priorities, is what you've got."

After the recess, Gillis said he met the other three men in Peabody on the morning of the twenty-second of March, 1973, having called in sick to work. He said he got into the car that would be used to rob the bank. He said he saw the other three men disguise themselves with cotton and sunglasses and bandages. He said he drove them to the bank, and that he waited outside with the motor running while they robbed it. He said he saw them come out, and get in the car, and that Donnelly said: "Get the motherfuckin' hell out of here," and that he did so. He said his state of mind at the time was one of fear.

At 4:05 P.M., Shanley said: "That's all I have of this witness, Your Honor." Judge Macarthur informed the jurors that the court would sit from 9:30 A.M. to 1:30 P.M. on the twenty-eighth, "so that everybody will have time enough to get where they're going for the Thanksgiving holiday," and that court would not be in session on the Friday following. He said the next session would be on December third.

At 4:20 P.M., Hunter went into Shanley's office and sat down, without being invited. Shanley was talking on the telephone, in a very soft voice, so that Hunter, seven feet away in the hard oak chair, could not understand what Shanley was saying. He noticed that Shanley's knuckles were white, on the hand that held the phone.

When Shanley hung up, he stared at Hunter. He did not say anything.

Hunter said: "We gotta talk, Dick."

Shanley shrugged. "Talk," he said. He looked down and began to move papers on his desk. There were lots of them, spilling out of manila folders, and stacks of manila folders in the In and Out baskets next to the green blotter on the light oak desk.

"They're probably gonna finish with Gillis tomorrow," Hunter said.

"Likely," Shanley said. He wore a brown cheviot suit, with a vest, and a brown tie with a blue stripe.

"That leaves you," Hunter said, "with the tellers and the guy from the camera store that developed the pictures."

"And Marr's statement," Shanley said.

"We already put that in," Hunter said.

"I haven't read it yet, remember," Shanley said.

"And then you rest," Hunter said.

"And then I rest," Shanley said.

"Which means," Hunter said, "that sometime around the first or the middle of next week, Donnelly's lawyer's gonna call Dominic Tessio, AKA Donnie Doyle, and put him on the stand."

"That's the way I understand it," Shanley said.

"What're you gonna do?" Hunter said.

"When Tommy gets through with him," Shanley said, "I'm gonna take the certified copies of the hospital records and demolish the fucker."

"And then?" Hunter said.

"Then I'm gonna sit down," Shanley said.

"Good," Hunter said, starting to get out of the chair. "But before that," he said, "I'm gonna find out who put the bastard up to it. And I got a pretty good idea the guy who put him up to it probably had a lawyer, that knew about it."

Hunter sat down again. Shanley said: "Deke, I

don't care. I really don't. Guys that're like that, Doyle or the lawyer, they're all the same. Sooner or later somebody whacks the Doyles out anyway, and nobody ever takes out the lawyers. So for Doyle it's just a matter of time, and for the lawyer, well, it should be.

"You think," Shanley said, "that Doyle's doing us a big favor, I guess you think because he likes us. Well, he doesn't. It's just a matter of him being more afraid of what we can do to him, right now, if he doesn't help us. Next week it'll be their turn again, and he'll come in and file an affidavit or something that what he told *us* wasn't true, and we'll have a new trial and go around again.

"You can't trust these people, Deke," Shanley said. "They'll go any way they think they've got to, that might help them right then. And then if something else, tomorrow, if they decide that something else'd help them more, tomorrow they'll do that, Even if it's the opposite of what they did today, and it wipes out what they did today. It's like hanging onto a weather-vane.

"You trust these guys, Deke," Shanley said, "and you're just asking for trouble. That's all you're doing. Because they can't, there isn't anybody who can keep them alive. That includes me, and it includes you.

"Well," Shanley said, "okay. So I don't get invited to the funeral. But the guys who really benefit from this're those goddamned lawyers that fuck around with everything, and nobody ever blames them for anything. So I'll tell you what I'm gonna do: I am gonna refuse to take out a mortgage on some rat's life that I can't pay, and don't want to pay, so I can protect some unethical son of a bitch that oughta be god-damned disbarred and put in the fuckin' clink so the rest of those bastards'll see that they can't keep on do-ing what they've been doing. I haven't got to do that, protect the bastard, and I'm not gonna do it, either."

For almost two minutes, Hunter did not say any-thing. Then he said: "I agree with you, Dick. They are gonna whack him, after you do what you say you're gonna do. And I'm gonna give you another one for nothing: you are gonna get a lawyer, maybe two of them. And they'll maybe have them whacked, too. I don't know who's gonna do it, and I don't know when, and I don't know where. But you're right: sooner or later, somebody's gonna ring the bells for them, and then they'll be dead.

"It won't be right off," Hunter said. "It's not like he was gonna come in here the day after you rest, and you clobber him so they know, they can tell, that you had it in hand long before, and they hit him on the way out the door. They'll take their time with him and they'll take their time with the other guys, and maybe, if we're lucky, it'll even look like it just might've been for something else. Maybe just that somebody got tired of having him, and them, around all the time. Making a lot of noise.

"But it'll take a while," Hunter said. "It could take years. And those years Doyle's gonna spend on the street, talking. Talking and talking and talking. And the lawyers're gonna be getting around also. Also talking. About how somebody took our word, and we double-crossed him, and got him out there all alone.

"Well, my friend," Hunter said, "I may be wrong, now, and if I am, I'll probably have time enough to be sorry for it, or else I'll be dead, in which case I won't give a shit. But my guess is, that kind of talk's gonna have a certain effect on business around here, and I don't think it's gonna be one that you're gonna like. Because the next time there's somebody who hears something that he thinks we might be interested in knowing about, that could save our pure white asses in another case, maybe, he's gonna think about it for a minute. And if he asks his lawyer, who's gonna have heard about what happened to the lawyer you get here, if you get one, and you will, his lawyer's gonna tell him to think about it for a week. Because they're all gonna remember what we did to Goat-ass, that got him dead, and they're not gonna envy old Goat-ass, I can tell you that. And what's gonna happen is that you're gonna come out of something looking like a horse's ass, that you could've come out of golden.

"Mister Shanley," Hunter said, "I'm trying to be a

friend of yours. You pay off the guy like you got in mind, there's gonna be a day when somebody pays you off, and if you don't believe that, Buddy, you're as big a horse's cock as everybody I know seems to think you are."

Richard Shanley's face got red immediately. He leaned far back in his chair. He steepled his fingers. He put his steepled fingers over his mouth and nose. He lowered his head and slid far down in the chair, and he stared at Deke Hunter. He tried to speak. Then he cleared his throat and spoke again. "I have been . . . ," he said, "I have been in this office for six years. Six years, Corporal. I was so wet behind the ears when I got in here that you could've washed a car with the water.

"I've learned things in six years," Shanley said. "I learned lots of things. And one of the things I learned is that the job I'm trying to do around here's not the same job that everybody else's trying to do around here. It's supposed to be, but it isn't.

"I have seen the people," Shanley said, "who got an apology from the Judge, practically, when they got convicted of stealing a million dollars, because they didn't use a gun and I guess that made them harmless. And I've seen guys that got fifteen years for stealing a hundred dollars, because they used a gun, even though they never fired it and nobody was hurt. And I've seen one little scumbag after another, protected because he once told a cop a dirty joke and the cop fell in love with the little cocksucker and decided to get married to him.

"When I came in here," Shanley said, "I thought I was going into law enforcement. And now I know, what I'm really doing's law adjustment. Hasn't got anything to do with making the punishment fit the crime, or even the criminal. What it is, it's making sure that the guy who could fit as a criminal, because he committed the crime, hasn't got some neat little reason why he oughta be ineligible for the position. And I don't like it.

"Deke," Shanley said, "for various reasons that I don't care to go into, I don't care anymore. I've got too many things on my mind, and this thing's about the crummiest one of the things I'm thinking about. And I don't care if you and Carmody think some shit should get special treatment. And I don't care what you think of me, if he doesn't get it from me. He's not gonna get it from me, and that's it. Now, do what you want."

"No special treatment," Hunter said.

"None," Shanley said.

"None for cops," Hunter said.

"Nope," Shanley said. "Take it up with the DA, you think you can blow it past him. Try it."

"None for witnesses," Hunter said.

"Nope," Shanley said.

"None for lawyers," Hunter said.

"None," Shanley said.

"And none, I assume," Hunter said, "for guys that're having some trouble at home, and're doing things."

"What do you mean?" Shanley said.

"Shit," Hunter said, "if I had a blanket made out of that material, I could cover most of New England."

"Who?" Shanley said.

"None for prosecutors?" Hunter said.

At 5:05 P.M., Richard J. Shanley said nothing. At 5:06 he said: "Are you threatening me, you son of a bitch?"

"No," Hunter said, "I really am not. I'm just asking you a question, and I don't care if you *give* me the answer, I just wanna know if you *know* it. Because I think you're basically an honest guy that doesn't listen to people a whole lot of the time, and you're maybe too busy. I dunno. Don't bother me. I'll put it on the street, how the guy got dumped, and as long as you're here, I won't get anything that'll help anybody, and we'll try every case and get so goddamned far behind we'll never dig out. But you'll be long gone, into your private practice, and besides, *when* you're gone, we'll start getting guys to trust us again.

"We're supposed to be on the same side, Richard," Hunter said, "and consequently, we are. Play it any way you want. Shave as many coats as you like. Understand: you gotta pay for it."

The Commonwealth Rested on the Afternoon of December Fifth

☐ 22

ON THE MORNING OF DECEMBER 10, 1973, Deke Hunter with a massive hangover arrived at the office in Salem shortly after ten. He hung up his overcoat and sat down in his chair and put his hands over his eyes.

"A little light table wine, perhaps?" Carmody said.

Hunter nodded, twice, without uncovering his eyes.

"Bad weekend, I take it," Carmody said.

Hunter put his hands down and sat slumped in his chair. "Since you ask," he said at last, "I had a lousy weekend. There wasn't one single fucking thing about it that I liked."

"What I saw in the paper," Carmody said, "I guessed it could've started out better."

"Five o'clock on Friday night," Hunter said, "the old bastard sends them out to deliberate. Will you tell me what is going on, inside his head, he sends a jury out on Friday night at five o'clock? Here's this guy, oh, sure, plenty of time, everybody nice and relaxed, week before last, quit early on Wednsday, take Friday off, digest the goddamned turkey, and then this week, nine-fifteen every morning, five, five-thirty every night, like the world's gonna end and we got to finish the case before the sun goes down. Holy Jesus."

"Very simple," Carmody said. "Peter Macarthur's son and his wife live in Burlington, Vermont, and Peter goes up there for all the holidays since his wife died. And he doesn't like to drive his Cadillac very fast, or after dark, so he quits early the day before the holiday, and drives up to Middlebury and stays overnight at the Inn, and then finishes the trip the next morning. And he plays with his grandchildren, and he feels nice and rested, and he takes all the weekend except for Sunday. Sunday morning he gets himself up and he has a nice breakfast, and then he drives down in daylight to Boston again, and on Monday morning he gets up, and he hasn't had anybody to talk to since the day before, and he's all nice and rested, and he spends the next week laying the lash to everybody in sight. I figured that's why you were never around."

"Whips the absolute shit out of you, those hours," Hunter said.

"How was his charge?" Carmody said.

"That much I will say for him," Hunter said. "His charge was beautiful. He as much as told that jury, if they didn't come back with 'Guilty as charged,' they should be all sent away for observation. It just didn't entirely work, is all."

"I saw a little of it," Carmody said. "I slipped in a couple of days."

"On Monday and Tuesday," Hunter said, "well, they finished cross-examination on Gillis on Monday. Macarthur thought they oughta finish on Wednesday, before we broke for the turkey, but for some unknown reason or other, Sam Wyman decided he wanted to screw around with Gillis for about a hundred hours, and so Killilea didn't get to him until Monday. But Fat John didn't take long, I'll say that for him. Then Tommy Hart, and he was less'n an hour, and I've got to say, Billy Gillis is a fink, and he only does the right thing when he's scared, but by Jesus, when he does it, he does it, dumb as he is. They didn't touch him.

"Then we had nine hundred tellers and people that saw getaway cars, and the guy from the camera store that runs the lab that develops the pictures. We did have some fun with him. I think Shanley kind of forgot how you get a photograph in evidence, and instead of just asking the guy, and then saving one of the tellers to look at the pictures and say if it was a fair and accurate representation of something he saw that day, he was going 'round and 'round with chemicals and developers and all kinds of shit. So we wasted Tuesday on that, and Fat John was having a glorious time for himself, driving Shanley crazy.

"Then on Wednesday morning," Hunter said, "we got the pictures in, and Shanley comes over to me and asks me what else we got, like he really didn't know, and I told him—it was a lot of small shit, really, guys from the Registry to talk about stolen cars and license plates and shit like where they were recovered, and so forth—and we blew the rest of the morning on that. Then we rested.

"Wednesday afternoon," Hunter said, "Fat John and Wyman argue their motions for directed verdicts of acquittal. Nice try. Waste a lot of time on that. Hart argues his motion, for Teddy. More time wasted. We take the afternoon recess. It's perfectly obvious to anybody ever stood in shoe leather; the Judge is not gonna take this case from the jury. Does Shanley care? He does not. He's got his argument to make, that the Judge shouldn't do what he's not gonna do anyway. The Judge tries to tell him. Shanley don't listen. If he does listen, he don't understand. Why the fuck do those guys talk so much?"

"They like to," Carmody said. "It's what they're trained to do, and it makes them feel comfortable, when they're doing it."

"Well, he did it," Hunter said. "Comes over to me afterwards, while Judge Macarthur's using the whole thing for an excuse to take his afternoon coffee recess, says: 'Whaddaya think?' I said: 'In my judgment, the whole goddamned thing's ridiculous.' "

"Shanley take it all right?" Carmody said.

"He agreed with me," Hunter said. "Then the Judge comes back in, and Donovan rests without putting on any evidence, and Wyman gets up to flog the duck about Marr. Puts Marr on the stand."

"For what the hell for?" Carmody said.

"I'm as confused as you are," Hunter said, "and Shanley was too. Andy tells this great cock-and-bull story about how he just knows Donovan from playing cards, and Leaper asked him to meet him at the motel, and he did it, and from robberies he knows nothing. I thought Shanley murdered him on cross. For some reason, Wyman didn't put Andy's prior record in, and have him look sorry about it, so Shanley gets to stand up and ask him if he's the same Andy Marr that did time twice before for knocking over banks, and then the Judge gives the instruction about how that doesn't mean he did the Danvers National, Ladies and Gentlemen of the jury; it's just on his credibility, because he's a convicted felon. They all kept a straight face, and at the time I figured it was because they were smart.

"Killilea don't cross-examine for Leaper," Hunter said. "Hart gets his chance to cross-examine for Donnelly, and he didn't want any part of that, so when Shanley's through, Marr steps down. Wyman rests, for Marr. Hart calls Donnie Doyle.

"Killilea got up faster'n I figure a fat man can do anything. 'Donovan rested, a long time ago. This is evidence coming in against Donovan, that Donovan can't rebut. It's unfair. It's reversible error.' Wyman screams the same thing about Marr. 'Marr's rested. This is unfair.' Jury's excused. That's the way we finished Wednesday: jury out, everybody arguing and making objections about how come Doyle shouldn't testify. Doyle, I assume agrees with them. The case against the other guys is closed. No more testimony. Shanley's going nuts.

"More of the same on Thursday morning," Hunter said. "Lemme tell you something, all right? It's not only Killilea was scared about Doyle. Wyman was too."

"They've tried a lot of cases together," Carmody said. "They probably haven't got a great many secrets."

"Big back and forth," Hunter said. "Judge finally gets fed up with the whole shouting match. Says Doyle can testify, and that's the end of it. They can take it up with the Supreme Judicial Court, on appeal.

"Then," Hunter said, "there's a big screaming session about *that*. If the Judge says it's gonna be appealed, it must be he's biased and prejudiced and he's gonna get them poor innocent fellas found guilty, so they *can* appeal. More carrying on. Judge finally shuts that down. Doyle takes the stand."

"How was he?" Carmody said.

"Horace," Hunter said, "on direct, Hart had him on direct, of course, he was Donnelly's witness, he was about as warm as a mother-in-law's kiss. Listless, he looked like he was bombed. . . ."

"He probably was," Carmody said.

". . . and he probably was," Hunter said, "you asked him if he saw the sun coming up in the north, I think he would've said: 'Yeah.' Limp as a soft dick up there. But he said it all, Donnelly's buying him drinks in the Good Time in Kelly Square, just about the time that the Danvers National's getting knocked over. I seen guys more convincing, telling bimbos they just met that it's really love, and now how about it.

"Tommy finished about in time for lunch," Hunter said. "Old Peter, I guess, wants his ham sandwich and his nap. 'Cross-examination after the luncheon recess.'

"At the time," Hunter said, "I was figuring that Shanley's the only one that's gonna do it. And that didn't bother me at all. Give him the hour to calm down. But when we get back, Fat John's gonna take the guy on cross. Even though he's rested. Hack him around a little. More of the same. Yeah, he's quite sure. Donnelly's buying the drinks. He never saw Leaper. Andy Marr? This is Wyman, now. Wyman sees Fat John rubbing it into the jury, how Goat-ass was having drinks, I guess he decides there's something to it. Wyman took an hour. We recessed on Thursday, with Shanley due up on Friday morning."

"And how'd *he* do?" Carmody said.

"Not a patch on him," Hunter said. "Went over the stuff about dates again, made him say he was very right well damned sure, showed him the record, he was in the hospital that day, and sat down."

"No Fat John?" Carmody said.

"No Fat John," Hunter said. "No Tommy Hart, no Charlie Thomas, no nothing."

"Son of a bitch," Carmody said. "Is the kid learning, or something?"

"On the way down the stairs," Hunter said, "he

told me I did a good job, and we're both on the same side, and if it doesn't come out the way we both want, it's his fault and not mine."

"When was this?" Carmody said.

"After the jury went out," Hunter said. "When Shanley got through with Doyle, Tommy Hart and Killilea for some reason I can't figure out decided they oughta take redirect and recross, just in case the jury didn't get the point, that the guy was lying. Then Hart starts bringing on the character witnesses, and he's got about ten sisters and cousins and stuff that *swear* Teddy reformed, a long time ago, and this minister that taught him to do an examination of conscience in the can, the last time he was in, and nobody even bothers to cross-examine them.

"Then," Hunter said, "it's almost time for lunch, and Hart finally rested for Donnelly. Shanley hasn't got any rebuttal. None of the other guys have, either. 'Arguments and charge after the luncheon recess,' the Judge says. Off for another ham sandwich and another nap.

"What you notice," Hunter said, "I didn't notice it then, but I noticed it later, old Peter didn't ask for any time limits. So we come back in at two, and Sam Wyman goes first.

"'A poor fellow,' he says, 'that trusted his friend, and his friend was in debt, from going to basketball games and betting on them, that he couldn't afford. Poor creature.' And he beats up on Marr for an hour or so, and says his client's an unfortunate queer— he didn't say that, but you would've hadda be a deaf-mute to miss hearing it, in what he was saying—that trusted a guy and the guy turned him in. Half an hour.

"Then there was Killilea," Hunter said. "Another forty minutes of how his client's a former great athlete, and apparently they got a license to rob banks.

"Tommy Hart," Hunter said. "Donnelly wasn't even there. He was someplace else. The fact that Doyle admits he lied don't mean a shit. If Doyle was mistaken, then Gillis was mistaken. Close to half an hour.

"Which," Hunter said, "is when we're supposed to

quit. Nothing doing. Judge Macarthur thinks we might finish. Shanley gets up."

"Bad job?" Carmody said.

"If it was," Hunter said, "I never saw a good one. He starts off bare-ass unprepared, and he's a perfect prick when you try to tell him something, but if it's a long trial, so he gets the time to learn what it's about, he can really put the boots to them when he sums up.

"You know," Hunter said, "maybe that's the biggest shame about the guy. He's really got it, when he wants to reach back for it, and really go to work. He can get in there and whale the shit out of you, when he takes the time to get ready. That guy could run the Pope in, if he put his mind to it. It's a goddamned shame, is what it is. If he only wasn't so interested in spinning his wheels. I was thinking that, anyway."

"Then what happened?" Carmody said.

"My guess is," Hunter said, "what happened was, it was Friday night, and it was late and it was cold and they were sick of all those mouthy bastards hollering and yelling. This was an experienced jury, Horace. They all sat on cases before. Civil cases, maybe, but they sat on them, and maybe the first time for each of them, they hung out all night when they had a disagreement, and then they got smart. And as a result there was enough people in there that knew, when they took that first ballot, that they had a problem.

"Now," Hunter said, "I'm gettin' awful generous, but I give them something, too. I think they must've really tried. They didn't stay out that long because they wanted to compromise. But, when they took the last ballot, the next-to-last ballot, they still had three guys that they hadda deal with, and only two of them that they agreed on. And things weren't changing, so they said: 'Okay, two guys in, one guy out, something for everybody. Time to go home.' "

"You don't think it was," Carmody said, "that you just had more on Donnelly and Donovan'n you did on Marr, and that was why?"

"Shit," Hunter said, "no. No, what it was, was, it was goddamned Sam Wyman and his emotional pitch.

Buddy on buddy. Guy's in financial trouble. Other guy
helps him out. Guy that helps him, turns around, the
guy that gets the help turns around and tips his helper
in. I don't care what anybody says: juries don't like
finks. Nobody does. If they can find a way to sink the
fink, they'll do it, and if you give them two guys they
can sink, and one guy they can leave go and rap the
fink on the mouth, by doing it, they will. We're all still
in grade school," Hunter said. "Nobody likes a rat-
fink. And we'll never get out.

"That jury?" Hunter said. "That jury, Horace, was
out six hours, plus. On a Friday night. They had real
troubles. I think Judge Macarthur thought they'd be
back in ten minutes. I think Shanley thought so, too.
But they didn't care what anybody thought.

"I went into Shanley's office," Hunter said. "It was
after six. They're still not back. And he's talking on
the phone."

"When he got off," Hunter said, "I said to him, not
really meaning anything by it, I said: 'Jesus, Rich,
you're on the phone more'n the telephone company.
What're you doing, running a small handbook out of
this operation? The DA'll be pissed if he finds out.'

"He leans back in the chair," Hunter said, "and he
really looked like he was exhausted. Kind of laughs.
'Shit,' he says, 'I know it. I oughta have an operation
and have one of those things stuck in my ear, so I
could talk and get something done at the same time.'

" 'That's good, though,' I says. 'Your practice keeps
you hopping like that, it must be bringing in an honest
dollar. Better that'n sittin' around, waiting for the
damned thing to ring.'

" 'Deke,' he says, 'there's practice and then there's
practice.' Then Fat John wanders in, and I want you
to know, I've seldom seen a guy that looked as thirsty
as Fat John did around six, six-fifteen last Friday
night, and Shanley clammed up.

"About an hour goes by," Hunter said. "Sam
Wyman comes in, and then Tommy Hart, and we're
sitting around, shooting the shit, nothing very heavy.
Judge has the deputy call up: they're feeding the jury.
We can go eat. 'Good,' says Fat John. 'Tell him we'll

be over the Pregnant Pilgrim, and we'll stay there until they get a verdict, if that's all right with him.'

"We get over there," Hunter said. "Fat John has three drafts and starts looking like a man who died and went to heaven. We're still shooting the shit. Wyman's not drinking."

"He had a little problem with the tea, a few years back, I heard," Carmody said.

"He's still got it," Hunter said. "We all had sandwiches, Fat John's acting like he's gonna make them tap another keg before that verdict comes in, I had a couple myself, Shanley's just sitting there with a scotch in front of him, making wet rings on the table with it. Tommy Hart found out they had some Wild Turkey at the Priscilla Puritan Bar and Grille, and he was drinking some of it, which improved his disposition.

"Eight o'clock," Hunter said, "eight-thirty, Fat John's giving me a whole mess of shit about how much of Gillis's story did I make up. 'All of it,' I says. 'You saw the guy. He's slow-witted, 's what he is. Has to have somebody help him in the morning, so he gets his pants on the right end.'

" 'Pretty slender reed for a case like this,' Fat John says.

" 'Not with the pictures and the money,' I says.

" 'You could lose it,' Fat John said. Jesus, does he like to get on a guy."

"He's a funny bastard to have around, though," Carmody said.

"He had me going pretty good," Hunter said, "and we're going along all right, every so often Shanley gets up and makes a phone call and comes back and sits down and looks like he's been carrying hod all day, and Wyman says: 'I think I'll have a drink for myself.' And he orders a Rob Roy.

"I didn't think anything about it," Hunter said. "Nine o'clock, nine-thirty, Wyman orders another drink. Bang, it's gone right off. Before the girl can set the beers down, that we ordered, and he's got this funny look on his face. Orders another one.

" 'Uh, Sam,' Killilea says, 'uh, you know, this could

be a pretty long deathwatch. Don't wanna get so you're not all right when you get in court.'

" 'Leave him alone,' Hart says. Killilea left him alone. Wyman had another one. Then he had another one. I can drink the beer pretty fast, but he was going faster with those dry Rob Roys, and I think there just might be a little more clout in those things'n there is in beer.

"Then Wyman clears his throat," Hunter said. "Except for when he was ordering drinks, this's about the first words he's said all night. 'At least it's not raining,' he says. I kind of looked at him. 'The thing of it is, you're always better off when it's not raining. Generally, when you get a slow jury on a night like this, it starts raining.'

"I looked at Fat John," Hunter said. " 'Sam's going to give us the weather report now, aren't you, Sam?' he says.

" 'It's the first thing that always happens,' Wyman says. 'It starts raining.'

" 'You know what I'd like to know?' Fat John says to me. 'I'd like to know when you guys got so efficient, and started checking records of guys that were in hospitals. You never did that before in your life.' And Wyman finishes his drink and orders another one. Close to eleven, now.

" 'I had a case down in Barnstable,' he says, Wyman, 'and it was many years ago. It was with Dan Gearey, Captain Dan Gearey, and the prosecutor was that reprehensible little Italian kid. I always called him "Citronella" because I could never remember his name.'

" 'Fortunato,' Fat John says. 'Billy Fortunato.'

" 'It rained the first day we were there,' Wyman said. 'It rained every day. We were there three weeks. It rained some part of every day. It was in August. The whole Cape became deserted. The hotels and the restaurant people were dying on the vine. Dying on the vine. Their establishments were deserted. They depend upon vacationers for their living, you see. It was a sad sight to see. That was a most regrettable case, with a most regrettable outcome. My client was convicted of murder in the second degree. He was ordered to waste the remainder of his life in prison. It was a miscarriage of justice. It was a sad sight to see.' Then he ordered another drink.

"I thought the best thing I could do, maybe, was talk to Fat John. 'My friend,' I said, 'you got to keep in mind, we're employing the methods of modern law enforcement around these parts now, and that guy's famous. You put him on there, well, the minute we heard his name, we know he's been in more'n he's been out. It was just a matter of calling up a guy to see if he was on a particular day. That was all. The odds were, he was, and that was the way it turned out.'

" 'I didn't put him on," Killilea says, 'that was the master stroke conceived by my esteemed colleague here, the eminent Thomas X. Hart, fabled in song and story as the uncrowned prince of the Massachusetts criminal trial bar.'

" 'Yeah,' Hart says. 'Lemme ask you something, Johnny-boy, all right? What's your honest opinion of your worthy client, Mister Michael Donovan?'

" 'A poor misguided lad,' John says. 'Lacks direction and purpose in his life. Easily led. Unable to make mature judgments. A victim of society. Just what I told the jury, which is obviously agonizing, even now, over the colossal injustice of prosecuting so misfortunate a fellow.'

" 'I said: your honest opinion,' Hart says.

" 'Ah,' Killilea said. 'Well, if pressed I might concede that he has tendencies which I have observed, that might to a less charitable person seem to warrant formulation of the judgment that he's a lazy, dishonest, crooked, lying little bastard that should've taken up passing bad checks instead of robbing banks, because I think the pasty-faced cocksucker'd be better at it, and he wouldn't be such a goddamned menace to society if he'd use pens instead of guns.'

" 'You think he'd shoot somebody?' Hart says.

" 'Only by mistake,' Killilea said. 'If the thing went off while he was holding it, he might kill you. If he aimed it at you, he'd miss.'

" 'Leaper give you any instructions about handling the case?' Hart said.

" 'He instructed me to get him off,' Killilea said. 'He protested his innocence in ringing tones, and when I mentioned the pictures he said he has a friend who can put pictures together so that you look like you've been someplace you never were. Reminding him of the necessity for candor with counsel, I told him of Mister Gillis's expected testimony. He was, I might say, most derogatory of Mister Gillis, and his reputation for truth and veracity. I believe he went so far as to allege that Mister Gillis had been *reached,* was the term I believe he employed, by Corporal Hunter, here.'

"I think Wyman'd gone to sleep," Hunter said. "He was sitting right next to me, so I couldn't watch him, and when Killilea says that, Wyman snorts and says: 'What?'

" 'I was relating,' Killilea said, 'certain rhetorical extravagances made to me in confidence, under the attorney-client privilege, of which I am not in flagrant breach, not that I give a particular shit, one of which was that Corporal Hunter, here, with the advice and consent of Richard Shanley, there, had *reached* Mister William Gillis, in order to embellish if not to invent certain statements to be uttered by Mister Gillis at trial of the case of *Commonwealth* versus *Donnelly, et al.*'

" 'Oh,' Wyman says.

" 'I reproved him at once for the harboring of the mere suspicion,' Killilea says," Hunter said.

" 'And what did he say to that?' Hart said.

" 'He manifested some displeasure at my reaction,' Killilea said, 'remonstrating with me to the effect that the whole thing is fixed, and your own lawyer won't even back you up because he's rigging it with the cops and the DA's office.'

" 'And what'd you say?' Tommy Hart said.

" 'I informed him,' Killilea says, 'that I was acquainted, as he suggested, with Mister Shanley, and that I had friends in the State Police who spoke very highly of Corporal Hunter, although I lacked personal

experience of the gentleman. I said I believed, therefore, that each of them was a man of complete integrity, who would die before stooping to so shabby a
practice. He said he wanted it looked into, and I
said that perhaps he should therefore give serious
thought to engaging new counsel. I also told him he
oughta start thinking about that anyway, because until
I saw fifteen thousand dollars on the goddamned
desk, he wasn't getting movement number one out of
me, and that I was not in the habit of having dead-
beat clients tell me how to run my cases, anymore
than I was in the habit of letting paying clients tell
me how to represent them, and that if he didn't like
it, he could go and fuck himself.'

" 'And what did he do then?' Hart says," Hunter
said.

" 'He stormed out of my office,' Killilea said, 'and
returned the next day with ten thousand dollars in
American money, which he placed on the table while
promising the remainder by the start of trial. I haven't
seen it, and I don't really expect to see it, which is
why I always ask for fifty percent more than I think
the case is worth. If they think they're beating you
out of a one-third discount, they're much more tract-
able when you tell them to do something. Unfortunately
for me, Mister Shanley, while a man of a great integrity,
is also a man of very deliberate speed, and the time this
goddamned thing took, I should've asked for twenty-
two-five. Ah well, live and learn.'

" 'That's about what I thought,' Hart says," Hunter
said. " 'I had a discussion with Teddy Donnelly, too,
about trial tactics,' he says, 'and I told him I was
very nervous indeed about putting that fellow Doyle
on the stand, and do you know what Mister Donnelly said to me?'

" 'Relying of course, only on hearsay,' Killilea says,
'I think I can imagine.'

" 'Save you the trouble,' Hart says. 'He looks at
me the same way a big old smart housecat looks at
a little old squirrel that made the mistake of getting
too far away from the old oak tree, and he says: "I
paid you your fee, Counselor, and you took it and

you put it in your pocket, and that means you're my lawyer, so you do what I say." And you know what I decided to do, since I do know quite a bit about Teddy Donnelly? You bet your bright blue arse you know. I decided to forget about even thinking about returning his twenty grand to him, and to do what he said. See, Johnny-boy, I go out every morning and I start up that Cadillac, and when I turn that key, well, the only thing I want going off's the ignition switch.'

" 'Very prudent of you,' Killilea says."

"What'd Shanley say?" Carmody said.

"Nothing," Hunter said. "Got up, very slow, went over and made another phone call. And he's just on his way back, the phone rings again, we've got a verdict. We got over there, it was almost midnight before they got all the ninety-year-old deputies located, and the defendants come in, and the jury comes down, and the foreman stands up and hands the papers to Mishawa: Teddy, guilty, guilty; Leaper, guilty, guilty; Andy, not guilty, not guilty.

"Nobody expected that," Hunter said. "Least of all Sam Wyman, I think. Biggest goddamned victory that he's had in years. His guy walks and the other two heavy hitters have to convey their sympathies to their clients."

"Compromise verdict," Carmody said.

"Sure," Hunter said. "Judge thanks them for their service on the jury. I turned around and looked at Andy. He gives me the finger. I hadda admit it, he got me. I gave him Thumbs Up. He beat me, just like he said he was gonna.

"So the jury goes out," Hunter said. "And old Peter says he doesn't need to wait for probation reports on Teddy and Leaper, he's gonna sentence right off. 'No point in waiting for the usual studies,' he says. 'You're both notorious men, and prison's the only thing we've figured out to do with men like you.' Then he gives them both life in the jug. Which kind of surprised me. I figured Teddy'd get life, but I didn't think Leaper was good for more'n twenty years. I'll give 'em both credit, though. They stood there and they took it like somebody was saying Good Morning to them.

"Then," Hunter says, "the Judge asks Sam Wyman if he knows of any other process on which his client's held, and Sam gets up.

"Now he doesn't *look* drunk," Hunter said. "He looks very impressive, just like he always does, maybe a little tired, but if you looked at him, nothing. And he says:

" 'My client has been wrongfully detained since his arrest nearly nine months of his irreplaceable life ago. Now, Your Honor,' and he starts looking around the place like he doesn't want to leave anybody out, 'I blame no one. Not this young man,' and he looks at Shanley. 'Not this officer,' which is me, 'and not even this honorable, ah, Court. All act in what they believe to be good conscience, and excuse what they do as necessary to what they conceive to be justice. Even when they lie, and, as I have reason to believe, procure, by fear and threats, others to tell their lies for them. But this is a travesty of our Bill of Rights, and it, and it, and it . . .' He was like a broken record. He must've said it five times. Then he passed out."

"What'd Peter do?" Carmody said.

"Looks at him," Hunter said. "Shakes his head. Then he says: 'Gentlemen, it's been a long day at the end of a long trial. We should all go home.'

"Me and Shanley went out the side door. Teddy and Leaper, like I say, no expression at all, they're getting the cuffs snapped on them, and on Andy too, of course, because he's still doing the rest of the bit they violated him for when we grabbed him for this. I oughta ask Shanley if he's gonna get out on that, now he's been acquitted on this.

"So we're coming down here," Hunter said, "and we're in the corridor, me and Shanley, just standing there, talking, and I told him it was my fault that Andy got off, and he starts to say something, and then Fat John and Tommy come down the stairs, practically carrying Sam. And he gets to the bottom, I guess he felt better, shakes them off and goes out the door, alone.

They come up to us. We're all telling each other we done a good job, and I started to say it was my fault that Andy got off, and Dick says: 'Deke, we don't always see eye to eye on a case. But you work your ass off, and you tell me what you think whether I wanna hear it or not, and if we only got the two of them, well, two out of three ain't bad. You're the one that got them.'

"Caught me flatfooted," Hunter said. "I was absolutely stunned. I don't think I even said 'Thank you.' Maybe I did.

"Then Fat John says something," Hunter said, "and then he said, 'Uh, Richard, you, ah, know, Sam was, well, he misunderstood what we were saying. Tomorrow, when he's sober, he won't remember it, probably, what he said. He doesn't really think that, you know, what he said up there. Sam was drunk. Don't hold that against him, willya?'

" 'Look,' Shanley says, 'okay? Sam was drunk. Deke's disappointed. You had a constant fight with your client, and Tommy's probably good and scared now, of his. Me? My wife's been having an affair for about three years now, on and off, and this past month or so's been one of the on times, and I call home and all I ever get is the babysitter, that the kids're lonesome and they can't go to sleep. There's nothing Sam, or Deke, or you or Tommy can do about any of it. The Judge is right. We should all go home.' "

"Jesus Christ," Carmody said, "I wonder who the hell she's banging?"

"Well," Hunter said, "I wouldn't waste a lot of time asking Charlie Thomas, I was you.

"Then," Hunter said, "I did what he said. I went home, and I got there about two o'clock, and what I wanted was a beer and what I got was, she got up and I got a good hour about how I should've gone down and fixed the cottage the Friday after Thanksgiving, like I was gonna, but I didn't because it was raining and I took the kids to the Trailside Museum instead and looked at the fuckin' woodchucks and stuff. So I said: 'Screw it.' And I went down there Saturday, and I put the boards back on the windows that the fuckin' little bikies ripped off, and I'll fix the glass next year that they broke, and that won't be right, either. Then, on the way back, I, instead of coming back, it was late, I stopped in East Greenwich and got a motel room and I got drunk Saturday night and went to bed without anybody yelling at me. And I got up Sunday, and I did some thinking, and then I watched the Pats game that was blacked out here, and I had about five nice cold Lowenbraus, and you know what I'm gonna do?"

"Anybody with you while you're doing all this thinking?" Carmody said.

"My goodness," Hunter said. "Horace, are you suggesting that I'd run around with boys or something? I decided, I am gonna take the exams. I am gonna take weekend details, so I can get some goddamned *money*, and also so, since she won't leave me alone, I can leave her, alone, and I'm gonna get one of those stainless steel Smiths. I called up this guy that I know down in Weymouth Landing, this morning, that owns a sporting goods store, and he's got two of them which he isn't even showing anybody. Eighty-four bucks apiece. Want one?"

"That's a very good price," Carmody said. "I could use it when I retire and go up to Vermont. Shoot all those guys that run around bothering their animals."

"Think it over," Hunter said. "I'm picking mine up tomorrow. If I'm gonna be a cop, and I am, I might as well go ahead and be a cop, and get it the hell over with."

"You're sure of that, then, finally," Carmody said.

"Yeah," Hunter said. "I think so. In fact, I know so. I'm sure enough so that if I wasn't really sure, I would say I was."

"There're worse things to do," Carmody said.

"There are," Hunter said. "I was talking to Gillis, the day he come in to testify, scared shitless of course, and I was trying to calm him down so he wouldn't crap his pants and offend the jury, which I guess he must've done anyway. He was worried about where we're gonna put him, to do the five he got for pleading and talking, if we hook Teddy, and I finally got him a little more relaxed. And he looks at me and he says: "Ah, fuck it. What difference does it make if he does? What you lose on the swings,' he says, Horace, 'you make up on the merry-go-round.' "

That night, Hunter went home.

The MS READ-a-thon needs young readers!

Boys and girls between 6 and 14 can join the MS READ-a-thon and help find a cure for Multiple Sclerosis by reading books. And they get two rewards — the enjoyment of reading, and the great feeling that comes from helping others.

For complete information call your local MS chapter, or call toll-free (800) 243-6000. Or mail the coupon below.

Kids can help, too!